CROSSED FIRE

by

KIM BACCELLIA

Lachesis
Publishing Inc

www.lachesispublishing.com

Published Internationally by Lachesis Publishing Inc.
Rockland, Ontario, Canada

A catalogue record for the print format of this title
is available from the National Library of Canada

ISBN 978-1-77359-011-0

A catalogue record for the Ebook is available
from the National Library of Canada
Ebooks are available for purchase from
www.lachesispublishing.com

ISBN 978-1-77359-010-3

Editor: Joanna D'Angelo

Copyeditor: Brenda Heald

DEDICATION

To Mom
(1938-2017)
You always believed in me.
I miss you.

ACKNOWLEDGMENTS

This book couldn't have been made without the help and support of a number of people. Louella Nelson, who has always been one of my biggest cheerleaders. Joyce Sweeney, who helped with brainstorming this story. My husband for all the times he told me never give up. To Christine Marciniak, whose suggestions and comments helped me so much. My fabulous editor Joanna D'Angelo, who loved this story and helped strengthen it!

And finally to my fans who told me they wanted more of Stephanie's story. This story is for you. I hope you enjoy revisiting Stephanie as much as I did!

ALSO AVAILABLE

Crossed Out

CROSSED FIRE

CHAPTER 1

Life hasn't been "normal" for me in a very long time. Not since I figured out that I could see and talk to dead people. Well, dead girls mostly. My name is Stephanie Stewart and I help dead teenage girls cross over into the light. I'm not sure why I've been singled out for this. I don't think I'm anyone special, but for some reason I've been given this "gift" and it has really thrown my life upside down.

My mom hates that I can do this. Big surprise. My mom and I have a volatile relationship. My dad doesn't know anything, and Mom wants to keep it that way. And I hate keeping important stuff from Dad. My best friend Cura doesn't know either. I'm working my courage up to tell her, but every time I try, I chicken out. And my boyfriend Dylan is having some trouble "adjusting" to my abilities, which is kind of weird because Dylan has a supernatural ability, too. He can sense auras—something he inherited from his grandmother. Speaking of which, Dylan took me to visit her recently and it didn't go very well . . .

The thought of being around hospital psych wards didn't exactly rate high on Dylan's Top 5 List of places to visit. But he agreed to go because it was the right thing to do. And my mentor, Dr. Anthony suggested it would help Dylan better understand his own abilities.

Dylan's grandmother rocked back and forth in a rocking chair, amusement crinkled in her faded blue eyes.

"Well, Dylan, what are you waiting for? The apocalypse?" she laughed.

I stared at Dylan, waiting for a reaction, but he just stood there, indecision in his gaze.

Her eyes pierced through the awkwardness.

"Uh—," he stammered, shoving his hands deep in his pockets.

"You girl." She turned in my direction. "Come here, I don't bite." She motioned me forward, her deep, blue veins pulsed on her hands.

I squirmed under her unwavering gaze.

"Any day now," she added. Her raspy chuckle filled the cramped room.

I moved closer to Dylan's side. I needed his reassurance I hadn't made a colossal mistake. It was unnerving being in her presence. Like if she wanted to, she could turn me into a toad. Dylan told me about her talent for reading auras, but my gut was telling me that reading auras was just scratching the surface with Grams.

He took my hand and gave a quick squeeze. "We can do this," he mouthed.

I nodded, dropping his hand and strolled over to his grandmother's side. I winced at the overpowering scent of lavender powder, the closer I got.

"Well." Grams said. "You're a pretty girl, but you dress like a tomboy." She looked me up and down, frowning at my high-top sneakers, black jeans, and Wonder Woman t-shirt.

I didn't know what to say to that, so I just smiled and said, "It's nice to meet you Ma'am."

She opened her mouth to reply and suddenly her eyes glazed over. Just like that.

"Mrs. Van Buren?" I asked. I reached out and tentatively touched her hand. It was like she was frozen in time. Worried, I turned to Dylan. "Shouldn't we do something?" I whispered to Dylan.

Grams' eyes seemed to roll back into her head, and a blast of cold air whooshed through the room even though the windows were closed.

I knew what was happening. It always happened the same way, when the spirit world was reaching out to me. Sure enough, the back of my legs began to itch something fierce. I resisted the urge to scratch.

Dylan walked to Grams' bedside. "I'm gonna call for help," he said, reaching for the emergency button.

Right then his grandmother jerked up, causing a loud creak as her rocking chair scraped against the floor.

Almost at the same time Dylan let out a groan and his hands went to his head.

"Dylan!" I helped him sit on the side of Grams' bed. I rubbed his temples and he seemed to calm down.

Seeing auras around people triggered headaches in Dylan, and the only thing that seemed to soothe the pain was either surfing off Half Moon Bay or cold water on his forehead. I thought about getting a cold cloth for him but that would mean stepping out of the room and I didn't want to leave him. "Don't do it!"

Shocked, I turned around to face his grandmother once more. Her eyes re-focused and she stared right at me. Goosebumps rose up my arms.

"Don't do what?" I asked, almost afraid of the answer.

"Grams," Dylan got up again. Holding his hand to his head, he went to her side. She didn't acknowledge him, or even glance in his direction. No, she fixed her cloudy blue eyed-gaze on me.

"You're at the crossroads," she croaked. "Choose wisely."

"What?" I choked out, now totally confused.

"Grams, you need to rest," Dylan said gently, covering his grandmother with the blanket. "We'll come back later."

"Rest?" She cackled. "There is no time for that." She

[3]

pointed at me again. "She needs to make the right choice or all will be lost."

A million thoughts ping-ponged in my head. Was she talking about my recent encounter with Mark the demon? I'd just sent him back to the dark depths where he belonged. I thought my run in with the undead had ended . . . A sick feeling settled over me. Was I in store for more demons? All I wanted to do was help dead girls find the light. Cross over. I didn't sign up for fighting demons and the undead. But maybe it came with the territory? I needed to talk to Dr. Anthony, about this. If there was anyone who could give me some advice about all this supernatural stuff, it was Dr. A.

"You know Dylan's right. You should rest." I said in a gentle voice to Grams.

Grams settled back in the rocking chair. She sighed, closed her eyes, and began rocking back and forth. "Stay true to who you are . . . And you'll make the right choice."

This was all so confusing and frustrating. I knew I shouldn't push it, but I couldn't help myself. "What choice should I make?"

When Dylan gave me the eye, I mouthed, "What? Shouldn't I know?"

Her eyes flew open again and she pointed at me. "Don't forget. Don't fall for the Devil in disguise, or there will be Hell to pay." Then her face froze, again, and she stared vacantly into the distance.

"Grams?" Dylan knelt at her feet and took her hands in his. "Frick." He glanced over at me.

"I'm sorry Dylan." Tears sprang to my eyes. I don't know why his grandmother had that reaction to me. But it was clearly a warning. I hoped she would be okay. I went to her bed and pressed the emergency button. After the nurses got her back into bed and gave her her afternoon medication, Dylan's grandmother seemed to relax. She didn't say anything more though, so Dylan and I left her to sleep.

Whatever it was that I had to face, I hoped I would be able to heed her advice and choose wisely . . .

* * *

A few hours later, I was in the car with my mom. On an outing. She said it would be good for us to spend some time together and she had my best interests at heart. Whatever that meant.

We were on our way to her former sorority house. She said it was going to be a secret ceremony to celebrate the anniversary of the sorority.

Seriously, who actually did things like this with their mother?

My best friend, Cura, and her mother, Melissa Stratton, were going to be there, too. Which was pretty weird. But the worst part was that Lisa Swanson would be there with my former BFF, her daughter Hillary. To say that Hillary and I didn't get along was an understatement. Hillary was my arch nemesis aka the Supreme Bitch of Sutter High.

Oh, this was going to be just wonderful, I could feel it. I blew out a breath, and grumbled that this was the last place I wanted to go to.

Mom gave me one of her looks and filled me in on the details.

Since Hillary's mother was a real estate agent, she could get access to pretty much any building in town, including the old Alpha Phi Sorority House that had been abandoned in 1990 after a tragic fire. Mom wasn't exactly an open book when it came to her college years, so I was surprised that she opened up to me about her former sorority house.

Situated close to Downtown Sacramento's J Street Bridge, near the campus of Sanders University, the building had been a sorority house for the Sisters of Alpha Phi until a fire destroyed it and caused two deaths:

Dylan's mom's sister and Hillary's mom's sister. That was certainly shocking, and it made me wonder if that was why Dylan's mom and Hillary's mom always acted strange around me. Mom only gave me the bare bones about the fire, saying it was an accident. So I had no idea why Mom would want to celebrate the anniversary of her former sorority house, considering what had happened there.

Getting out of the car, my first impression of the former sorority house was that it must have been a beautiful building at one time. But now, over-grown vegetation strangled the house's former elegance. Soot blackened what had once been a pristine white stone facade, several signs posted on the front door warned us to 'KEEP OUT" and "TRESSPASSERS WILL BE PROSECUTED."

The crumbling appearance of the house and the meandering American River that ran behind the property was like something out of a gothic novel. Or the setting of one of those CW paranormal TV shows where teenage vampires and witches plot the demise of their enemies when they're not working on their school term papers.

"Let's just get this over with," Hillary said in her usual snarky tone. Her head was down and she was texting on her smart phone. Big surprise. Word at school was that she broke her previous phone mid-fight with her mom. She threw it against the wall and it smashed into bits. Of course "Mommy Dearest" replaced it, because fight or no fight, Hillary always got what she wanted. She glanced up, dissing me and Cura with one of her trademark snooty looks. "This place is giving me the creeps." She directed that comment my way, letting me know what—or rather who—really gave her the heebie jeebies.

I glared back.

"Stop complaining," Hillary's mother shot back. I could tell where Hillary got her attitude from.

My mom and I were dressed in pretty white dresses. Mine was short sleeved, and had a simple boat collar and a hemline that reached my knees. My mom's dress was sleeveless, calf-length and had a row of silver buttons that marched up the front. Both of us looked like we'd fit right in at a garden, tea party, but we paled in comparison to Hillary and her mom. Both of them looked like they'd just left a Versace show at New York Fashion Week. Both were dressed in nearly identical tight, white, mini-dresses that clung to them like a second skin, and both wore matching sky-high heels. Cura and her mom on the other hand, were the very definition of "alternative" style. Cura was dressed in a cute, white, poodle skirt and matching white knit sweater she must have bought at one of her favorite thrift stores. Cura's mother wore a long flowing white skirt accented with pastel-colored flowers and a flowing white peasant blouse, that looked like a Stevie Nicks throwback to the early '80s. I guess the apple doesn't fall far from the tree when it comes to fashion in the Swanson and Stratton families.

My mother cleared her throat, but not before giving me one of her warning looks, "We have something *special*," she emphasized that word, "to show you girls."

Even though I'd rather be hanging out with Dylan and Cura at the mall, my interest hiked up a notch. Hillary kept on texting.

"Well, ladies," Cura's mother interrupted, taking our silence for agreement to whatever awaited us inside. "Ready?"

Hillary snorted, her gaze glued to her phone. "Yeah, whatever."

After our mothers handed out flashlights with a strict warning not to wander away. I followed behind, careful not to trip or fall on the loose boards in the rickety, wrap-around front porch.

Inside, the building reeked of decades-old smoke-damage, rotting wood, mold, and other things I didn't even want to think about. Soot-colored dust coated the tattered drapes and garbage was strewn all over floor. Spider webs hung from the rafters like a canopy. I sneezed more than a few times.

"Do you think it's true?" Cura whispered.

"What?" I asked, trying not to trip over the warped floor boards.

"That this place is haunted?" she whispered a tad bit louder.

That got Hillary's attention. She put the flashlight under her face, the yellowish glow giving her skin a ghoulish look. I rolled my eyes at how annoying she was being. At least her outside now matched her insides. I almost said it aloud but stopped myself. I didn't want Mom to scold me in front of my arch enemy.

"Up to another Bloody Mary, Steph?" she snickered. Apparently, Hillary had no such restraint. Figures she'd bring up the sleepover, which my mother forced me to attend. She'd dared me to play the supernatural game with embarrassing results. Only I hadn't shared with anyone at the sleepover how that game had unleashed a paranormal presence into our world. The more I thought about it, though, the whole atmosphere inside this house would be the perfect setting for playing that game again.

"Girls, this way," Mrs. Swanson broke the tension. Hillary cackled.

I couldn't resist a parting shot.

"Are you trying out for Ghoul Number 3 in *Halloween: The Musical*?

"Screw you," Hillary hissed.

Cura and I giggled as she stormed off, tripped on a loose board, and then let out a string of curses that, according to my grandmother, would "make a sailor blush." I guess sailors were always cursing. Although, I had no idea why.

We carefully made our way up the rickety stairs,

which seemed to groan in protest. When we reached the top floor, I stopped and stared in amazement. Although the bottom floor had been trashed big time, the second floor looked almost normal. A few posters still hung on the walls announcing a Valentine's Day Dance, Alpha Phi news, and an upcoming kegger.

"Creepy, much?" Hillary asked. She bent in closer and whispered, "How weird is it that our mothers actually partied?" She shuddered.

Everyone in town had heard the rumors about the ongoing battle to save the building versus tearing it down. I'd have thought that after the fire, and the deaths of two of the sorority sisters, the county would have been quick to demolish it. But I guess there were people out there who desperately wanted to hang on to the past. I snuck a glance over at our mothers and wonderd if, in fact, they were in that category.

"Girls," Mom's voice interrupted my thoughts, "this way."

My mother strolled over to two huge oak doors, somewhat scarred but still sturdy, and opened them to reveal an altar-like stand in the middle of the darkened room. A large white-etched inverted star had been drawn on the gray floor. Tall, white-tapered candles in slender holders had been placed at each point of the star.

I hung back, taking it all in, my senses being sucker punched by the extreme decorating, which looked odd in the otherwise empty room.

"Wow!" Cura gaped wide eyed.

My sentiments exactly.

Hillary stepped into the room and pinched her nose, waving her hand in front of her. "My God, don't you think decorations are overpowering much?" she said in a nasally tone.

"Button it, young lady," her mother hissed. "I've had enough of you today."

"Yeah, yeah. Whatever."

And my mother thought *I* had a 'tude problem.

Mrs. Swanson straightened her shoulders and marched over to her daughter, and with one quick movement, snatched Hillary's phone and dropped it into her purse.

"Hey, what's your problem?" Hillary protested.

"Enough. This is important and you will shut your mouth and listen. Understand?"

Hillary glared back at her mother, who stood with her feet slightly apart and her hands on her hips. Showdown time. I expected a huge hissy fit, but after a few tense moments, Hillary flipped her long, over-processed blonde hair over her shoulders. "Whatever. Let's just get this over with." She swung around and glared at us, waiting.

When we didn't say anything, she added, "I know you guys are thinking the same thing."

I only shrugged, which got me yet another snub.

Mrs. Stratton and my mom lit the candles while Mrs. Swanson lit what smelled like sage, in a silver bowl on the altar. The scent of sweet coconut and burning sage filled the air. This was getting weirder by the minute. And definitely not in tune with what I knew about my mom. She wasn't exactly a fan of my ability to communicate with the dead nor my work with Dr. Anthony in helping murdered girls cross over. In fact, my mom hated it so much, she'd wanted me to see a shrink about it last year and almost had me committed. So why the witchy set-up?

"Girls, you're probably wondering why we're having this gathering," Mrs. Swanson said. "Before we get to the actual ceremony, we need to discuss something. Something important." Her voice went down a notch. The muted candle light cast eerie shadows on her features, which added a menacing tone to what she was saying. With one bejeweled hand, she waved to something over in the corner of the room. A large tarnished silver bowl filled with rose petals sat on a small wooden table. Beside it, a smaller bowl filled with what looked like water had a few rose petals floating in it.

"No way," Cura said. Her eyes widened. "Is this some kind of witch-thing?"

"No!" All of our mothers protested at once.

"Not that there's anything wrong with that," Cura's mom said.

Mrs. Swanson narrowed her eyes and glared at Mrs. Stratton.

"Okay..." Cura stepped back. "Come on, even I think this looks a little weird."

"It looks like some kind of initiation rite," I added. The chips and chocolate milk I'd gulped down before we left rumbled inside my stomach.

"Isn't this right up your alley, Cura?" Hillary asked, only reaffirming what everyone knew: Mrs. Stratton loved New Agey stuff. Though I knew better. My own paranormal gift might be considered dabbling with dark magic.

Cura rolled her eyes at Hillary's comment. "Uh, Stephanie meant sorority initiation." She turned back to our mothers. "Isn't it too soon for us, considering we're only juniors in high school?" Crossing her arms she continued. "I didn't know mothers organized stuff like this? Isn't it just, uh, for college girls?"

Cura had a point there.

"Another reason why I'm applying out of state." Hillary stepped away from us. Her nose wrinkled in disgust. "I knew you all were weird. This just verifies it."

Mrs. Swanson scowled, but Hillary ignored her. "Well, am I right?"

Cura nodded. "I have to agree with Hillary." She shrugged. "Sorry," she muttered, suddenly interested in her bracelet.

Lovely, I could just see how this would be played out on social media tomorrow morning.

You know Stephanie Stewart, aka Itchy Steph? Well, it looks like she's not the only girl with secrets in this town.

Then again, Hillary would have to admit she'd been here, too, along with her mom. Well, maybe not, considering how resourceful she could be with her lies and all, but still, that didn't make me feel any better. I wish I could just snap my fingers and send her wherever rude, annoying witches—substitute 'b' for 'w'—went.

"We thought you girls would like a head start on this," Mrs. Swanson said. "We loved being sorority sisters. The best part of college."

"But why here? Isn't this place condemned?" Cura asked, scrunching her eyebrows.

"Serious?" Hillary asked, moving farther away from us, as if we had the plague. "When I join a sorority, it won't be here. Or with them."

"Be nice," her mother hissed.

As if I wanted to be anywhere with Hillary anyway. Her endless whining was annoying to say the least.

I raised my hand, ignoring Hillary's dark glare.

"Count me in," I said. "I mean, yeah, this is kind of creepy, but I'd like to know what kind of initiation you guys had when you were in college. And I've heard of stranger things, why not have a ceremony?"

I turned to face Cura. "Don't you think?"

Cura frowned, glancing back and forth between me and Hillary. Then she sighed and said, "Sure, why not?"

Relief flashed over our mothers' faces along with what looked like the jitters. Curious, I waited for our mothers to tell us more of what transpired and why the place was set up like a shrine. Instead, Mrs. Swanson broke out in a nervous smile, rubbing her hands together.

"Good, now that that's been settled," Mrs. Swanson said, directing us to the silver bowl, "Please wash your hands in the basin. We must cleanse both our physical and emotional selves before we begin."

Hillary snickered. "Jeez Mom." She rolled her eyes. "Could you sound any more *Witches of Eastwick*?"

I couldn't resist snickering too.

"Enough," Mrs. Swanson said. She glared at both Hillary and me. My mother's frown seconded that.

Hillary's lip rose up in a half-smirk. "Fine."

First Hillary, then Cura dipped their hands in the bowl. When my turn came, I shot my mother a quick look and she gave me a reassuring nod. I peered into the bowl and noticed the rose petals had curled under and the edges had turned a light brown. I guess you can't always get fresh rose petals at a moment's notice. I placed my hands in the lukewarm water. Ugh! The water felt a little slimy. Where was hand sanitizer when you needed it? At least you couldn't catch any germs from ghosts. Oh, they usually showed up with a missing arm, or a hole in their chests—and my personal favorite, half-blown out brains—but no germs.

"What's next?" I asked, shaking my hands dry.

"Go stand over there." My mom pointed to the bowl on the altar.

"Are we going to sing Kumbaya next?" Hillary smirked.

Cura started to giggle.

Hillary's mother scowled.

My mother frowned.

Cura's mom let out an exaggerated sigh. "Let's just tell them now."

"Tell us what?" Hillary asked.

The moms glanced at each other as though they were hesitating over who should start talking first. "Have you noticed anything out of the ordinary happening lately? Things you can't explain?" my mother asked. "Around town? At school?"

I glanced at my mom suspiciously. What was she

getting at? She knew very well that I helped dead girls cross over. Was she planning on revealing my secret to everyone in the room?

"Come to think of it, yeah, there have been," Hillary said, giving me a pointed glare. "What's that have to do with us being here?"

My face burned.

I shot my mom a panicked look and waited for her to share the whole burning coffee house incident where I'd sent Mark, the demon, back to hell, or where ever damned souls go. I hated that I'd been tempted by Mark's good looks, only for him to try to take away my ability to help the dead by kidnapping and harming Dylan. I shudder thinking what would have happened to Dylan if I didn't confront Mark.

"Something happened, back in 1990," my mother said, then surreptitiously gave a quick head shake my way with a warning look in her eyes. "And with what's been happening recently, we felt we needed to do something."

Relief washed over me that my mom wasn't going to "out" my paranormal activities, but now my curiosity shot way up. Before I could open my mouth to ask what happened Hillary jumped in.

"What exactly happened?" Hillary asked.

My mother and Mrs. Swanson squirmed. Usually I'd think this would be funny, but not now. Resentment gnawed at me that my mother felt she had to drag my best friend and former friend to this meeting in order to answer my questions. What did they have to do with all the paranormal stuff going on? Everything was connected to me, not them.

"Well that night of November 3rd, 1990—something happened. Something terrible. We did something that night that kind of changed things," my mother said, avoiding our eyes.

"Speak for yourself, Jean," Hillary's mother said. "It

was *you-know-who's* big idea to actually call on the dead."

Hillary gaped at her mother. Clearly, she had no idea Mrs. Swanson had dabbled in witchcraft in her youth.

"It didn't stop you from agreeing to do it," my mom retorted, surprising me with her back bone by standing up to Mrs. Swanson.

Mrs. Swanson looked embarrassed. Mrs. Stratton sighed again.

"Anyway," Mom resumed speaking, "*we* didn't know that it would actually work. The spell that is. Somehow, when we messed with the spell, it affected us and we're worried you girls might also be affected. We need to stop it from happening again."

Oh, just flippin' great.

"And you think repeating that spell won't do the same thing it did back then?" I asked.

Before any of the moms could answer, Cura spoke up. "Wait, you mean a dead person actually showed up like a real ghost?" She looked nervous. "And from what you're saying, it must have been an evil ghost right?"

Hillary turned back to me. She had that smug, squinty look in her eyes that she always gets when she's about to pounce. "Oh, I get it. This has something to do with you, doesn't it?"

"Seriously? I wasn't even born yet."

Her mouth thinned. "I'm not talking about back then. I'm talking about what's been going on now . . ."

Mrs. Swanson saved me from an angry retort by stepping forward. The candlelight played tricks over her cosmetic-surgery-enhanced face, giving her a ghoulish appearance. "We don't want any of you to go through the same thing," she whispered. "That's why we need to do this right."

Oh, my god, this did have to do with me. Whatever spell they cast in 1990 had already screwed with me, and they were worried it would mess up Cura and Hillary.

That's what this was all about. At least, now I knew where I got my "ability" from.

"So, they weren't lying," Hillary said, her gaze drilling holes in me. "I thought everyone was just joking, but they weren't. So, you really saw Allison? Wait," she held her hand up. "I don't want to know."

"Huh?" Cura asked. "Allison? Our friend Allison? She's dead. What are you talking about?"

I took a deep breath and faced both of them.

"Ghosts. Spirits. Yeah, whatever you call them, I can see them," I said. "It started after Allison died." Allison had been my best friend when we were thirteen, and she was the first dead girl to ask for my help. I braced myself for the laughter and snide comments, sure they'd be thrown my way.

Cura's eyes widened. "You didn't think you could share something like that with me? She looked shocked and angry and sad at the same time. "I'm your best friend."

"Now Cura," her mother jumped in, "it's not Stephanie's fault. "

My friend folded her arms across her chest and turned to her mom. "I can't believe she'd think so little of me to not confide in me." She glanced back at me, a world of hurt reflected in her eyes. "I thought we were tight. Apparently not."

I winced. How could I even begin to explain all of this to Cura? *Sorry, but I didn't want you to think I was a freak and that's why I didn't tell you?*

"Are you saying, we're going to become like-like *her*?" Hillary said, pointing at me like I was some sort of freak.

"Uh, hello, my name's Stephanie," I said. I knew this would happen. My worst nightmare was coming true. My best friend Cura was upset with me about not telling her about my so-called gift and my worst enemy Hillary was gleeful about the potential gossip she could spread around school. So much for keeping a low profile. I had my mom's sorority sisters to thank for that. I wonder if it was Mom's idea or theirs? It didn't matter anyway, the cat was out of the bag as they say.

"Whatever." Hillary turned back to her mother, waiting for confirmation.

"We hope not. That is—" Mrs. Swanson backtracked no doubt, to cover up. The damage was done anyway, since Cura was still giving me shade. "We hope that with this ceremony, we can erase their presence and they then can't bother you," Mrs. Swanson finished and clasped her hands together with finality.

"And hopefully, Stephanie won't be bothered anymore either." Mom added, reaching out and squeezing my shoulder.

"Seriously, that's the best you can say?" I shrugged off her hand. I was beyond furious. Pissed was more like it. It was obvious that my mom didn't think that helping murdered girls cross over was worthy of respect or support. She clearly thought I was a freak, too, and wanted to put an end to my visions.

"Steph, why don't you at least listen?" Cura finally spoke up. "Maybe they can help."

One part of me wanted to get the heck out of there, but if, just if, this so-called ceremony did work, would I be happy to go back to the way things were before? What would happen to those lost girls who couldn't find the light? Who would help them cross over? "Can you actually do that?" I asked, looking at my mom. "Make them go away?" When my mother didn't say yay or nay, I added, "Forever?"

My mom smiled encouragingly. "Why don't we find out?" My mother strolled over to the table. A glow radiated from the silver bowl. It was engraved with markings that looked like Celtic symbols I'd seen in a book at the library when I had to do some research for an art project. "Lisa, you start," she said.

Mrs. Swanson motioned to Hillary, "You can be first."

Disappointment hit. You'd think since I was the only one of us seeing dead girls, I should be first, but I didn't want to jinx anything so I kept quiet.

Hillary's eyes widened and for a moment I thought for sure she'd waltz right out of the room and leave us. "You sure this will really help?" Then she narrowed her eyes and pointed at me. "You know, for us not to be like her?"

Typical snarky Hillary.

"Just get your behind over here," Mrs. Swanson hissed.

"Fine. Anything that will keep me from turning into Miss *Sixth Sense* over there. I'll do it."

As Hillary passed me, she slowed for a moment. Our eyes locked. Anger and resentment flared in her gaze, like she blamed me for all this trouble she had to go through. It wasn't my fault I could see dead people. Heck, if truth be told, it was our mothers who were to blame for all this. I clenched my hands together, my fingernails biting into the soft flesh of my palms. How I wished I could smack her.

Mrs. Swanson motioned to the chair facing the table. Hillary scowled but sat down. Her mother dipped her finger into the silver bowl with rose petals and water and traced a wet finger across Hillary's forehead.

"We initiate you with this water, and make you pure and clean," Hillary's mom said, while her finger traced the shape of an eye. "Let this third eye see the truth and not be a vessel for the Evil One. Not now. Not ever more." She finished by making a cross-like motion with her finger on Hillary's forehead.

Cross. Why use a cross and not another symbol? I made wooden crosses to help the dead cross over. I squirmed as a sick dread swirled in my stomach.

The third eye thing was different, though. Hanging

with Dr. Anthony had exposed me to a bunch of different spiritual things including Tibetan prayer wheels.

Cura went next. And then me.

My mother and Cura's mother then gave us each a lit candle. Mrs. Swanson motioned us to kneel on the floor, around the pentagram. Hillary took out a tissue and wiped the chair before she sat. Her mother then handed her a candle.

The flames from the candles danced back and forth.

"You need to repeat this chant together now," Mrs. Swanson said, ignoring Hillary's eye roll.

"Whatever darkness might be here, we summon lightness to drive you out."

This was all a little too simple. I hoped it would work, but I wasn't holding my breath.

"Girls?" My mother asked, "You need to repeat it three times, in unison."

"Okay, let's just do this and get it over with," I said, taking a deep breath while trying not to extinguish the flame.

"Whatever darkness might be here, we summon lightness to drive you out."

Cura's voice blended with mine. I gave a pointed stare in Hillary's direction.

"Fine, this is so lame," she said.

"Whatever darkness might be here, we summon lightness to drive you out."

Just then I felt an icy blast of air. Each of our lights were snuffed out. And a buzzing sound erupted at the back of the room. It sounded like a bunch of bees. I turned to see if anyone else had heard it. Nope.

Hillary's eyes opened. A half-smile crept up her face. If I didn't know any better I'd think she was actually enjoying this. Or maybe she was just planning her next attack on me?

The backs of my legs started to itch and burn big

[19]

time—the signal that the dead were about to show up. I was still trying to get used to that feeling. It was kinda weird, but then again, seeing dead people was pretty weird. The fact that the creepy, crawly, burning feeling was kicking into high gear did not bold well.

The temperature plummeted even more.

I blinked once and then my eyes widened.

No, no, this couldn't be happening! Not now!

I saw a girl. Omigod, I knew her! Leaves and broken twigs matted her dark, brown hair. I gasped. A huge gash cut clear across her forehead. Blood dripped onto the floor, leaving a messy puddle.

She stumbled toward Hillary, whose face went completely white. Could Hillary see her too?

"Where am I?" the girl asked. I searched my memory for her name . . . And then I remembered: Emily Jones, a friend of Hillary's and head of the cheerleading squad, or she had been until she transferred to a high school in Florida so she could live with her dad and his new family. The gossip around the school was that she and her mom were always fighting because of her mom's revolving door of boyfriends and constant drinking, so her dad got his lawyer involved and they came to an arrangement that she would live with him for a while.

It sounded like hundreds of fingernails scratching down a chalkboard in Dolby Surround Sound. NOT good.

The moldy scent of old, forgotten things filled the air.

"Oh my God." Hillary jumped up out of the chair and pointed to the corner. "Why is Emily Jones here? Is she . . . . dead? She turned to her mom in a panic. W- what did you do to me?" She screamed.

"This isn't supposed to be happening," Mrs. Swanson shouted. "We were trying to prevent you from having visions."

"Well, that's not happening is it?" Hillary sounded like a screechy mouse. "I thought you said this would help?"

Emily the ghost, opened her mouth and began to scream. Hillary's response was not helping. The screams echoed around the room.

Cura scrunched her eyes shut and covered her ears as she slid to the floor. "Stop. Please, make it stop."

I wished Hillary and Cura would stop their screaming so we could help Emily and find out what had happened to her.

Cura's screams increased.

I took a step toward my friend, wanting to help her. At this point, I was sort of used to seeing and hearing weird, supernatural stuff, but Cura wasn't. And take it from me—the first time it happens is pretty darn scary.

"You." Mrs. Swanson's long, French-manicured finger pointed at me. Her eyes venomous.

I froze at the look of scorn on her face.

"You're just like your aunt," she hissed. "You channeled this evil to prevent us from completing the ritual. Monster."

What? First of all, I was pissed off that my mom's friend just called me a *monster*. Considering they were the ones who started all of this. Second of all, I had no idea what she was talking about. What did my mom's sister have to do with this? Mom told me she died a long time ago. I glanced at my mother, who looked terrified. I knew that all three moms couldn't see or hear the ghost but they could certainly see how we were reacting to it.

Mrs. Swanson lashed out at my mom. "Wasn't it bad enough Karen dragged us into this twenty-five years ago?" Her face was red and mottled with anger. "She played with fire and paid the ultimate price. And now, your daughter is going to do the same to these girls—"

Another scream from Emily Jones cut off Mrs. Swanson's next words. High pitched and shrill, it persisted until I thought I'd go crazy. I'm not sure why she was screaming. Dead people were kind of odd. Sometimes they hummed, sometimes they cried and cried, sometimes they laughed. Emily had been a cheerleader and was used to shouting cheers, so maybe that had something to do with it.

"We need to get out of here! Now! I shouldn't have brought you." Mom grabbed my arm, trying to pull me away.

I wanted nothing more than to get the heck out of there, but I knew I couldn't. "No." I shoved her hand away. "I can't leave Cura. I know what to do, she doesn't."

"Leave it," my mother said.

"No Mom! You leave it. You obviously had no problem messing with the supernatural when you were in college, now you want to run away?" With that I turned on my heel, leaving her gaping. I had to help Cura. That's all that mattered to me right now.

Emily hovered close to Cura, her bony hands reaching for her. "Why aren't you saying anything?" Emily cried out. "Why isn't anyone?"

Cura was curled in a fetal position, her hands clasped over her ears and her eyes closed.

I barreled through the ghost making her vanish.

An icy chill cut through my body, as I felt the ghost splinter around me. "Cura?" I crouched down next to my friend, laying my hand on her shoulder.

She opened her eyes and glanced up at me, mouthing, "Ohmigod."

"It's going to be okay—" A tight grip on my shoulder stopped me.

"Stephanie." Cura's mom said. "Maybe you'd better leave with your mom, I'm taking Cura home." Unlike Mrs. Swanson, sympathy was etched on her face.

She pulled Cura up, who muttered some nonsensical words. Pain lanced my heart, worse than anything I'd ever felt before. It was hard enough for me to accept what I was, but now that Cura knew, would I lose her too?

"Help me." Emily reached out to touch me, but her hand went through my arm. I shook my head and muttered, "I will help you, but I can't right now, it's too nuts here. Look for me later." My mom grabbed my hand and pulled me out. Hillary and her mom had already left and so had Cura and her mom.

As we rushed out of the room, I glanced over my shoulder at poor Emily standing there with her head cocked to the side, looking so lost . . . But I knew she would find me again.

Dead girls always knew how to find me.

CHAPTER 2

Funny how a little thing like a dead chick showing up at a witching ceremony can really clear the room. Or in this case, a condemned sorority building. I'm sure there was a cheesy horror movie idea in there, but I didn't want to stick around to figure out the ending.

Emily's screams bounced down the staircase after me like a rubber ball from Hell. I dashed down the rickety staircase, on my mother's heels. I almost toppled us both the rest of the way after I tripped on a loose board.

Mom yanked me out the front door and we ran to the car. Getting in, Mom quickly pressed a button and I heard the reassuring thwack of the door locks sealing us in. Whew. She gunned the engine of our Toyota Rav4 and sped away. I swear she must have left tire marks.

Neither of us spoke. I knew she had to be pissed at me for trying to "do my thing." Well, whatever. I was pissed with her for lying to me.

After a few minutes, I peeked at her from the corner of my eye. Her face was a frozen mask that had nothing to do with her bi-monthly trips to the dermatologist. She didn't look my way or comment on the mess back at the sorority house. They should have realized that they were playing with fire. I mean, it didn't take a rocket scientist to figure out I was one huge ghost magnet. The ceremony only made things worse, not better, because now Cura and Hillary could see dead girls, too. The I-5 exit quickly flashed into view. The car swung to the right, merging into traffic.

"Why?" I muttered. "Did you actually think you could strip me of my ability? You know the crazy thing is, even though I was starting to get used to this whole Rescuer thing, a part of me just wants to be like I was before. Just a normal teenage girl whose biggest worry is an upcoming math test and not getting a zit on her nose before the next school dance. I slumped down in the seat, "I should have known better."

Still nothing. Mom kept driving as if we'd just finished an all-day shopping spree and couldn't wait to get home to try on our new clothes.

"Mom?" I whispered, when I really wanted to scream and shake her.

She tapped her acrylic nails against the steering wheel.

Tap. Tap. Tap.

One of her nails broke halfway off. Ouch, that must hurt considering her real nails were thin and brittle.

"Mom . . . MOM!"

"Okay, I was wrong. I was worried the ceremony wouldn't work, but I had to at least try."

"How could you betray me like this? How could you let them all know about my abilities?"

More silence.

"It's not like that," she finally said. "You wouldn't understand."

I snickered. "Oh, sure. Typical lame-o excuse."

"It's not an excuse but the truth. And no, I didn't betray you. I only agreed to this because I thought it would help you and the other girls. Never did I think it would go off the rails like this."

I snorted. "That's an understatement."

"I didn't think—"

"That a dead girl would show up and ruin the show?"

"We did other spells when we were in college, but we never experienced anything like this."

"That's what Hillary's mom said. This has something to do with that fire at your sorority house, doesn't it? You guys called on the dead."

She blew out a breath. "Yes."

I clenched my hands together. This made absolutely no sense. My mother had been so against my Rescuer work while the truth was she was responsible for my abilities. Cura probably won't ever talk to me again and Hillary will probably spread gossip about me all over school.

Then Dylan's grandmother's warning flashed back: *You're at the crossroads. Choose wisely.*

Did she know what would happen? What else could she have meant by warning me to "choose wisely?" If that had been the case, I failed big time.

Why hadn't I listened? Too late now.

"Mom," I directed my anger at her. "I don't know what happened, but I do know those dead girls need my help."

My mother narrowed her eyes. "That's one reason why I brought you. Admitting the dead need you is . . . well, it's not normal."

"What exactly is *normal*, anyway?"

"Trust me when I say this. Nothing good comes from communicating with the dead."

"As if I have a choice in the matter," I said. "Trust me, if I had a choice? I'd rather not be helping dead girls cross over. I'd rather be home working on my term paper. But I can't. I have to help them because they are drawn to me. They need my help."

"You do have a choice. Or at least I hoped you did."

"No, it's clear from what happened back there," I pointed back to the sorority house we'd left behind, "that I don't have a choice."

My whole body trembled with anger and frustration. For a blip of a moment back there, I'd actually thought my mom had the ability to make things all better, like

[26]

she used to when I was a kid and a had tummy ache or a cold. But that sure as heck didn't happen. Chicken soup and a bedtime story were not going to fix this.

My mother threw a glance my way, her eyes drooped in sadness. "Sorry. I really had hoped this would have gone better."

"That's all you can say? You're sorry?" I stared out the window watching the passing scenery. "You heard Mrs. Swanson," I grumbled. "According to her, I'm a monster." I glanced back at Mom, my eyes filled with tears. "D-do you think that too?"

"Honey, you know I don't think that."

"Well," I wiped my face with my sleeve, "You could have fooled me."

I slouched down, and turned back to the window.

My mother did the whole exaggerated sigh thing. "I didn't think the gals would still be holding it over me—us. If I'd known they were going to react like that, I wouldn't have dragged you there."

"Was Aunt Karen a Rescuer too?"

The elusive aunt that no one spoke about at our house. I knew she must have done something really bad because Mom always got upset whenever her name came up. I didn't realize how much of a black sheep she was until tonight.

Mom sighed. "Yes." She reached for my hand and squeezed. "But, honey, you're nothing like her."

"Did she start that fire back in 1990?" Somehow, I kind of knew she must have, but I had to hear it from my mother.

"I don't like talking about this."

"Come on, Mom. You've got to tell me. This has to do with me, too." I glanced at her. "And BTW, I'm sick of how everyone pussyfoots around any mention of Aunt Karen. Did she or didn't she do a bad spell that backfired and killed people?"

Mom said nothing at first. She stared through the

windshield and drove on. I figured end of discussion. Then she spoke. "Karen and I were a little older than you when she told me she saw the dead, but at first I didn't believe her. Then she suggested a "fun" game one night and asked a few friends to come."

A few friends who happened to be Hillary's and Cura's mothers right?

"Yes, and a few others."

Curious, I waited for her to say who else, but her lips were tightly shut.

"I take it that whatever Karen did worked? That you all saw the dead?"

My mother nodded.

"One thing led to another. So, Karen decided we should have our own secret group."

A foreboding overcame any surprise I had at my mother's confession. Something must have happened to make them all so scared. I wanted to know exactly what that had been, but one look at my mother's tight face and I knew I had to go about this in another way or else she'd clam up.

I settled back against the car seat. "So, what did you do after that?"

"None of us could believe what we'd seen. At first, we were each hesitant to admit we'd actually seen a ghost, but once we all fessed up that we had, it changed everything. We all felt special that we could do something that no one else could do." A small smile tugged at her lips.

"I bet."

Mom's eyes started to tear up. "At first I loved the fact that Karen was no longer "the outcast". That my friends began to accept her. And she was thrilled that they all looked at her like she was cool, you know?"

I nodded, knowing how superficial girls could be, but I couldn't fault my aunt for savoring the sensation considering how most teens want the same thing—to have friends and be part of the group.

"Then Karen started coming up with these strange ideas." Mom said, shaking her head. "Karen suggested we go further. We had a responsibility to help not only the dead but others with this new-found ability we now shared. She even thought we could actually go to the Other Side without dying."

I stared at her. "Seriously? You actually thought you could do that?" I had to admit that idea never crossed my mind. Would I want to try it? It seemed way too out there for me and way too dangerous.

Each rescue I did had a big positive impact on me. It's pretty cool being touched by the light, but what would it be like to actually walk into that light?

My mother continued, "Karen told us she found a ritual from some old dusty book in the archives of the CA State University library."

"They actually have books like that there?"

"You'd be surprised."

I didn't know whether to be freaked out or curious.

"She had us try a ritual that she claimed would help us communicate better with the dead. But it went terribly wrong." Mom shuddered.

"How?" I whispered.

"She brought back a dark presence. We all felt it. I should have spoken out, stopped her from continuing the spell, but my sister was very strong-willed."

"Omigod, so she messed with a demon."

Memories of Mark resurfaced. My previous boyfriend who turned out to be a demon. I hadn't summoned him, but his attraction to me had almost cost me my soul and Dylan's life.

"Yes and it caused the fire and . . . deaths."

Wow. Could that be one of the reasons behind the animosity? My aunt had been the catalyst for a horrific event that killed one of Hillary's family members. Not to mention Dylan's mom's sister.

Mom's hands gripped the steering wheel. "God, what I'd do for a cigarette right now."

Whenever Mom gets upset or anxious, she smokes. Dad hates that she does it, and so do I, but it's understandable. I bet she gave Marlboro tons of business in the last month alone, thanks to my new-found calling.

"Mom, that girl back at the sorority house? I know her or knew her."

She turned back to me. "Who?"

"The dead girl who showed up. I think she was a girl who used to go to our school. But that doesn't make sense. She moved to Florida a year ago. I only help girls who are killed here in Sacramento."

"Oh, honey, I hope it wasn't her."

I nodded. "Yeah, maybe I'm wrong . . . I hope I'm wrong."

Mom let out a loud sigh. "Let's just get home. I think we've had more than enough excitement for the day."

I placed my hand over hers. "Mom, I'm not like your sister. I'm not being foolish and I don't have any crazy notions about going to the Other Side. Okay, maybe I almost did fall for a demon, but I learned my lesson. I won't fall for a trick like that again."

"My sister didn't start out that way either . . . She really wanted to make a difference," Mom whispered, mostly to herself. When I didn't say anything, she focused her attention back on the road, "When you don't know what kind of dark stuff is out there, especially with demons, how can you protect yourself? Karen wasn't able to stop herself and look what happened . . ."

"Mom, I'm smart. I won't let that happen to me."

Mom skidded to the side of the road and slammed on her brakes. As I grabbed the dashboard, my stomach lunged.

"Mom! What's wrong?"

She grabbed my shoulders. "Don't ever for one

moment think you're evil." She gave my shoulders a squeeze. "You're not. Okay?"

I stared back at her. Dark smudges lined her otherwise perfect makeup. Pain and worry and, maybe, fear flashed in her eyes. For a brief moment, I wanted to be the perfect, normal teen daughter just to make that look go away. But how could I ignore the dead girls when they come to me for help. How could I shut myself off from those girls when they visit me looking so confused and lost and not knowing what to do? Whatever kind of gift I had, it attracted dead girls. Girls who had been murdered or killed in some tragic way. Girls who couldn't find their way to the light on their own. They needed help. I was some kind of beacon for them. I couldn't turn my back on them. I just couldn't.

"But if you insist on rescuing those lost girls, you know that you'll put yourself at risk to the evil on the Other Side, and sometimes an evil entity can lure someone good into doing something dangerous or bad."

"Mom, it's not like that for me." Frustrated, I pulled back. "You weren't there at the coffee house when I had to battle Mark. I know it's possible to help spirits cross over and drive back the undead. "That's not evil!"

Mom put the car back into drive and got back on the freeway. For a while she said nothing but her hands grew white from her grip on the steering wheel.

"That's the same dangerous thinking that got my sister in trouble," she whispered. Then she looked over at me. "You have to be careful or else..."

"Or else what? I'll become some undead chick? Ain't gonna happen in my life time."

Mom let out a loud sigh. "I hope you're right."

We finally pulled into the driveway. "Just be careful, please." She grabbed my hand and squeezed.

I released the seatbelt and opened the door. "Fine, will do."

I was so tired of all these big dramatic "reveals." My

life was turning into some kind of '80s night-time soap. Was my mom telling me the truth about Aunt Karen? Did she die because of getting mixed up with the dark side? Or was Mom just trying to scare me? For all I knew, my aunt Karen might be in some mental hospital, just like Dylan's grandmother, doped up and shut away.

Mom tried to put me away before. No way would I let that happen again.

CHAPTER 3

Once inside my room, I quickly stripped off the white dress and hose, kicking them to the corner. I rummaged through my dirty clothes pile and threw on a pair of shorts and a Sucks-to-be-Me t-shirt.

How do you spell fool? S.T.E.P.H.

I grabbed my pillow, holding it tight and screamed into its softness. I directed all my anger and hurt into the cotton cover.

I was furious at my mother and her friends for what they had set in motion all those years ago, and then for thinking they could fix it now. But I was also mad at myself for thinking that they could actually help me. Don't get me wrong, there is something awesome about being able to help a lost spirit find her way, but it comes with a heavy price. Especially when your best friend now thinks you're a freak.

My anger boiled over and wouldn't leave me. I felt as if I'd guzzled a six-pack of Red Bull and couldn't sit still. I tried to use my pent-up energy to finish my homework, but I couldn't stop thinking of the look on Cura's face. Shock and hurt and, probably, disgust.

She couldn't accept the truth of who I was and what I could do. When Hillary had spread those rumors about me being able to see dead Allison, Cura had bugged me to tell her if I had an ability to see the dead. I'd said no. I'd kept the truth from her. Should I have told her? No matter how I rationalized keeping my secrets from my best friend, deep down I felt like crap. I could have at least trusted her enough to confide in her. Now, it might be too late. That look of hurt in her eyes was haunting me. But I was also mad about her reaction, and mad at myself for not telling her earlier on.

I strolled over to the bedroom window and yanked the partition blinds open. I snuck a peek at Dylan's house across the street. I glanced at my watch and saw it was almost 11 p.m. I knew I probably shouldn't bug him this late, but I needed to feel his arms around me right now. I longed to snuggle into the warmth of his body and get a whiff of his tangy scent that reminded me of the ocean.

Plus, I needed someone who believed in me. Rescuer or not.

I took another peek, first checking for the familiar Beemer that meant his mother, alias Ms. Crazy, might be home. I didn't want to chance that she might have heard from either Cura's mom or Mrs. Swanson about the disastrous evening.

That familiar uncomfortable feeling of not being wanted over at their home shot through me, but left once I noticed Dylan's mother's car missing.

Whew.

Instead, a lopsided happy antenna topper smiled at me from the beat up Toyota Truck that I'd grown to love. Faded, red paint and gritty sand from Half Moon Bay caked its tires.

I rushed to the night table, grabbing my cell. There were some unanswered texts from Dylan. I didn't want to waste time reading them when I could just go over and tell him what had happened.

I texted: *R u there? Can we talk?*

A minute later a message came up: *Sure.*

I grabbed my trusted black hoodie and shoved my cell in the pocket. Opening the window, I climbed out and shimmied down the lattice.

As I crossed the street, I could see Dylan's silhouette through a half-parted curtain, in his bedroom. My body grew very warm, as I remembered our last kiss. Long and sweet. His kisses tasted like Half Moon Bay. Everything about him made me think of the beach and the ocean. Soothing.

"What's so urgent?" Dylan leaned out the window sill, while slipping a faded Peace Out t-shirt over his head and teasing me with a flash of his killer abs. Too quick they were covered up. I longed to run my fingers down that buff chest of his, kissing the valley . . .

Jeez, Louise. I looked down, shoving my hands in my pockets. Heat scorched my face, along with other parts that tingled, begging to be closer to Dylan.

"Uh." I shuffled some loose leaves around, ignoring the sudden warmth spreading throughout my body.

"Well?" Humor touched Dylan's voice. "Somehow I doubt you came over to rake the leaves."

I looked up. "Can I come up?"

"Hasn't stopped you before." He nodded to the side, and then walked back inside his room.

Propped behind the huge oak tree was a ladder, hidden from view of the street. I scrambled on up. We'd been doing this ever since we were kids.

Posters of the latest surfing competitions, along with a few trophies, cluttered his room. Dylan kicked a couple of balled-up shirts into his already crammed closet, which threatened to explode at any moment. An open chemistry textbook, a notebook, and a stash of Cheetos sprawled across his desk.

I plopped down on the cozy blue comforter on his bed, surprised that he'd taken the time to straighten it up. Usually it was just a crumpled mass of sheets and blankets. Although I was still feeling crappy from the mess back at the abandoned sorority house, being this close to Dylan, and in his room, sent other messages throughout my body. I found it hard to resist spooning into his warmth. Even more comforting than chocolate. And that was saying a lot.

"So. What's up?" he asked, wrapping his arms around me as we leaned back against the headboard.

"You won't believe what just happened."

He cocked his head. "Try me."

I sighed. "I just got back from the weirdest meeting—if you could call it that."

"So that's why you didn't answer my texts?"

I turned to him. "Yeah, it was next to impossible with what I was going through."

"So, it has nothing to do with chem?" He grinned, but when I didn't say anything he continued, "You know we have a test tomorrow, right?"

I thumped my forehead. "Just great. Figures. Today has been a totally weird day and I completely forgot about the test."

"What's weird? I'd think you'd be used to things out of the norm." He brushed off my concerns as if stuff like seeing dead girls was an every day occurrence. Okay, yes, it was, but when your best friend and ex-friend could see them, too—it classifies it as weird. I didn't know whether to share this latest development with him.

I smacked him. "Gee, thanks for reminding me what a freak I am."

He raised his hands up in protest. "Hey, just saying it as I see it."

"Believe it or not, there are other people out there who can see the dead." I stopped and waited for his comment.

"What are you saying?" He frowned. "There's more people like you out there?"

I sighed. "Yup, you can say that again." I picked at the black polish on my thumb.

Dylan got up and walked to his desk. He started flipping through the pages of his chemistry book as though he were looking for answers there. I fidgeted in place, debating whether or not to leave.

Then Dylan slammed his chem book shut and

muttered, "I kind of figured if you saw them and the good doc did too, then it only meant others could, too, like..."

"Your grandmother," I whispered. Now would be the time to fill him in on how she'd been right, but after our visit at the hospital. Dylan had refused to speak about her. So, I said nothing.

"Yeah, like her," he muttered, picking up his pencil and tapping it on the book.

"No, this is different," I finally said. "I kind of told Mom what I do and well, she said she could help. Only her definition of helping turned into a disaster."

"Man, I'm sorry Steph." Dylan pushed the half-eaten bag of Cheetos aside and sat next to me again. "You already knew your mother must have had some idea about your abilities."

"Yeah . . . and I kinda wished she could have helped me. . ." I hung my head. "But now I wish she hadn't even tried because everything is worse."

Dylan stared at me. "I hate to ask. How worse?"

"Cura and Hillary worse."

"They were there?" Surprised, he pulled back. "Why?"

"So were their mothers. We all met at that abandoned sorority house. You know the one by the bridge."

He nodded.

"Well, they did this weird ceremony thing and then a dead girl showed up. I think it was Emily Jones. It looked a lot like her, but it was hard to tell because—you know—she was dead and a ghost."

"But she's in Florida with her dad," Dylan said. "Don't tell me you're now doing cross country rescues."

"No, not that I know of. Maybe I'm wrong, though Hillary did say her name."

Dylan let out a low-pitched whistle. "You're kidding me, right? He shook his head. "But you know that kind of makes sense in a weird way considering all the rumors about that deserted sorority house . . ."

When I didn't say anything, he went on, "They were in that sorority weren't they? When that big fire happened?"

I nodded. I mean, what else could I really say? Finding out my mom and her gal pals were involved in some kind of dark witchcraft stuff back in the day was weird enough, but realizing that their actions may have triggered this "ability" I have is too much for me to handle right now.

"Man, that's totally wacked," he said.

"Tell me about it."

Dylan pushed back a stray lock of my hair. "Steph, you know I'm with you on this, right?"

"Yeah, but what about—?"

"Shush, you talk too much." Dylan leaned in and kissed me. Slow at first, then more intense.

Then he pulled away. "Dang, girl. We can see this through, okay?"

Staring up into his eyes, I melted.

How I hoped he was right.

CHAPTER 4

Any warm fuzzy feelings I had from my visit with Dylan dissolved into vapor the next morning when I got to school. My stomach was doing back flips knowing that I had to face Cura and Hillary. No matter how much I wanted to skip school, I knew that would only prolong the inevitable. I just hoped they wouldn't mention our version of *Nightmare on Elm Street*.

Right now, I needed positive thoughts—the rainbow and puppy-dog kind. Just to be safe, I brought a can of Cura's favorite sugary drink: strawberry Fanta. I concealed the smuggled beverage in my backpack to avoid the over-zealous "good" food police, aka the teachers, who were constantly confiscating any junk food and candy they saw and lecturing us about the "perils of too much sugar, fat, and preservatives." *Sheesh.* Like we didn't already know. And with all the stress in my life, what was so bad about having a soda every now and then?

A sudden chill caused me to snuggle inside my jacket. The gloomy weather tail-gated me right to the entrance of Sutter High. The hallways weren't so packed this early in the morning. I made my way to my locker bay, head down, avoiding any eye contact. Maybe no one would bother me if I pretended I wasn't there.

A couple of kids were chatting about the upcoming Cone concert. Posters announcing the event were plastered everywhere on campus. Retro-looking with black-on-red, they stood out next to the usual posters of club meetings: Chess Club, Drama Club, Computer Club, aka geek central.

I sighed.

Cura had hinted earlier she'd wanted to go to the concert scheduled to take place over Christmas break. At the time I thought it would be a great way to get out and have some fun that wouldn't involve a cross or a dead chick.

I glanced around but saw no sign of Cura. Maybe she was at my locker, popping gum and fidgeting, as per Cura's usual routine.

A few lockers down, a guy and a girl were bringing new meaning to saying good morning. You'd think the guy was going to swallow her whole. *Ugh!* I kept walking. If Cura had been walking beside me she'd probably say "TMI for that PDI" while snapping her gum, machine-gun style. I needed her spunk and positive outlook on things right now. I made my way down the crowded hall and spied Cura in front of her locker. Maybe I could try talking to her? A group of kids were milling around her, so I couldn't see if she was in a good mood or a bad mood or just neutral.

I dragged my feet, wondering how I was going to broach the subject. Should I state the obvious—*Yeah so, I see dead people*—then roll my eyes, and laugh? Nah, probably not a good idea, considering she was mad at me for not telling her in the first place.

All these thoughts vanished when Cura turned in my direction. I stopped in shock. Cura's usual retro-thrift-store style, army boots, torn stockings, mini skirt, and denim jacket was noticeably absent in favor of a short-pleated dress in a daisy, floral print, a pale yellow-knit sweater, and cream-colored, suede, lace-up, ankle boots. If I didn't know any better I'd think she raided her fashionista cousin Courtney's closet.

I hesitated, not sure whether to turn around and forget I even entertained the thought to talk.

No, that's not what a friend would do. I took a deep breath, counted to three, and marched over.

Cura didn't look up, but instead rummaged around in her locker, through the crumpled candy wrappers, rainbow-colored pens, and glittery notebooks. A few old York Peppermint Pattie silver wrappers fell out. Photos of her family and the cute guy Erick, from the latest Vampire TV show, hung on the inside of her locker door, but not the photo of us together from a trip to Disneyland last summer.

I suddenly felt sick to my stomach, wishing I could just erase the last twenty-four hours. I may as well get this over with.

I cleared my throat. "Uh, Cura?"

She whipped around, her smile quickly turning into a frown. Make-up failed to cover the dark circles under her eyes. She turned away, pulled a huge, science textbook out of her bag and plunked it down on the bottom shelf. The loud thump made me wince.

I took another tentative step closer.

"Ok, I know you're pissed and all, but come on, can't we talk about this?" When she persisted with the silent treatment, I added, "Right?" I gulped, searching for any acknowledgment. None came.

She banged her locker shut, making the other lockers rattle. Whirling around, she faced me. Her narrowed eyes and frown told me all I needed to know.

"I don't know what's going on, but you are mega freaking me out," Cura said, folding her arms. "And frankly I don't want to know."

"I tried to tell you, really I did."

She shook her head. "You know I would have listened, and even believed you, if you told me that you actually saw dead people. That's what hurts. That you didn't trust me enough to tell me what was going on with you."

"That's not fair," I protested. "I was trying to deal

[41]

with that nasty Hillary gossiping about me. There was so much going on . . ." I bit my bottom lip to keep it from trembling. "I was having a hard time coping and I just wanted to try to have a normal life and not have my best friend look at me the way you looked at me yesterday at the freak fest."

Cura's face looked like a stone statue. Silence.

"I'm sorry I didn't tell you. I'm so sorry . . ." I knew my eyes were tearing up and I couldn't just start bawling in the hallway. So, I took a deep breath. "Can we please start over?" I asked.

Cura shook her head. "I don't know . . . " Then she let out an exaggerated sigh. "I wish it were that easy."

Just then Cura winced, covering her ears.

I stared at her, then scanned the hallways to see if any ghosts were walking around.

Nope.

"What's going on?" I asked, touching her shoulder. "Tell me."

She blinked once, twice, before lowering her hands. She glanced over her shoulder, checking out the area. Then she faced me. "I just..." she shook her head. "I can't deal with this—any of this right now."

"Okay, that's fair."

She held her hand out in front of her, interrupting me. "I can't talk about this right now."

"Cura, can't you let me explain? Please?"

"Not now." She turned on her heel and rushed off, mingling in with a crowd of kids going through their notes for the upcoming chem test.

Well, so much for trying to explain things. A sudden rush of vertigo hit with the realization Cura had blown me off. She'd never done that before. Sure, we'd had our share of fights and disagreements, but never did she tune me out. I held onto a locker, closing my eyes to will it away.

Just when matters couldn't get any worse, Dylan skidded to a stop.

"Wow, did I miss something?" he asked, his forehead wrinkled in concern.

"Don't. Want. To. Talk. About."

"Is this about what happened at the sorority house yesterday?" Dylan said. "You okay?"

"I've had better days." I relaxed against the locker and gazed up at Dylan, swallowing back the tears.

"Man, she's royally pissed," he said, glancing at Cura's stiff-backed stance. "Her aura is pulsating red big time."

Dylan's ability to see auras usually helped figure out the truth about people. It was one of the reasons I trusted him and why we had such a strong bond. That, and he was super cute. But at that moment, I didn't want to think about Cura's aura. It hurt too much "Not now, please," I sniffled.

"Give her time. She'll come around." He flashed his amazing smile that usually melted me on the spot. "Didn't I?"

"Did you? Come around that is?"

Dylan winced. I wished I could have taken that comment back, but to be honest, I didn't really know how he truly felt about my "abilities," considering how he wavered from being all supportive, like the time when I had released him from being chained by Mark down in the coffee house basement, to giving off mega negative vibes when he had left me alone after witnessing a crossing.

Dylan took a step toward me. He reached for my hand and squeezed it, leaning close. "You know I'm here for you."

I nodded, sniffling back my tears again. "T-thanks."

Then my worst nightmare parted the sea of mingling students. You know that scene in *Mean Girls* when the Plastics are walking down the hall in slow motion and their hair and outfits are perfect, and everyone stares at them in awe because they know that they own the school? That's what Hillary Swanson and her besties looked like strutting down the hall.

She sauntered over with her flock of groupies around her. You wouldn't know she'd had a huge mega fit the day before at the dead-head session my mom and her mom had set up with Cura's mom. Looking at Hillary's dyed blonde hair and Pretty-In-Pink designer duds, it was like yesterday had never happened. A mix of confidence, sass, and "nasty" oozed out of her whole body. Hillary ruled the Sutter High hallways.

"Hey, look everyone. Ms. Freak decided to grace us with her supernatural presence," Hillary announced.

Shock, confusion, and then anger spiked through me. I couldn't believe her! I'd hoped—Nope. I tossed that thought aside. What did I expect? A miraculous change of heart in my high school nemesis? If Cura couldn't deal with yesterday's supernatural Sunday, no way in Hell Hillary could.

I balled my hands into fists, wishing, not for the first time, that I could smack that smug look off her Kylie-Jenner-copycat-made-up face.

Dylan released me and glared back at Hillary. "Not cool, Hillary," he said. "Didn't your mother teach you better?"

"Right," I said. "I think she left her manners back in kindergarten."

Oohs, filled the cramped hallway. I pushed down my nerves. Standing up to Hillary was something no one did at Sutter High.

Dylan grabbed my elbow, trying to steer me away from the face off. "Ignore her."

The crowd had grown by now and even a few started chanting "girl fight."

I couldn't back down now. I glanced at Dylan, and whispered, "It's okay, I can handle it." Dylan let go of my arm and I turned back to Hillary. I squinted my eyes and took a step closer to her, ready to have it out with my former childhood friend. Hillary flinched and, as her mask of indifference slipped, I saw a flicker of fear in her eyes.

That one moment strengthened my resolve not to take any more shit from her. "You'd know all about freaks, now, wouldn't you, Hillary?" I taunted. "Want to tell your wannabes what fun they missed out on yesterday? Or do you want me to tell them?"

I swear Hillary's face went white, like she'd fallen into a vat of baby powder. "You wouldn't dare," she hissed.

"Wouldn't what?" Ashley, one of Hillary's clones, asked. She flung her salon-tinted, caramel-colored hair over her shoulders and batted her mega-sized fake eyelashes at Dylan.

Dylan slipped his hands in his pockets and gave Ashley an uncomfortable half-smile.

The rest of her group looked puzzled and, might I even say, a tad bit nervous?

Just as quickly, Hillary's smug expression came back. "Dylan, I can't believe you hang with her, especially after what her aunt did to our families. Aren't you afraid she might do more damage?"

I clenched my hands, anger flushing my face. How dare she?

As if it was my fault. As if I messed with Hillary's aunt back in 1990 and had caused her death. I hadn't even been born yet! Bad enough her mom had rubbed it in my face only yesterday. And bad enough my mom failed to inform me that my own aunt Karen had been the catalyst for all the dead and undead problems in town, but I certainly didn't need to hear it from Hillary in front of the whole student body.

Dylan disregarded the snide comment. "Jeez, Hillary, give it up," He tugged my elbow. "Don't listen to her, Steph. She's just being her usual annoying self."

Hillary staggered back, clutching her hand to her

heart. "Oh, I'm so wounded." Her cronies cackled, while their fingers frantically texted the whole exchange.

"Maybe you are the one who should be worried," I said. She wanted a war? She sure as heck would get it. I glanced at her besties. "You all want to know what went down yesterday?"

One of her newbies, I forget her name, eyed me up and down. Her bright frosted pink lip curled in disgust. "As if Hillary would hang out with you!"

I shook my head. Wow! Imagine if high school kids learned to think for themselves rather than trying so hard to be popular, we'd all be better off. "Yeah, fun times, wouldn't you say Hill?" There was no stopping me now. "Too bad we didn't film it, we could have posted it online for the whole friggin' world to see."

"Shut up, freak," Hillary hissed again. She turned to her friends, who were fidgeting and looking more confused. "I don't know what she's blabbering on about."

"Steph," Dylan warned, his voice deepening. "Chill."

"Do you want me to spell it out, Hillary?" I asked, ignoring Dylan. My heart was racing a bazillion miles a minute. I clutched my hands so hard, I swear my fingernails ripped through the skin.

"You. Wouldn't. Dare!" Hillary whispered, venom dripping from each word.

"Stephanie," Dylan said, drawing out my name. "Leave it. Let's go."

Hillary regained her composure and laughed. "As if I'd ever go anywhere or do anything with Ms. Freak!"

Her friends' giggles sounded strained. But Hillary wouldn't leave it alone. "Seems like your bestest friend, Cura, is realizing the truth about you," Hillary lashed out. "She finally smartened up." She tossed her hair back. "Besides, who'd want to ever be seen with someone who dresses like you?"

Okay, maybe I didn't do the whole Nordstrom thing and buy only the most expensive clothes, but my long, layered t-shirts, faded jeans, and high tops were comfy and I liked to feel comfortable in my clothes, not like I was walking a runway.

"Well, at least I don't have to worry about keeping up with the Kardashians like you do every second of the day," I said. Nervous energy pulsed through me. I wanted to smack her bubble-gum-pink lip gloss right off her face.

"Well, at least *I* don't get my clothes from the hardware store." She snickered along with her friends and then, all of a sudden, her laughter turned into a gurgling sound. Clasping her throat, her eyes widened and all color drained from her face. She wobbled backward against the lockers and almost fell.

Ashley ran toward her while everyone else started buzzing about what was wrong with Hillary.

The temperature dropped. I began to feel that familiar creepy, crawly, itchy feeling up and down the backs of my legs.

Great. Just great.

I followed Hillary's shocked gaze. The ghost-girl from the mommy/daughter fiasco was there, hovering above the floor, her body fading in and as students moved about. Her face had changed to a deep blue hue with ghostly vomit dripping out of her mouth. She reached out to Hillary with her ghostly hand. "Help me . . ."

Omigod, it is Emily Jones!

The nearby trash can flipped over, sending the garbage flying everywhere.

Dylan stepped back, and grabbed my hand. "What's going on?" he whispered to me.

A chorus of screams filled the air as the garbage flew all over the place. A few brave persons starting filming the whole thing. A rotting banana peel smacked

one of Hillary's Barbies in the face. Discarded candy
wrappers, half-eaten sandwiches, and half-finished lattes
literally floated in mid-air. Then, as if someone had
snapped their fingers, the garbage all swirled back into
the trash can, which righted itself and resumed its spot
on the floor. To say that everyone was surprised by that
display was an understatement. In fact, the entire hall
was full of gaping mouths and wide eyes.

"Hey, Hillary, you all right?" Ashley asked. Out of
Hillary's so-called friends, Ashley at least seemed
genuinely concerned.

"Yes, I'm okay." Hillary sneered in my direction.
"It's nothing."

Ashley put her arm around Hillary, guiding her away
from us. Hillary's other friends wobbled after them on
their impossibly high heels while frantically texting.
What they were texting, I could only guess.

I looked around the locker bay, making sure ghost-
girl was gone. Sure enough she had disappeared.

"Did a dead chick just show up? Dylan asked.

"Yup."

I almost said Emily's name, but just couldn't. I made
a mental note to do some research online about her,
almost dreading what I'd find.

"So, you weren't joking last night." He blew out a
breath. "Judging from Hillary I knew I should probably
fill Dylan in on everything that had gone down at the
initiation ceremony. I hesitated, chewing my bottom lip.

"Well?" He moved in closer.

"Yes," I whispered. "She saw a ghost."

Dylan blinked, then shook his head. "I'd hoped you
were exaggerating when you mentioned that Hillary
might see the dead, too." A worried look flashed across
his face.

"Seriously? Did you think this might have just been
a phase and all of us would turn back to normal?" I
sighed. "Now, it's just gotten worse because Hillary and

Cura can see them, and who knows what's going to happen next?"

Dylan stared into my eyes. A mix of emotions flashed over his face, but not the one I'd hoped for. Acceptance. He pulled back. He may as well have stabbed me in the heart.

"My mom, Cura's mom, and Hillary's mom knew where I'd gotten this ability to see dead people and they tried to do a ceremony to make it go away." I slipped my hands into my pockets, suddenly feeling more alone than ever. "Only they made it worse and now their daughters sense ghosts too."

Dylan's eyes widened.

"Is that what Grams meant when she…?" He shook his head. "No, that's just totally wacked."

Figures. Once again he brushed off the obvious— that his grandmother had known something would go down. Even though he had his own paranormal intuition, at least he wasn't haunted by ghosts. I couldn't really blame his reaction. Who would want this so-called "gift?" I'd rather be normal, thank you very much. I sighed, figuring I should get to class so I wouldn't risk detention, which would be the icing on my chocolate-fudge-crap day.

Dylan had another idea. He pulled me closer. I resisted for a moment and then gave into the comfort and safety of his arms. My head nestled against his chest, feeling the steady beat of his heart. Dylan sure was confusing. Just when I was worried that he didn't accept me, he showed me he did.

The class bell rang, breaking the spell. Reluctantly I pulled away. Dylan stared at something over my head, then back at me.

"Seriously, Steph. The drama and all, man, it just drags the energy out of me."

And he did it again. Ruining that feeling of safety and acceptance with just a few words. I looked down, picking at a loose thread on my sweater.

"Sorry, if this is only drama to you," I said, glancing back up. "But it's not to me. For better or worse, I seem to be stuck with this ability to see the dead. And these lost girls need my help. They'll keep popping up and making the garbage do air ballet, or worse, if I don't help them. Even though my mom and her friends tried to make this gift of mine go away with that little ceremony, it didn't work. So, I'm back where I started, except now I have Hillary and Cura to deal with, too." I swallowed the lump in my throat at the thought that Cura might never talk to me again. "Maybe this is what I'm supposed to do. My calling. My destiny. My purpose. If that sounds cliché so be it."

Dylan nodded, but he didn't say anything. Instead he shoved his hands in his pockets and scuffed his shoes.

The warning bell rang, signaling us to get to class or risk detention after school. But to be honest, I didn't care. I wanted Dylan to get me and get what I was doing. And yet he kept flip-flopping . . .

"I thought you, of all people, got it." I sniffled back the tears that threatened to escape.

"Man." Dylan let out a huge sigh. "I didn't say that."

"Well, what did you mean?"

"Never mind, okay?" He shrugged and gave me his one dimpled smile that shot right to my heart. I traced my finger across his cheek, stopping at his mouth. The full bottom lip begged for me to kiss him.

I needed Dylan. I couldn't lose him right now, not after possibly losing my best friend. I wanted him to accept me and what I did to help the dead cross over and find peace. I didn't want him to feel like I was a drama queen. Even though the way my life was going lately, it sure must seem that way to him. I sighed. He did have a point. "Sorry for all the drama crap," I said.

"Nah, don't spaz over it. You know I believe in you." His words felt more forced than meaningful.

The final bell rang. Signaling the end of our conversation. Rushing to get to class, I wondered if Dylan would leave me, too, the way Cura had? Was my calling worth it if I only ended up alone?

CHAPTER 5

The rest of the day felt like a cross between a B horror movie and a Saturday morning cartoon from the '80s. *And the award goes to Hillary Swanson, for her role of the-childhood-friend-turned-frenemy-turned-popular-girl-at-school-who-is-pretending-that-she-can't see-dead-people-but-I-know-she-really-can.*

Emily Jones showed up several more times and caused the same minor tornado of flying paper, pens, notebooks, and half-eaten sandwiches. The speculation around school was that these weird events were either some sort of nerdy prank by the Science Club or some nerdy prank by the Audio Visual Club. Either way, the nerds got blamed. But Hillary was over-the-top in trying so hard not to react. She would grimace and flinch as if she were having a major case of constipation. Her whole face blanched, eyes bugged out, while she frantically muttered under her breath, "Go away. Just go away."

Although not my favorite person at school with her obvious flirting with Dylan, I had to give Ashley credit. She clung to Hillary's side like a best supporting actress. The others? Not so much.

Hillary loved her popularity, but I seriously doubted she craved this kind of attention. Especially when her freak-outs were being filmed by everyone who had a tablet or a smart phone, and posted on who-knows-how-many social media feeds. The rumor mill was working overtime. For the first time in her high school career, Hillary was finding out what it meant to be the "weirdo."

All right, I admit it, I was kind of enjoying the

"Karma's a Bitch" thing. But that feeling was short-lived because I knew the ghost-girl needed help, and I knew that if this continued, a lot worse things could happen than just some flying garbage.

Once the nerd-theory antics was rejected the haunted school rumors resurfaced. And everyone started buzzing again about the strange behavior of the teachers, last year that included our boring algebra teacher, Mr. Nelson, suddenly jumping up on a table and rocking out like some middle-age wannabe rock star on an air guitar.

I said nada. I had to keep my thoughts to myself for the time being and figure out what to do. Emily hadn't reached out to me, she'd reached out to Hillary. I mean, I could see her, but she acted like I wasn't there. So, I had no idea what to do about that. Besides, I wasn't exactly feeling perky after Cura's rejection that morning. If she'd only give me a chance to explain why I hadn't told her. Why I couldn't tell her. I mean, how do you tell someone you can see dead people and you help them cross over? I couldn't help but think our friendship was strong enough to overcome any crap that came its way.

My stomach growled. Not even the ghostly craziness on campus could dampen my appetite. After World History class, I wandered over to my locker, musing over the sudden turn of my life.

"Ready for lunch?" Dylan propped up against my locker, his half-dimple smile making me slightly giddy. As always. I wrapped my arms around him.

"Hey, happy to see you too," he said, then leaned down and kissed me. I pressed closer, craving his warmth. I loved his strong guy-soap smell. I savored the tingly taste of peppermint on his breath.

He pulled away and flashed another smile. So adorable and, even better, all mine. "Unless you want to finish…" he kissed me again, "this somewhere."

I giggled. "You're so bad, you know that?" I gave him a playful punch. "I'm starving."

He grinned. "Starving for this?" He kissed me again, only this time his tongue made its way in. Shivers of pleasure wormed their way throughout my whole body. I leaned into his hard frame, longing for the promise of where this could lead.

"Get a room," someone shouted.

We pulled apart and laughed.

"You were saying?" Dylan asked, running his hands through his hair and glancing away.

"I'm famished."

"Me too." He waited while I placed my backpack in my locker. "Wonder what they're passing off as food today."

"Well, as long as they have whatever passes as a salad, I'm fine." I banged my locker door shut.

"Hey, have you checked out all the photos of you-know-who?" he swiped his smart phone, revealing Hillary huddled over by the staircase, a crazed expression plastered on her face.

Suddenly no longer hungry, I grabbed Dylan's hand, which felt warm and safe. "Yeah, seen," I said. "Let's just go, okay?"

"Sure." With his other hand, he shoved his cell into his back pocket. "We already know she's whacked. Why encourage it?"

"Exactly," I said, pushing down a slight queasiness. Still the icky feeling clung to me. I needed to do something about Emily Jones, or things could get worse. The question was, what was I supposed to do if Emily hadn't come to me? How was I supposed to cross her over? I knew I needed Dr. Anthony's help with this dilemma, but that would have to wait until later.

We merged into the growing throng of people. The smell of grilled hamburgers and fries collided with a cauliflower and cabbage soup that smelled like my bathroom at home after my brother got done with it. Why couldn't the school make their healthy food options more appetizing? It was no wonder most of the kids still stuck with the fast food. It tasted good and it didn't risk you farting your way through US History.

A line of people had already formed. Dylan grabbed two trays and handed me one.

"Hey, there's Cura." Dylan said, inclining his head to the other side of the food line.

Sure enough, up ahead stood Cura, her tray loaded with the usual—plain hamburger, small tossed salad with ranch on the side, and a water bottle with the Sutter High logo plastered on it.

Dylan nudged me. "Now's your chance." He took my tray then nodded toward Cura, who, at the moment, fumbled around in her wallet. "Ask her to eat with us."

"I don't know," I hesitated, not really sure if now would be the best time to chat. "She asked for space. I should respect that."

"Since when do you do that? This is Cura." Dylan gave me a little shove. "Seize the moment or whatever that famous dude said."

"Great now you're going all literary on me," I said, but I found myself moving toward Cura. My heart pounded and my hands felt all slimy. I wiped them on my pants.

"Hey, want to eat with us?" I asked.

"No." She bent close to me and whispered. "You know very well Hillary's not crazy like they're all saying."

A guy standing behind us walked around us. Others in line avoided us too.

"What am I supposed to do about that? If you ask me it's about time she got a dose of her own medicine."

Cura scowled. "The Stephanie I used to know would never wish anything like that on anyone, including Hillary. Are you going to do the same thing to me?"

My eyes narrowed. "What do you mean?" I said in a louder voice than I intended.

Cura's eyes widened in warning and she pulled me farther away from the line. "I hear them," she whispered. "Ghosts. Spirits. Whatever they are."

I blew out a breath. So, Hillary was seeing ghosts and Cura was hearing them? Was it the same ghost or a different one? Life was getting more and more complicated by the minute. I wished we could go back to when it was only me who could see and hear dead people. "Look, let's pay and eat." I nudged my head over in the direction of the table where we always ate. Dylan waved.

"What for?" she snapped, "Can you stop what's happening to me?"

I glanced away, unable to meet her eyes.

"Yeah, didn't think so." Cura shook her head.

I swear I could feel everyone staring at me. A few were texting. Oh great, just shoot me and get it over with.

"Why are you acting like this is all my fault?"

Cura gave me her pissed off look again. She was mad at me for not telling her about my abilities, so she was blaming me for the fall-out after the sorority ceremony fiasco. Message received, but I wanted her to try to see my side of things. "Come on. Can't we talk?"

"Didn't you hear me?" she muttered, her voice growing louder and attracting yet more unwanted attention. "Not now. Please move out of my way. I'm hungry."

I slid to the side while she grabbed a container of chocolate milk and a brownie.

"Wow, a double dose of chocolate and it's only noon," I said. "Like to live on the edge, huh?" I teased.

She shot me a dirty look. "Who could blame me considering what's been going on." She dug in her small charge purse, "at least you could have warned me. I thought we were best friends."

I scanned the area, nervous how much others in line

had heard. But I shouldn't have worried. Most had either passed around us or muttered, 'go hog the line somewhere else.'

I took another deep breath. "Of course we are," I said. "Can't we go somewhere quiet and talk about it?"

Cura frowned then moved farther down the line. Dumb me, who couldn't get a hint, followed. On second thought, I went over and grabbed a container of chocolate milk. Not pure sugary bliss, but it would do for now.

"Well?" I asked again, not willing to give this conversation up.

Cura paid, then looked over her shoulder. "Does Dylan know too?"

"Yeah . . ."

"Oh, that's just lovely. Both of you have this 'little' thing going on. But oh no, we can't let Cura in on it. Yeah, and you probably have your own mentor too."

"What?" I looked down, embarrassed. Now, so wasn't the time to tell her about Dr. Anthony.

I glanced back up. Cura glared at me, clearly realizing that her sarcastic reference to those popular teen supernatural shows was actually the truth.

"Hmmph, just like I thought. Great, just great." With that she stormed away, leaving me standing there like an idiot.

You'd think I was used to keeping secrets. But keeping them from my best friend Cura had been a mistake. One that I was paying for big time. Right now, I felt lower than dog poop on the bottom of my shoe. Unfortunately, unlike the poop, I couldn't scrape it off.

How could I fix this? Could I explain all of this to her? Would she even accept anything I might share with her from now on, considering I hadn't exactly been truthful about not only seeing the dead, but also my ability to help them cross over to the Other Side?

And what did she mean, when she said she could

hear them? Did that mean she only heard the voices of the dead? I didn't think it was possible to only be able to hear them. It must feel pretty creepy to hear a dead girl whispering in your ear.

I paid for my milk and turned to look for Dylan . . . And saw Ashley chatting with him. Flirting was more like it. She was gazing at him like he was the lead singer of a British boy band. He didn't seem to mind the attention, either. And then another thought hit me. Would Dylan get fed up with my abilities? Would he turn his back on me, too? I was having a hard enough time dealing with this mess with Cura, how could I handle losing Dylan too?

CHAPTER 6

Three o-clock couldn't have come fast enough. Once the final bell rang, I skedaddled off campus. Between all the craziness at school with Hillary, my fight with Cura, and my test (which went okay, I guess) I was anxious to get home to make a talisman for Emily Jones. Not that I knew for sure that it would help her, since she hadn't reached out to me, but it was all I could do at this point.

Believe it or not, the place that gave me some peace was my garage. Armed with a Diet Cherry Coke and some dark chocolate, I was ready to get to work. I rummaged through my "tool box," which consisted of an old make-up tray jam-packed with paints and an assortment of Sharpie pens. I also kept an assortment of wood in behind the garbage bins. It was my job to take out the trash, so it was a good hiding place. In some weird way, the scent of the pens plus the grainy feel of the wood in my hands helped to relax me. It also reminded me of my purpose—helping people, albeit dead ones, find their peace.

I sat cross-legged on a blanket on the floor of the garage and leaned over the cross I had made, trying to draw some type of flower, but I couldn't stop thinking of Cura. Her words in the cafeteria hurt like hell. She had a right to be upset though. I should have told her about my ability. I swiped at my tears, more frustrated than angry.

Constantly thinking about it had given me a whopper of a headache. I sighed. Right now I had more important things to deal with, which included trying to help Emily Jones.

I stared at the cross beams trying to figure out what design I'd use, since I didn't have any info to go on—not a dream, or a vision—to guide me at the moment. I closed my eyes and saw nothing. Usually after a ghost-girl makes contact with me, I have a dream that helps to guide me in my design. It seems kind of weird, but Dr. Anthony explained to me that the dreams are just my mind working out how to help the girl cross over. Somehow, the design that I draw on the cross helps guide them to the light. Dr. Anthony calls it a "talisman" that reflects the girl's essence or spirit.

Frustrated, I whipped out my fine-tipped Sharpie pen and sketched rosebuds around the edge of the cross beam. It seemed most of the girls I crossed over liked pink. I just had to hope Emily liked it, too.

"Another crossing?" Mom's voice startled me. I messed up the drawing so it looked more like a frog than a flower. *Flippin' great.*

"You aren't upset that I'm making a cross?" I asked, not giving into my urge to be flippant because, to be honest, I just wanted to get the cross done.

"Why should I be?"

"Well, after you guys tried to erase my abilities at that intervention, I'd think you'd be going all ballistic."

"Stephanie, it's complicated, okay?" Mom squatted down next to me. "Those flowers you've drawn look very pretty. You're a good artist."

I stared at her in disbelief. How could she sit there so nonchalantly and discuss my cross building like it was an art project, especially after everything that had happened yesterday? I mean, she and Mrs. Swanson and Mrs. Stratton tried to hold a supernatural ceremony to prevent me, Hillary, and Cura from seeing dead people. I took a deep breath trying to calm down.

"That's it?" I whispered. "You're not even going to talk about what happened yesterday at the abandoned sorority house. Or afterward when you told me about

Aunt Karen?" Then I added in a grumbled whisper, "Why doesn't that surprise me?"

"What do you want me to say that I haven't already said?" Mom snapped.

"Well, did you know Cura can now hear dead people talking to her? And I won't even go into what's happening with Hillary."

Mom shook her head. "Honey, why do you do this to yourself?" she asked.

"What? All I'm asking is for you to talk about what happened? You hung onto the Aunt Karen secret for years. How can I figure this out if you won't talk to me?"

"It's complicated."

"Yeah, yeah, complicated." I did air quotes. "Your favorite word. But you know what's even more complicated? Finding out you know the dead girl, but she moved to Florida. I never did a rescue out of state."

"You're sure that this girl was from here?"

"Yes, but it doesn't make sense, all of my rescues have been local girls." I threw my hands up, "But none of this does. Make sense that is."

Mom looked down at the cross, her long nails tracing the pattern of the flowers I'd drawn. "I'm sorry honey." She looked back up at me. "Is there anything I can help you with? I mean, I can't help you do a crossing for that poor girl in Florida but there must be something." When I didn't say anything she added, "I really want to do this, okay?"

I bit back another retort because to be honest, I hated fighting with Mom. If I'd been in her shoes back in 1990, and knew my sister had caused a lot of damage and death, I don't think I'd be too open, either.

"Okay, any help would be nice. Though, I'm still confused about that ceremony the other night. If the one you guys did with Karen had backfired so bad, why chance it again?"

Mom squirmed a little and threw a quick glance at the opened side door. Dad wasn't home from work yet, but you could never be too careful, right? She stood up, brushing off her pants and strolled over to the door. She closed it, and sat down on the steps.

"We wanted to protect you girls from seeing those . . ." She avoided looking at me."

"Dead people. Just say it, Mom."

"Yes . . . Spirits. But you already knew that."

She reached out and grabbed one of my sketch pads and a marker and started doodling. "Let's just say we—Hillary's mom and Cura's mom—the others and me, found out the hard way that being around the supernatural can have tragic consequences."

"The fire, right?"

It all came down to that fateful night about twenty years ago. Even though she'd already told me this, what was she holding back??

Mom kept sketching on the pad. If it helped relax her to doodle while I tried to get some answers, then I was all for that.

I forged ahead, "What exactly happened on that night?"

A painful look crossed mom's heart-shaped face, adding years to her youthful looks.

"Karen wasn't exactly what you'd call a popular girl. She desperately wanted to be a part of my sorority at Sac State, but they rejected her at first, even though she was my little sister. That was hard on her and made me feel torn because, although I loved being in the sorority, I also loved my little sister. So, one day we were having an open house and she showed up and came up to me—telling me she'd figured out a way to impress the members . . ."

Yes, this was old news, but I didn't want to say that or else Mom might stop talking. I needed to know everything so I repeated, "So Karen wasn't a cool kid?"

"No, she was definitely not cool."

I could only imagine. A rush of empathy surfaced. I knew all too well the feeling of being a pariah.

"Against my better judgment, I set up a private meeting with the membership committee. Karen did something that blew everyone away. She wasn't faking or anything."

I winced at that, knowing how others, including my own mother, had thought I was "faking." Karen felt like a kindred spirit more and more . . .

"So, she made ghosts appear?" I asked.

Mom nodded, then elaborated: "We, I mean I, didn't exactly see them but I could sense and feel them." She shuddered, pulling her cardigan closer. "She became an overnight sensation. She got all kinds of requests to hold séances and, long story short, the sorority welcomed her in. For a while everything was great for Karen. She started making friends and was more confident, more sure of herself. There was even a rumor she had a boyfriend who dabbled in the same thing."

"So, what went wrong?"

Mom stopped sketching and closed her eyes. "She wanted more. Much more."

"What did she want?" I whispered, afraid to hear the answer.

Mom's eyes opened and I could see the fear reflected in her gaze.

"It wasn't enough for her to just summon the dead, she wanted to experience their world."

"You told me about this already, but what exactly happened on the night of the fire?"

"We thought we could actually conjure up the power to increase our abilities to see the Other Side." Mom shook her head, sadness and regret were in her eyes. "Karen actually thought that if we worked together, our abilities would strengthen to the point that we could do just about anything, maybe even cheat death."

"Are you serious? No one can cheat death." I would have laughed if I didn't know the severity of what Mom had just shared.

"She told us, 'Imagine all the good we could do to those who died tragically. It would be like a paranormal super power as we could vanquish the evil too.'"

"Two for the price of one," I retorted. "Couldn't she just leave well enough alone? Why mess with something you can't see?"

I'd only had one experience dealing with the dark side of the paranormal world and that had scared me enough to never want another one. Ever again.

"Honey, you have to promise me that you won't try anything like that. What Karen did was dangerous and it not only caused a fire but it killed two girls. Both of whom were my friends."

"Mom, I would never be that naïve or stupid."

"It's easy to say that now. Believe me, I know."

"Mom . . ."

She raised her hand, silencing me.

"Let me finish. Karen wouldn't leave well enough alone . . . and well, you know what happened." She paused, and bit her trembling lips. "I-I should have stopped her. I f-failed." Mom wiped the tears from her eyes and added, "I won't make that mistake again."

"Just because your sister messed up big time doesn't mean I'll make the same mistake."

Mom sighed. "That's what she said. And look what happened." She put her hand on my shoulder. "The fact that you can see the dead, opens you up to the evil out there, too. We had to try our best to replicate the spell, but we needed five people. That's why Cura and Hillary came."

"But there were six of us. Do you think that was the reason why it failed?"

"I don't know," she whispered. "We thought it might be good for all of us to try the spell together. Maybe then it might actually work. We didn't want to chance our luck again."

"But it didn't work," I reminded her.

"Right."

"Mom." I reached out to grab her hand. I remembered how easy it used to be to reach for my mom's hand. Crossing the street. At the grocery store. It was always so comforting to me knowing that all I had to do was reach out to hold her hand, and everything would be better. Now, it was me trying to make her feel better. "It's going to be okay. I'm getting pretty good at this helping-dead-people thing, and I can handle it."

When her eyebrow arched up, I said, "Yeah, so I messed up once, but I learned my lesson." I'd learned to trust my instincts, especially when dealing with the dead. If your gut tells you to run the hell away from trouble, do it. Even if, in my case, that trouble happened to be a cute guy, who turned out to be an undead demon.

The garage door creaked open and Mom said in a rushed whisper, "You have to keep this quiet. Don't let your father know about this."

"But why?" I sat back. "It might be a good idea to tell Dad about my abilities and what happened to Aunt Karen."

"Your dad is a particular kind of guy. He's not like us and wouldn't understand. Best to keep this between us for now."

I frowned. I didn't like keeping secrets. I knew what that could lead to. Case in point: Cura. I didn't want that to happen between Mom and Dad. "Just for now though," I added. "I'm sick of all the secrets."

"Well, you can be sick of them for a while longer."

And just like that, my mom's face settled back into her usual bland, Mom smile. At least, when she was crying she was being honest. Now, she just looked like robot-Mom again. I slipped the cross I'd been working on underneath some old newspapers so Dad wouldn't see it.

Dad's familiar silver Honda Civic drove inside. I swear the temperature dropped at least ten degrees and it had nothing to do with ghosts. The recent tension between my parents hadn't let up since the coffee house incident. If Dad got wind of the messed-up initiation meeting, I knew it would get worse.

"Hey, why's everyone in here?" Dad said as he got out of the car with his gym bag. "What's for dinner? Oh," He gave both Mom and me the awkward are-you-talking-about-girl-stuff look, "Am I interrupting something?"

Dad smiled, waiting for an answer. Unlike some men his age, my father prided himself on staying in shape. He went to the gym every day after work. Aside from his balding hair, he still looked pretty youthful.

"No, that's okay, we're done." I would finish the cross later. Maybe Emily would appear to me before then, so at least I could get a better sense of how to finish decorating it. Not to mention I needed to figure out where to go to help her cross over. After all, she had moved to Florida. This was certainly a tricky situation. In my haste to cover the cross, I forgot to put my tool box away. One of my sketches of roses fluttered next to it.

"You know, pumpkin," Dad continued, "I admire your artwork. Maybe you should take an art class?"

If only he knew. I smiled, "Yeah, maybe next year, Dad."

He glanced at Mom, who only shrugged. "Let me put the potatoes in. Dinner should be done in twenty minutes or so."

"Great, I need to call Cura anyway. Later." After I put my tool box away, I went back inside the house and scooted up to my room. Even from there I could hear Dad asking Mom about what we were talking about.

I'm sure she replied with the usual "it's that time of the month" thing, which would get Dad flustered and put a quick end to his questions.

I was feeling so frustrated I wanted to scream into my pillow. My mom didn't trust me. She thought I was like her reckless sister Karen. She'd told her friends about my abilities, and they'd all decided what would be best for me was stopping this supposed curse/spell that Aunt Karen had put in motion that enabled me, and now Cura and Hillary to see and hear the dead. For some reason, I'd gotten this ability first. Maybe because I was directly related to Aunt Karen. But since the ceremony debacle at the burned down sorority house, both Cura and Hillary were now affected. Mom and her friends had tried so hard to "cure" me that they'd ended up making things worse. But was it so terrible? I'd been getting used to my abilities, even feeling good about helping lost dead girls cross over and find peace. What was so wrong with that? I was helping those girls, not interfering with life and death? I blew out a big breath. Would any of this get any easier?

My ringing cell phone interrupted my musings. I fumbled through my blankets in an attempt to find it. Sure enough, it was under a pile of squished up pillows at the end of my bed. *Hello, my name is Stephanie and I am addicted to throw pillows . . .*

I snuck a peek at the caller ID—

Dylan.

My stomach did the usual weird fluttering thing it did whenever he called. Do I answer and seem too eager or leave it and call him back?

My cell kept doing its vibration dance across my bed. I waited, still debating what to do.

Then it stopped.

For some funny reason, I felt relieved. Don't ask me why, considering how much I was into him.

But maybe it wasn't the best time to be talking to my boyfriend. He had that uncanny ability to read auras. Did it work over the phone? Who knows? But I didn't want to chance it. After what happened at school today, I was worried that he might already think I was Miss Drama Queen.

I connected my cell to the charger next to my night stand. I would see him tomorrow at school and come up with some excuse about crashing early. One thing for sure, Emily needed to appear to me soon, if only to direct me to the site of her murder. Time was ticking. I only had a little more than a day to help cross her over. Usually I only had 48 hours to do my job. Otherwise, the dead girl would end up stuck here in limbo or worse. I had no idea why it worked this way. It was something Dr. Anthony had told me and he knew about this stuff way more than I did.

I shuddered to think what would happen to Emily Jones if I didn't cross her over.

CHAPTER 7

The next morning, I woke up not feeling refreshed.

I'd had a weird dream where I was the guest on a TV talk show and the host was Aunt Karen. She patted my hand and told me that she was going to help me. Then the audience started to clap and I turned and saw they were all ghost-girls. But no Emily.

Grumpy, and groggy-eyed, I took a quick shower and threw on a pair of loose pants. I completed the look with a lacy tank top and a hoodie. I pulled my hair back into a high ponytail. Light makeup, some lip gloss, and of course some under-eye cover cream to mask the dark circles from my restless night.

My stomach growled. I rushed downstairs, hoping not to run into the 'rents as I didn't want to deal with Mom after our little chat yesterday afternoon.

I turned the corner and stopped. Sitting at the table, Dad was perusing the *Sacramento Bee*. Most people used their cellphones or iPads to check out on the news. Not my father. His oxford shirt, tie, dress pants, along with his smartphone close by, completed his look as an effective senior auditor evaluator. He worked downtown with countless other State employees, which meant he had to leave early in order to miss the nightmare traffic.

As I made my way to the fridge, I snuck a quick peek over his shoulder to see if there was any mention of a murdered girl, which would explain Emily's ghost on campus yesterday. Nope, the only headline that jumped out at me was a politician caught cheating on his wife.

Dad smiled my way.

"Hey, pumpkin, you're up early."

"Yeah, tell me about it."

I grabbed a bottle of cran-apple juice from the fridge and took a few sips. A quick glance in the "carb" cupboard revealed a vast selection of high fiber and low glycemic cereals. Yuck. Mom and Dad really needed to get off their health kick. I was only sixteen, after all. I still required a healthy dose of sugar and caffeine in the morning. I moved the bird seed and found my pot of gold: Pop-Tarts. It was a toss-up between cookies 'n cream or strawberry. With a nod to the benefits of fruit, I chose the strawberry and popped two in the toaster.

Dad looked up from the paper, his eyes inquiring. "Must be something important to get you up this early."

I shrugged. "Have a yearbook meeting."

I avoided his gaze and I made myself busy stuffing a banana and a chewy granola bar in my bag. I swear, sometimes I think I inherited my psychic abilities from Dad, with those sharp eyes of his.

"Is there something going on with you and your mom?"

At that moment, the toaster spit out my Pop-Tarts. I grabbed them and plopped them on a paper towel.

"No, just the usual," I said, blowing on the hot pastry before taking a tentative bite. "She's just being Mom."

Dad opened his mouth, but I cut him off. "Sorry Dad, but if I'm late, the editor is going to put me in charge of the chess club write-up."

My father's brow furrowed. He looked disappointed and maybe a little hurt. *Damn.* I hated this secret-keeping business. But I promised Mom.

I wrapped up the tarts in another paper towel and zipped up my bag. After giving my dad a kiss on the cheek, and offering up a cheery "see ya later," I made a quick getaway and decided not to text Cura but walk the few blocks to campus alone.

Once I got to school, I dumped my books in my locker, hoping that the day would not feature a supporting cast of ghost-girls floating around campus. I hadn't lied to my dad about the yearbook meeting. Since Dylan had chosen not to volunteer this year, he lucked out and could sleep in.

I hurried to one of six portables located on the other side of the parking lot of the high school campus. The portables had been installed ten years ago to deal with overcrowding. I loved having classes in the portables because it meant being able to walk outside to get to class, which kind of felt like being in college. But as I scurried to the yearbook meeting, I hoped I didn't get checked off for being tardy. Of all my recent troubles from Mark the demon, to the recent sorority house fiasco, I didn't want to add Saturday school to that list. Vice principal Hatch loved to enforce the whole "Breakfast Club" thing. I swear, he probably oversaw Saturday school so he could get out of doing yard work.

I rushed into the room, and plopped down in a chair next to Cade Reid, the editor in chief and head-geek of campus. Jade Willow, the school photographer and deputy editor, sat close to him. Both were hovering over Jade's laptop.

Jade's Nikon camera sat on the table next to them. She never went anywhere without her expensive equipment.

"Wow, can you believe it?" Cade asked, pushing his rounded Harry Potter glasses up his narrow nose. "I wonder if she ran away or something nefarious happened?"

I glanced over their shoulders trying to see who they were talking about.

Omigod. I shouldn't have been shocked considering I'd seen her spirit not once, not twice, but three times. Still actually seeing her picture on the newsfeed took me off guard.

"Isn't that Emily Jones?" I asked, an all too familiar feeling of dread coming over me.

"Yeah, she's gone missing," Cade said.

"She was at the annual cheer camp," Jade added. "We were going to do a story on it for the yearbook, but no one from our school was scheduled to go. Now we find out Emily Jones was there."

"We could have covered it even though technically she's no longer at Sutter High," Cade said. "We could have gotten a scoop about her going missing."

"A wasted opportunity." Jade shook her head.

"Cheer camp?" I asked, trying not to the think about the cut-throat journalists Cade and Jade would make someday.

"Yeah, the one at Sacramento State."

"Well, apparently Emily's mom picked her up to take her to the airport for her flight back to her dad in Florida and she wasn't in her dorm room," Cade added.

I guess I looked confused because Jade piped in with, "Her mom and dad are divorced. Emily was living with her dad since last summer because she was having problems with her mom. She's an alcoholic and has a constant revolving door of boyfriends in and out of the house."

"How do you guys know all this stuff?" I asked them.

Jade and Cade looked at each other as though I were from the former planet, Pluto.

"Uh, it's our job to know everything."

"Right. Sorry." Their job? Boy, scratch that, they were already cut-throat journalists.

I slunk to a desk at the back of the room and rooted around my bag for my iPhone. Quickly scanning the most recent local headlines I read the following article: *Emily Jones, sixteen-year-old former residence of Sacramento, California, has been reported missing by her parents, David and Diane Jones. Emily had been attending the annual National Cheer Summit for head leaders, which was being held this year in Sacramento.*

Recently moved to Naples, Florida to live with her father after her parents' divorce, Emily had been appointed as head cheer leader at Seaview High School, a prestigious school in Naples. Emily had won a coveted spot at the week-long event and, according to her parents, was set to fly back to Florida on Sunday, the final day of the Summit. But when her mother arrived to pick her up to drive her to the airport, Emily was nowhere to be found. A search by local police has commenced and the participants and organizers of the Cheer Summit are being questioned by local authorities.

So, she died here. No wonder she showed herself. But why to Hillary and not me? Then I remembered they'd once been tight.

This put a whole crimp in any plans I had to help her cross over. I blew out a breath and leaned back in my seat. Lizzie Dexter sat next to me. She was in my art class and was super-talented. She was intently doodling on her ever-present sketch-pad. Probably a design for another one of her tats. You couldn't get one at sixteen without parental permission, but Lizzie's mom and dad were really cool. They ran their own tattoo parlor and were covered in tats themselves. In fact, they did all of Lizzie's tattoos. Too bad I couldn't ask her to help me decorate the talismans, as I could totally use her talent. For some reason, when I had a "visit" from a dead girl it usually came with a vision of a particular kind of flower or plant connected to her. I always decorated the cross with what I saw in the vision. When I did the crossing with Dr. Anthony, the girl would always appear at the spot where she had died. She would be drawn to the talisman and then be able to cross over. It was kind of weird, but who I was to question it. I still didn't understand the extent of my abilities, and without Dr. Anthony's guidance I'd probably be in a hospital ward on a rotating round of meds.

I glanced around the room. Hillary and Cura weren't there. Strange. If anything, Cura prided herself on being involved with the yearbook. She wanted to get into the Columbia School of Journalism and was totally building her extra-curricular activities. I, on the other hand, hadn't given much thought to which college I wanted to get into, let alone what I'd be studying. I was far too busy helping dead girls cross over. The only reason Hillary was on the yearbook committee was because it guaranteed her face would be plastered on more than one page. I snorted to myself, prompting an odd look from Lizzie. I covered up by pretending to be reading from my phone.

Ashley, Hillary's new BFF, slid into the desk on my other side. Usually those two were joined at the hip, so I wondered why she was here and Hillary wasn't. Because Hillary and I were frenemies, I avoided anything to do with her, but considering we were both on the yearbook committee, that proved almost impossible. And now my life was even more intricately tied to hers because of the sorority ceremony from hell and the definitely-dead Emily Jones. Since Emily had reached out to Hillary, I'd have to talk to Hillary about it, if I wanted to help Emily cross over. That didn't mean I had to like Hillary though.

Curious, I leaned over, tapping Ashley on the shoulder. She went on texting. I tapped her again. Harder this time.

"What?" She looked up, annoyance laced her question.

"Where's Hillary?"

Ashley frowned, checking her cell again.

"Not sure."

"Isn't she afraid we might overlook one of her photos?" I asked, sarcastically.

Ashley only shrugged without glancing back up. "How should I know? It's not as if she's gone MIA like Emily. She probably slept in."

I bit back another smart-assed retort, knowing it wouldn't get me any answers. I settled back in my chair. Would Hillary have confided in Ashley about seeing Emily's ghost? I decided to test the waters. "Yeah, that's terrible," I said. "About Emily and all."

When Ashley gave me a pointed glare, I added, "Well, considering Hillary and Emily were friends, it must have been upsetting for Hillary when she heard."

Ashley went back to her texting. "I wouldn't know anything about that, Hillary never mentioned Emily."

Hmm . . . did Hillary and Emily have a fight? Could that be why Emily had reached out to Hillary?

Not much later Mr. Johnson came in. While most teachers only endured extracurricular activities, Mr. Johnson was really into working with us on the yearbook committee. Apparently, he'd written for the *Hollywood Reporter* years ago, before going into teaching. Now, he was all about turning the yearbook into a big splashy affair. Right now, I needed some of his enthusiasm to get through this meeting. He sauntered in with his Fossil leather satchel over his shoulder, a big Starbucks latte in one hand, and his iPad in the other, and excitement all over his face. No doubt due to the fact that this was the 50th Anniversary of Sutter High. I kicked myself for not grabbing a coffee on my way to school, but I was in such a rush to avoid talking to Dad that I forgot. I inhaled the delectable aroma of hazelnut swirling with caramel . . .

Even though I'd missed my morning quota of caffeine, pent up energy surged through me. I tapped my pencil on the desk, impatient, yet at the same time dreading my assignment. Figures my part of covering this 50th Anniversary yearbook was a retrospective photo essay on the cheer leaders. Mr. Johnson prided himself on getting us all out of our comfort zones and shaking things up. So rather than covering the Art Club which I did last year, I got thrown into the Cheer Squad. *Oh, joy, I get to take photos of Hillary and her friends.*

When the bell rang, I couldn't get out of there fast enough.

I scanned the parking lot for Cura's little Jetta bug, but it wasn't there. I made my way across the packed lot to the back door of the main building. The bustle of kids on their way to class tuned out the worrisome thoughts circulating nonstop on how I could help Emily cross over.

Midway through my inner debate about whether or not I should approach Hillary and ask her if ghost-Emily had spoken to her, I spotted Dylan leaning against my locker, waiting for me. My heart did its usual somersaults whenever I saw him. And seeing him first thing before class was a definite boost to my morning.

"Hey, rough night?"

"Yeah, you could say that."

He stepped away from my locker door so I could unlock it, concern etched on his face.

Dylan didn't say anything, instead he took my hand, leaned in, and kissed me. I closed my eyes, relishing his warmth and guy smell. I kissed him back, lingering longer than I probably should have. His kiss tasted like peppermint chocolate. Even the slight roughness of his recently shaved face, was comforting. I could get so used to this.

My birthday wasn't until January 30th, which was only in a few more weeks. What better gift to myself than to plan a special day with Dylan. We could be together without any distractions. I definitely wanted to make that happen. All I had to do was cross Emily over and make Cura forgive me.

I opened my eyes. Dylan smiled back. "You kiss great in the morning," he teased.

"Thank you. It must be all the excitement about the yearbook that's just coursing through me."

Dylan traced his finger across my cheek. I wanted to stay there forever, but I had to get to history class.

Sighing, I searched for my textbook under a pile of hoodies. I had no idea how so many of my hoodies got in there. I should talk to Dylan about what I'd read about Emily, not to mention my little chat with Mom yesterday, but something stopped me.

"Want to talk about it?" he asked.

I turned. One glance into Dylan's beautiful hazel eyes and I forgot my first name. I bit my lip, mulling over what to say. I mean, we were boyfriend and girlfriend, right? So why was I hesitating? "You know me. Just the usual Rescuer stuff."

After the words came out, I wanted to erase them. Hurt clouded Dylan's eyes. Then his expression hardened. Why did I just do that? My life was becoming one mess after another. When I confided in Dylan about the sorority fiasco on Sunday night, I could sense something off in him, like it was making him uncomfortable. Then Emily Jones showed up yesterday and kicked up a tornado of garbage. Then I had to deal with Ashley making goo-goo eyes at Dylan, my best friend Cura giving me the cold shoulder, my mom not telling me everything about Aunt Karen, lying to my dad, and now I had to possibly seek out Hillary to ask her if Emily's ghost had told her anything that I could use to help her cross over. I didn't know where to start with Dylan.

"Got ya," Dylan stepped away from me, surveying the corridor. He shoved his hands inside his pockets. "Don't need to spell it out."

The warmth I felt after our hot kiss vanished and it was suddenly chilly between us. But then again, why should I be surprised? I had an ability to see lost dead girls and help and help them cross over. I'm sure that wasn't exactly top on the list of every guy's dream girl.

I threw my book into my bag, ignoring Dylan's scowl and trying not to think about Mr. Warner and his boring World History lectures. I grabbed a notebook.

Dylan shoved his hands in his pockets, suddenly interested in something at the other end of the hallway. I followed his gaze.

Sure enough, Hillary stood alone. She clutched her books to her chest, not making eye contact with anyone. Her designer outfit didn't have the usual immaculate feel. It seemed as if she'd just thrown something together. Strands of blond hair escaped a loose ponytail

"You sure she's not using?" he finally asked.

"Jeez, Dylan."

"And no fan club?" Dylan added. "What's with that?"

Sure enough, her usual entourage was missing. Maybe they finally came to their senses.

"She missed the yearbook meeting too," I said. "Mr. Johnson wasn't too happy." A slight itch began on the back on my left leg, warning of another ghostly encounter.

Just flippin' great.

At that moment, Dylan bent his head, shielding his eyes. Could he sense the ghost too?

Sure enough, a presence faded in and out next to the lockers. Broken twigs, dirt, and something disgusting (*omg, was that pepperoni?*) now covered Emily's hair and clothes. Confusion filled her startled eyes.

Drip. Drip. Drip.

A thin stream of blood trickled down her forehead pooling into a puddle at her feet. Other students walked right through it, trailing the ghostly blood through the hallway. It still amazed me how no-one but me, and it looked like Hillary, could witness the ghostly encounter.

Emily's greyish-blue lips opened and closed as she stared back at all of us. I swear I caught a glimpse of an enlarged tongue. *Yuck.* I should be used to all of this considering I saw the dead, but the sight of blood and guts nailed me every time. I swallowed the vomit that threatened to erupt.

"Holy hell," Dylan's voice broke through my concentration. "Something's scaring her."

I stared at Dylan. He was watching Hillary's reaction to Emily. But could he see Emily's aura?

"Omigod, Emily?" Hillary asked.

"Yeah, it's her," I whispered.

Hillary's face paled and I thought for sure she'd hurl whatever energy bar she'd eaten for breakfast.

Emily floated closer to Hillary, reaching out to her. Her hand went right through Hillary, making her shiver.

Hello ghost-girl, I'm right here! I can help you cross over. I tried to talk to her with my mind, hoping she would turn around. Isn't that what psychics on TV shows did? I'd have to ask Dr. Anthony about that some time.

Hillary's books crashed to the ground. "No way. No way." she whispered. She backed away, then ran like hell into the nearby bathroom.

I blew out a breath. Just great. This was going to be another stellar day.

A group of girls huddled next to their lockers giggled and pointed at the bathroom door.

Dylan glanced at me, his eyes concerned. I'm sure I had the exact same look in mine.

I banged my locker shut. "I probably should go check on her." Mostly, though, I needed to know if Emily had said anything to her. The sooner she crossed over, the better for everyone.

Until, Dr. Anthony came along, I was sort of winging the whole Rescuer thing on my own. When my dead friend, Allison, had appeared to me, I was definitely scared. Just as scared as Hillary was now. Although I wasn't a fan of Hillary, I didn't want her to go through the fear and second guessing over whether she might be having a mental breakdown.

Maybe I could help her get through this and she could help me cross Emily over. We could help each other out.

[79]

I squared my shoulders, mentally psyching myself up to talk to Hillary.

"Is that such a good idea?" Dylan leaned back, folding his arms. "It's not as if you two are tight or anything."

"What can I say? Maybe my mother did teach me some manners," I said.

He raised his hands up. "Ok, shoot me." He lowered his hands. "Million-dollar question. You think she'll talk to you?"

"Well, I won't know unless I try, right?"

I took a deep breath and walked toward the bathroom. On the way there, I picked up the shoe Hillary had lost in her haste to get away from Emily's ghost. A few girls rushed out. One stopped and said, "Jeez, what's with her anyway?" She didn't stay to hear my answer.

As if I'd have one.

CHAPTER 8

I paused, my hand on the bathroom door. I asked myself again, why was it I had to talk to Hillary, the girl whose life mission included making my life miserable?

I sighed, knowing the answer to that question. I had to help her. I, more than anyone else, understood what it was like to see dead people, even if that meant incurring her usual snark. And somehow, she'd channeled Emily Jones. I nudged back the sting of being rejected by a ghost and settled on a more important matter—getting through to Hillary.

I pushed the girl's bathroom door open, ignoring the urge to apply some antibacterial sanitizer on my hands. Although, I have germophobic tendencies when it comes to public bathrooms, I needed to do two things: help Hillary and cross over Emily. Besides, ghosts didn't carry any germs, as far as I knew. Still, it was pretty gross seeing the trail of ghostly blood spattered on the bathroom floor.

My eyes did a once over, scanning under the stalls. Sure enough, I spotted two familiar feet in the last stall. Only one designer shoe, though. I held the other one in my hands.

"Hey, missed you this morning," I said, directing my words to the occupied stall. "Remember? We had a year book group meeting. Although, not much happened, other than Mr. Johnson reminding us that we all had to get our assigned school club write-ups done by next week."

Now wouldn't be the time to mention how Emily had been the real talk of the meeting. I figured I'd take it easy and then I'd ask Hillary what she knew.

A sigh let me know she'd heard.

I walked over to the stall door and tapped on it.

"Hey, you okay?"

The door suddenly swung open. I jumped to the side to avoid getting hit.

"Go. Away." Hillary scowled at me. She hobbled over to the sink, limping with only the one shoe, but her head was still at its usual snooty angle. I had to give her credit for trying to hold on to her supreme façade.

She snapped open a small designer cosmetic bag, removing her favorite Pink Sapphire Stila lip gloss and a lip liner. She moved in close to the mirror and applied the lip liner to her lips, then filled it in with the gloss.

"Take a picture, it'll last longer," she finally said, rolling her eyes.

I dangled her shoe from one finger. "Missing something?"

"I bet you think this is hilarious, huh?" Hillary snatched the shoe out of my hand. Turning it over, she frowned at the broken heel. "Just great. These cost two hundred dollars."

"I might have a pair in my locker that you can borrow," I volunteered.

She gave me another once over. "Yeah, as if I'd wear your knock offs." She turned back to the mirror and pulled out a hair brush. A slight tremor in her hand, she removed her hair band and brushed out her hair.

Okay, this so wasn't working. I needed to try another tactic.

"Look, I'm just trying to help." I took a deep breath, mentally counting to five in Spanish, because I had Spanish class later, then started again. "Can you tell me what you saw out there?" I pointed to the door. "In the hallway?"

"You mean 'who' don't you?" Hillary went back to brushing her tangled hair.

"Who?" I acted innocent.

"Don't play dumb with me. You know who. Emily Jones, that's who."

I sighed. Finally, some honesty. "She moved to Florida last year, right?" I asked.

"Yeah. She and her mom were having some issues, so her dad stepped in and said she could live with him and his new wife and baby son." Hillary paused and met my eyes in the mirror. "Why is she following me?"

"The only reason why she would be following you," I said gently, feeling sorry for both Emily and Hillary, "is because she's dead and she needs your help."

Hillary eyes widened. She shook her head. "No, no, no, this can't be happening."

"You guys used to be tight, right?" I asked.

"We were on the cheerleading squad together and I saw her last Friday night. She was back for the cheer camp. She'd made head squad leader at her new high school in Naples. Hillary forgot about brushing her hair and turned to me. "She can't be dead. Omigod, you're the one that sees the dead. Not me! I'm not a freak. I'm not!"

I reached out to Hillary, touching her arm.

"Just get out." Hillary jerked away. "And stay away from me or else you'll be sorry."

"Hillary, can't we get past this? We have to work together if we want to save Emily."

She froze and for a moment I thought she'd be all on board. "Why are you still saying that? She's not dead. She's missing. Why are you saying crazy shit like that?"

I sighed. "You know I'm right. Emily's dead. How else can we see her spirit?"

She narrowed her eyes. "Your crazy aunt couldn't leave well enough alone."

"Oh, for the love of . . ." So much for being nice. If

she wanted to be a bitch, then I would return the favor. I jammed my finger in front of her face. Hillary stepped back, fear replacing the earlier arrogance. "I'm trying to help you. Okay? You have no idea what you're talking about."

Hillary's eyes widened. "Yes, I do. Mom's right. You're a freak."

"Really?" I smirked, wanting to get back at her for that remark. "Then why is everyone laughing and pointing at you?"

Hillary glared, if it were possible, venom would be dripping from her eyes.

Just then the door opened. A couple of first year girls took a few steps inside, gushing about Greg McCallum, the captain of the football team.

"Get the eff out of here," Hillary snarled, flinging her hand toward the exit sign. "We're busy."

The girls didn't need to be told twice. They scooted out of there fast.

"Oh, that's real mature, Hillary," I said.

"Shut up." She turned back to the mirror and finished brushing her hair.

"Jeez, I only came in here to see if I could help." I picked up one of her lip glosses that had fallen on the icky floor, washed it clean with soap and water, and handed it to her.

"Thanks," she grumbled, taking the lip gloss from me.

"So, what happened last Friday night? Did you guys hang out at the cheer camp?"

Hillary pulled her hair through the hairband, high up on her head. It looked sleek, shiny, and blonde with no roots showing. She had a good colorist, I'd give her that. "We all went to party in one of the dorms. We hung out. She was liking it better with her dad than living with her mom, but she missed all her friends here, including her boyfriend Greg."

Ah, yes, Greg McCallum, the captain of the football team. Tall, blond, and handsome. And the most conceited guy in school. "Didn't they break up last year, just before school ended?" That had been big news around campus for weeks. "Word around school had it that she was fighting with her mom about Greg."

"He wanted to go all the way. Her mom found her birth control pills and got into a huge fight with Emily." Hillary re-applied her lip gloss with the expertise of a Hollywood make-up artist.

"And that's why she moved to Florida?"

"That's partly why." Hillary turned to me. "When she told Greg about the fight with her mom, he dumped her. He didn't want to be part of her drama, he told her." Hillary rolled her eyes. "He wanted a mature girlfriend who wasn't going to let her mom walk all over her."

"So, her fight with her mom and then her break-up with her boyfriend was the last straw."

"Yup. She packed her stuff and flew down to Naples, last July. She only came back up here to attend the cheer camp." Hillary swept her mascara wand over her lashes.

"Was Greg at the party?"

Hillary slipped the wand back into its tube and dropped it back into her bag. Zipping it up, she turned to me. "Yes, he was there."

"So . . . ?"

"So what?"

"What happened?"

Hillary narrowed her eyes, her hands going to her hips. "Why does any of this matter to you? She wasn't *your* friend, she was my friend."

"I'm trying to help *your* friend cross over."

"You keep saying that, but she's been declared *missing*, not *dead* . . ." Hillary's eyes widened and she looked at me like she'd just figured out it was Miss Scarlet with the candlestick in the library. "You're obsessed with the dead, Steph. You think she's dead but maybe you're just projecting all of this into my head. You're like some kind of weirdo witch like your Aunt Karen."

"What the hell are you talking about?" I couldn't believe she was blaming me for seeing dead Emily's ghost.

"Look, just leave it alone. "She threw her designer makeup bag into her designer shoulder bag and swung it over her shoulder." And leave *me* alone. Or you will be sorry for playing your twisted mind games on me."

I shook my head. Sheesh. I was trying to be nice and she throws it back in my face. Well, two can play at this game. "Or else what?" I couldn't resist shoveling back some of her crap. "Get your friends to post crap about me online? You're the one everyone is gossiping about."

Hillary scowled. "Don't mess with me. I know your secret."

"Hey, that goes both ways, doesn't it? I wonder what your so-called friends would think if I shared what I know about you?" I gave her my best smirk. "That *you* see dead girls."

Hillary's mouth thinned and she tried to walk past me, but almost tripped with her one shoe.

Damn. Now, I was feeling sorry for her again. Why do I have to be such a good person?

"Look," I said with a sigh. "I don't want to fight with you. If you want help with Emily then you know how to reach me."

She continued to ignore me and kept walking to the door.

"Fine. Just keep spending your days running down the halls like a crazy person. But if you really cared about Emily, you'd want to help her. Even if that means working with me."

Hillary snorted and shoved open the door.

"Just remember what I said. The time is ticking down for Emily."

The bell rang for class.

"Saved by the bell," I muttered. No good deed goes unpunished, as the saying goes. If Hillary was seeing her fellow cheer squad bestie then that meant trouble. But what could I do about it? Emily's ghost hadn't reached out to me. I turned to look at myself in the mirror. Was I doing the right thing trying to reach out to Hillary?

CHAPTER 9

The rest of the day went by in a boring blur. It turned out Hillary wouldn't be my only confrontation of the day. Mom was waiting for me outside, sitting on the old porch swing. When I approached, she looked up from her tablet. All my feelings of the day jumbled together, threatening at any moment to just hurl out. I took a deep breath.

"Dr. Anthony called," Mom said, flipping the cover over the tablet. "He texted you, but when he didn't hear back from you, he called me. He wants you to call him back."

"Just great. As if I didn't have enough excitement today," I mumbled, opening the front door.

Seriously, could this day get any worse? I'd been avoiding Dr. Anthony's texts all afternoon. I knew he wanted me to check in with him about Emily Jones. How could he not? It was all over the news, so he most likely assumed that she had appeared to me. Even though I'd seen her, she had officially appeared to Hillary, and I had no idea how I would be able to connect with her if Hillary wasn't on board. I strolled into the kitchen like a zombie in search of food, preferably sugar-based, to perk me up. Opening the fridge, I grabbed a Cherry Coke. From the cupboard, I snatched a chocolate pudding cup. That should do the trick.

Mom had followed me into the kitchen, her face creased with her usual look of concern. She lay down the tablet on the kitchen table, went over to pour herself a cup of coffee, then she sat down. She was dressed in her usual mom uniform: pressed jeans and one of her revolving, pretty, patterned blouses. Even Mom's casual clothes were always put together.

She cleared her throat. "Stephanie, can we talk?"

Mom flipped open the tablet and scrolling, landed on an article. She tapped on it and handed me the tablet. Curious, I took a step closer. The newspaper headline read: *Former Local Girl Missing.*

I glanced up at Mom, then back at the news story. It had been the buzz around school all day. A group of seniors had gotten together with some teachers to help with the police search.

"Honey, is this the girl you saw?" Mom looked like she wanted to start crying any second. I knew why . . .

"Yes. It's the same girl who showed up at the sorority house and everyone at school's been talking about it," I said. No need to mention that I'd seen the ghost-girl today, and that she'd approached Hillary and not me.

Mom frowned.

"Mom, sorry I should have told you, but to be fair, I only just got home and all." I flipped open the tab on the Coke and took a sip, avoiding her worried gaze.

Mom sat back and wrapped her shaking hands around her coffee mug. "She could have been you."

I swallowed, totally getting what my mom was saying. I get so involved in helping these dead girls cross over that I forget they are—or were—like me, with families, homes, boyfriends, part-time jobs . . . before their lives were cut short. Goosebumps threatened to erupt again.

"Things have been different since the sorority fiasco," I said.

My mom looked at me, her eyes filled with tears. "I'm so sorry about what happened the other day."

I nodded and took another chug of Coke to push

down the lump in my throat. Sometimes my mom could be all high-and-mighty like she was the boss and other times, like now, she was all soft and mommy-like. The mom from my childhood. But something nagged at me.

"Thanks Mom." I took a deep breath. "Do you remember the spell that Aunt Karen used at the sorority?"

My mom's eyes widened. "Why?"

"Because I don't know if Mrs. Swanson said it the right way. Maybe that's why everything went off the rails?"

"Why revisit that? Didn't it do enough damage the first time around?" She took another sip of her coffee.

"Yeah, right. Sorry."

If I wanted my mother to open up to me, I had to try another approach. Getting her upset would only make her shut down and I needed to know more about what exactly happened that night.

I sat down across from her and sipped my Coke.

"Mom, sorry I brought that up."

"Will you be able to help her?"

"I don't know." I shrugged. "Emily hasn't appeared to me. She reached out to Hillary. I mean, I saw Emily, but she didn't connect with me, so I'm not sure how I can help her cross over."

Mom shook her head.

"That poor girl. She probably doesn't know what is going on, does she?"

"Yeah, you could say that."

"Poor, poor girl." Mom stood up and placed her coffee cup in the sink.

She was shaking and she wiped the tears from her eyes.

Damn. I got up and gave her a side hug. "It's okay, Mom. Everything will be okay." Here I was acting all mature. That was supposed to be her job.

"I can't believe I'm saying this, but please call Dr.

Anthony back, he can help you cross Emily over and then maybe we can fix whatever happened at the sorority house.

Dr. A was pretty brilliant; he could always help me figure out where we needed to do to connect with the dead girl, so we could cross her over. Now, there was a glitch to that, considering I hadn't had a dream or vision helping to direct me to the site. Maybe he'd know what to do.

I rushed up the staircase to my room. Once inside, I closed the door and dug out my cellphone from my bag. When chatting with Mom, I'd ignored the vibration, which signaled I'd missed a call. Sure enough, my phone was flashing.

Cura. I speed dialed her number. On the first ring, she answered. "This is nuts. What did our mothers do to us?" she whispered.

Even though I could totally relate about the mom thing—I was thrilled that Cura had called me and had answered on the first ring. Progress!

"Did you read the news article?" I asked.

"Uh, kind of hard not to considering everyone at school was talking about it. Then I get home and my mother shoved it in my face."

"Yeah, my mom did too."

"Steph, my mother is going all ballistic about this. So is Hillary's mother. Seems Hillary told her that she saw Emily today."

"Yeah, we both saw her."

"And you're only telling me this now?"

"Come on, be fair. I tried talking to you this morning and you gave me the Arctic-cold shoulder. Remember?"

Cura sighed. "It's just that Mom never, I mean *never* gets upset. Hell, she looks for positivity in everything even clueless people. So, when she goes off, I know something is bad. And this is bad, isn't it?"

"Yup, really bad."

"Can I tell you something and promise you won't,"—I heard a gulp—"think I'm nuts?"

"Sure," I said.

"I keep hearing this voice, asking for my help. When I look up, I don't see anything," she whispered.

Silence.

"If it's who you say it is, Emily? I never knew her. I mean, yeah, I saw her on campus and all but we never actually spoke. How can I help someone I don't really know?"

Seriously, what else could I tell my friend?

"I'm so sorry, Cura. I should have told you about everything."

"Am I going schizo, or what?"

"Trust me. You're not."

Cura let out a bitter laugh. "You know kids at school talked about how weird you were and I stood up for you. I thought it was just the usual Hillary brand of gossip. Now I find out they were right. But you know what's even worse? That I have the same thing you have."

"It's not like that."

"Whatever. So, are you going to tell me everything? Or are you going to keep your secrets? That seems to be a pattern with you."

Ouch.

"I deserve that, but Cura, I really need your help right now."

A laugh. "Now you need my help?"

I took a deep breath, "Yes, Emily is dead but the problem is she's not reaching out to me."

"I thought you said you saw her too?"

"Yes, but this is different. In order for me to help her cross over, she has to send me some kind of vision showing me where she was killed but she hasn't done that."

"Why don't you ask Hillary since she's the one Emily showed up to."

"I tried, but Hillary gave me the shove off. I need to figure this out or Emily will keep haunting you and Hillary, and she'll never be at peace."

"You're joking."

"I'm dead serious."

"I wish you had told me all of this from the beginning. Then maybe we could have stopped our moms before they did that ceremony.

"Well, it's too late now, isn't it?" I said. I knew I was losing my cool and I should have been more sympathetic to Cura, but I'd been living with this ability for a while now and I was doing okay. Cura was acting like it was the end of the world.

"If you'd just been up front with me—."

"I know, I know," I interrupted her. "Look, how many times do I have to apologize? What we need to do now is work together otherwise this won't go away."

"You know for someone who lied to her best friend, you're certainly acting like a jerk." A loud click echoed in my ear. She may as well have rubbed salt into my already open wound. I tried to explain it to her but only made things worse. I was in deeper than before.

I swiped at my tears. I was a regular leaky faucet lately. No, I couldn't dwell on this right now or I'd be a soggy mess. Instead I dialed Dr. Anthony's number.

He answered after the first ring. "Stephanie. I need you here. Now!" he said.

"Wow, no hello or anything?"

"We need to talk about the missing girl." Then he hung up.

Jeez, get right to the point, why don't you?

I glanced over at my backpack flung over in the far corner of my room. Papers had spilled out and were now scattered on the floor.

I sighed.

Mr. Johnson, also my English teacher, had promised a pop quiz on *Fahrenheit 451* sometime this week and I knew I really needed to study or else I'd get a big fat D to add to my growing list. Plus, I needed to start working on my Spanish American War essay for World History.

I sighed again.

Unlike other kids who could go home, relax a bit, have dinner, and do their homework, I had to rush off and save a dead girl from wandering in ghostly purgatory for eternity. Yup, it was tough being me.

I checked my cell, debating whether I should call or just text Dylan.

Nah. Let Dr. Anthony do that. It's not as if he hadn't done that before. Dylan was sort of becoming an unofficial member of the Rescuer's club. The last time Dylan helped with a rescue it hadn't exactly gone great, but I thought after the run-in with undead Mark, he might have changed his opinion on the supernatural world.

I glanced longingly at Angelina, my cherry-red laptop. Yup, I named my lap-top Angelina because I love actress/humanitarian Angelina Jolie. Since Mom wouldn't tell me more about that night with Aunt Karen, I was itching to do some digging on my own. But that would have to wait until after I met with Dr. A.

CHAPTER 10

Borrowing my mom's car, I turned on Morse Avenue where Dr. Anthony's office was located close to Kaiser hospital. My mentor. And he was probably the only person who really understood me. Mom had been the one to introduce us and, at first, I resented him because, *hello, Mom,* but after he saved my butt back at the coffee house? I knew I could trust him. Several oak trees had been planted around the perimeter of the building and two large stone lions were positioned on either side of the entrance to the thirteen-floor office building. Dr. Anthony's office was located on the thirteenth floor. No surprise there. I resisted the urge to squeeze in a grande mocha latte from the Starbucks across the street, even though I knew it might be a long night.

I parked and went inside. On his office door was a sign that read: *Light Bringer's Family Support Services.* The familiar marquee, with the half-moon shooting out beams of light, may have said family services, but what he really did was help cross over the dead, although I wasn't sure how he got paid or if he was independently wealthy. It was all kind of mysterious. Dr. Anthony was a licensed psychologist and he *did* provide counselling but his "hobby," so to speak, was helping lost souls cross over. I didn't know what else he did. And I didn't ask. Maybe one day I would, but that day was not today. I wondered if the other people who worked in the building knew what really happened behind this door. It gave a whole new meaning to the phrase helping those with "unresolved issues" move on.

I blew out a breath and went in. Framed diplomas from Stanford and several other prestigious universities decorated the dark blue walls. They mentioned degrees in cognitive neurology and psychology, but I knew the truth of Dr. Anthony's vocation. Underneath one of his many degrees was a certificate from the Koestler Parapsychology unit. Yup, he was definitely an expert in the paranormal.

In front of Dr. Anthony's large mahogany desk were two plush, dark green chairs. Dr. Anthony's desk sat in the middle of the spacious office in front of a huge window with a dark green shade that was pulled down at the moment. Two big, green, leafy plants stood on either side of the window. A black leather sofa with a bunch of magazines in a wooden slot sat against the wall beside the door. On the far wall across the room was an amazing built-in bookcase with an assortment of books about psychology, cognitive memory, and some college journals with the title *Parapsychology Association*. An old-fashioned round wooden table with chairs sat in front of the bookcase. When I had some time, I promised myself, I'd go through the books, if only to satisfy my morbid curiosity on the paranormal world. I mean, it was one thing to have abilities, but it was another to have knowledge. Good knowledge. Not the kind that got you into trouble like my Aunt Karen.

Sitting at his desk, Dr. Anthony waved me forward without glancing up. His tousled brown hair looked as if he hadn't combed it that morning and he seemed to be completely absorbed in whatever he was typing on his laptop. His brown eyes were all scrunched up and his Clark Kent glasses sat low on his nose. He was wearing a black turtle neck sweater and a gray-tweed jacket with those patches on the elbows that professor-types like. A gray scarf was looped around his neck, hanging lower on one side than the other. If I could compare him to someone famous, I'd say he kind of looked like Benedict

CROSSED FIRE

Cumberbatch. Definitely not my type. He was young-ish looking but was probably around my dad's age.

"Hey," I said, "so I'm here for my appointment." I sauntered in, kicking myself for not picking up that mocha latte. I'd brought my cross along to see if he could give me some insight into what to add to it to help Emily. I left it on the table against the wall, opposite the big bookcase at the other end of the room. It had another door leading to an adjoining room, which I never went into. I think he kept his top-secret paranormal stuff in there. The table had several plain wooden crosses of various sizes scattered haphazardly across it. Dr. Anthony didn't decorate them like I did. For some reason, I had a "talent" or "gift" for sensing a particular image that attracted the dead girl and helped her cross over. Even though my mom had wanted to reverse my abilities, I was pretty proud of the work that Dr. Anthony and I did. Yes, it was a little strange, and yes, I didn't know much of the theory behind it. Certainly nothing that could compare to Dr. Anthony's vast knowledge about the paranormal. But I did have an ability to connect to the dead and, in particular, young girls who had been murdered and needed help to cross over. The crosses I constructed helped guide them. And that made me feel pretty special. Yup, you could call me a ghost artist, and in a way, my artwork was a tribute to the lost girls out there.

I leaned over to the corner of Dr. Anthony's desk and lifted the lid of the oversized glass candy jar. I swear he must re-fill it every day because it was always bursting with different candies every time I had a session with him. All individually wrapped of course, because ewwww . . . germs. Dr. Anthony said he kept them on hand for the kids he counseled. But I knew better. Dr. A had one mean sweet tooth. It must come with the territory. Once again, he didn't disappoint me. Today's selection featured caramel Werther's and Mini-Tootsie

Rolls. I snatched a couple of Tootsies. Not coffee, but it would do for now.

"So?" I asked in between bites, waiting for his reply. The chewy chocolate nougat stuck to my teeth but I didn't care. I crumbled the wrappers and tossed them in the nearby tin wastepaper basket. Perfect shot.

"I'm sure you've seen this by now?" he asked, moving a pile of books to the side and picking up a copy of the newspaper. What was it with older guys and newspapers? Emily Jones' pretty face stared up at me. The same picture that Mom showed me in the online news article, and no doubt the same picture Cura's mom had shown her. She looked like an all-American cheerleader in the picture. Pretty, blonde, and with a gleaming, toothpaste-commercial smile. Nothing like her horror movie appearance at school today.

"Yeah, she's been the talk of the whole school. But not only that, her ghost graced the halls of Sutter High today," I said hesitating about telling him everything.

Dr. Anthony settled back in his oversized high-backed chair, waiting for more.

I hated when he gave me that penetrating-raised-eyebrow stare. It made it so hard to hold back any info from him. I had to fess up.

"Well, um, I saw her at school but she didn't appear directly to me. And I usually dream about the ghost-girls, but I didn't this time either."

He frowned, pursing his lips together.

"And there's another thing. She hovered around someone else on campus." I gulped, knowing I had to share this little fact. "Hillary."

Dr. A didn't bat an eye. "Did Hillary have some connection with Emily in this life?"

"They both were on cheer squad last year. I'm not sure if they were besties or not, but they did hang out." I bent forward, fishing around for another Toostie Roll amidst the hard candies.

"Then it might make sense that Emily is choosing to try to contact Hillary and not you."

I stopped and mused over that.

"But Hillary isn't a Rescuer. She can't help Emily."

"You didn't know what to do either when your friend first appeared to you." He tapped his chin with his finger, seeming to debate his next point. "Tell me again what exactly happened at school?" he prodded. His voice had a slight accent to it. I didn't know where he was born. For that matter, he could have been from a foreign country and moved here when he was a kid. He was a pretty mysterious dude.

Even after working with him for the past few months, I still felt unnerved by his intense gaze. Like he could read my mind. I looked away, my gaze skittering to the built-in bookshelf. I knew there was a hidden cabinet behind it. You had to push a book and it opened. It's where he stored the tools of our trade—wood, hammers, nails, and some other things that I had no idea what they were for. But I'm sure he did.

I stopped mid chew, almost choking on the candy.

"The girl popped up right when..." I stopped. How could I tell him how the ghost had appeared without revealing the part about Hillary and the ceremony that our moms concocted the other day? I'd promised Mom I wouldn't squeal on her.

Dr. Anthony's eyes narrowed, like he could tell I was hedging. "When?" he asked.

"When I got out of class." I shrugged, brushing it off as no big deal, although I'm sure he knew better.

He settled back in his chair. "Maybe she'll come to you later in one of your dreams. The veil between our world and the Other Side is thinnest during the dream state. If she doesn't visit you, then maybe we can speak with your friend Hillary."

"She's no friend of mine," I said. "Besides, Hillary would never in a million years help us." I blew out a breath, worried that my ability might have been altered considering that now Hillary and Cura could see and hear the dead. Did that mean I wouldn't have any more dreams of the victims? Without the dreams, I couldn't see the murder scene or get a glimpse into the essence of the victims.

He cleared his throat. "I know you say you need to have dreams of the girls, but given your history helping lost girls cross over—I think we can still help Emily. In the meantime, I need you to help me with someone else."

I almost sighed in relief that he'd dropped the whole Hillary thing, but knowing Dr. A, I somehow knew this wouldn't be the last of it.

Dr. Anthony opened his drawer, and pulled out a news clipping. "Here's someone who's been missing for a couple days. She's currently listed as a Jane Doe."

I leaned over, pulling the clipping to me. A black and white photo of a girl around my age, with shoulder length hair and a rock band t-shirt, stared back at me.

I touched the photo, wondering about her. A sudden flash of insight came to me. "She's a run-away, isn't she?"

Dr. Anthony nodded. "A lot of the Jane Doe cases usually are. They often get put on the back-burner or thrown at the bottom of a pile of other cases. "I want you to try something, Steph."

I looked up from my perusal of the article.

"I want you to close your eyes, relax, and let your mind float free. Picture yourself taking a walk in the park, the birds are chirping, the wind is whistling through the trees . . . "

I knew where he was headed . . . If the rules had changed, why did I have to rely on dreams? Maybe all the stress of the past few days was making it hard for me to connect with these dead girls in my dreams. Maybe I just needed to relax and focus . . .

I closed my eyes and took a deep breath, sitting back

in the plush chair. An image of daisies fluttered through my mind. "I see it." I opened my eyes as relief swept over me. At least that "ability" hadn't deserted me. I was still surprised when these images appeared to me seemingly out of thin air, but that usually only happened after a dream. I didn't know why or how—just that somehow these pretty images of nature and animals would pop into my head and I would know instinctively that they were somehow connected to the spirit of the girl who was murdered. And drawing those images on the cross created the talisman for them to find their way to the light. It left me a little in awe of the entire process. It wasn't me, really, it was some greater force out there in the universe that was using me as their "Sharpie" and through me, helping those girls cross over.

Dr. A grinned and inclined his head to the work table. "Good girl. Time to get to work. I have to finish up some paper work and then we can go."

I got up, went to the table at the far end of the office, and picked up one of the two-and-a-half-foot wooden crosses. Already prepped, the smooth surface just lacked my own contributions. Over to the side lay a collection of acrylic paints and some colored Sharpies. My hands itched to get to work.

I fumbled through the paints, settling for yellow. With a black Sharpie, I carefully sketched a cluster of daisies and forget-me-nots. A delicate burst of leaves added to the girl's essence. Another image came of small hummingbirds poking their long beaks into a coral hibiscus flower.

I concentrated on sketching the delicate bird. Strokes of fine lines captured the bird in flight.

Just then the door flung open and slammed closed. Classic Dylan. My pen slipped, creating a droopy beak on my pretty hummingbird.

I bit back a sarcastic grumble and concentrated on fixing the blobby mess.

[101]

"Did I miss anything?" Dylan strolled over, looking over my shoulder and then stopped. "Whoa, Dr. A, you called me over to help with another one of those Rescue things? I thought you said you had something important to tell me."

"Next time, don't slam the door okay?" I snapped, then went back to work. So much for supportive boyfriends. If Dylan was going to act like this, then he didn't deserve a nice hello from me.

Dylan blew out a breath and walked over to Dr. Anthony, who was busy pouring over some notes at his desk. "So, what's up Dr. A?" he asked, obviously ignoring my snarky comment.

Dr. Anthony held up the picture of Emily from that day's paper. "I'm sure you've heard about this missing girl?"

Dylan glanced at me, as though asking me if he should mention what happened at school with Hillary and her "visions." I gave him a "look" and a slight shake of my head, hoping the counselor's sharp eyes hadn't seen our exchange.

Shoving his hands in his pockets, Dylan muttered something. "Do you mean did I hear about her going missing? Yeah, so did the whole school," he finally said in reply.

"Stephanie told me that she saw Emily's ghost on campus. I guess I just wanted to hear if you were able to sense her aura, and what you could tell me about it." Dr. Anthony laid the paper back down. "That is, if you were close enough to her."

"If anything, it was just the usual, 'mad jive.'" Dylan shrugged. "Is this why you called? I have a big test to study for. Some of us are serious about school."

I snorted. The last thing Dylan was serious about was studying. He was more likely upset about having to be called away from his latest video game obsession—the one with the armies and the zombies or cops and the zombies? I couldn't keep up, but it usually involved fighting zombies. Dylan glanced back at me again, almost daring me to argue. *Nope. Not gonna give into my urge for sarcasm.* I snickered to myself and kept drawing. Dylan was super cute and his kisses made me melt, but sometimes he was such a "guy."

"This is important, too," I said, finishing the daisies on the cross. The paint didn't skip on the smooth wood finish like it did on the crosses I made. I made a mental note to be sure to spend a little extra time sanding the wood I used for my own crosses.

"If it's true, and Emily's dead," he commented, "I doubt she'll appreciate the cross where she is."

I dropped my brush and placed my hands on my hips, ready to battle. "Jeez, Dylan, that's the point. Something's happened to Emily. I don't know what, considering she didn't show up in a dream. If you don't want to say it, I will. She was murdered or else she wouldn't have appeared."

"You don't know that. You might be mistaken. That ghost you saw might have been someone else."

"No, it was her." I shook my head. "I wish it wasn't."

Ever since I helped to cross Allison over, it all felt too close to home.

"Still, I doubt Emily would care what you drew on that cross."

I glared back at him. "This cross isn't for Emily, it's for another girl." I frowned at him. "And if being here bugs you so much, go home to your 'studying,'" I said making air quotes.

Dylan stepped backward, raising his hands in protest. "Jesus, don't be so touchy. I know it's important. I was just trying to lighten the mood."

I rolled my eyes at his attempt at humor.

"Dylan, given your uncanny ability with sensing auras, I was hoping you can help us find out more about the girl we're working on crossing over." Dr. Anthony intervened in a smooth tone, clearly trying to put a stop to our bickering.

Dylan nodded. "Right." He then gave me a sheepish grin. "Sorry, Steph. Okay?" Puppy dog eyes followed. "I'm here to help, honest."

My heart softened. I nodded and gave him a reluctant smile.

His grin went from sheep to wolf. And he winked at me.

I sighed. Sometimes he made me so mad. And other times he could make my heart do back-flips. Dylan picked up the clipping Dr. A passed to him, flopped down on the chair opposite the desk and started reading. I shook my head and went back to my drawing.

CHAPTER 11

True to his word, Dylan stuck around and helped me dry the freshly painted crosses with a vintage, teal-green fan that Dr. A had in his "magical cabinet of curiosities." I tried not to think about Cura and Hillary and when I would tell Dr. A what was going on. That could wait until later. We had a crossing to do.

We hurried over to the site of the crossing after I texted Mom that I might be running a little late and not to wait up.

The crossing was right off the I-5 freeway, across the street from Old Town Sacramento. A heavy fog hung over the Sacramento River, giving it a ghoulish feel. I glanced at Dr. Anthony, who was checking his watch in between staring out into the distance.

"So how much longer?" Dylan asked.

"Not much longer." Dr. Anthony checked his watch again before scanning the freeway. I don't know how he did it. But one of his abilities as a Light Bringer was being able to pin-point the exact location of the crime scene. Usually, we started with one of my dreams and worked from there. Sometimes I had a dream that came out of nowhere and then we'd find out about a missing girl and we put two-and-two together. He called this "precognition" or using my dreams of the future to determine the sites. But this time we were kind of going in "blind." Dr. A told us he had to call in a few favors from the police department. Not sure what that meant, but here we were, at this lonely stretch of highway. "Stephanie, tell me when you sense her."

Dylan took a sip of water from his water bottle. He looked nervous. I took hold of his other hand and squeezed it. He sometimes got crippling headaches when he sensed an aura from a dead girl.

"Yes, I came prepared this time," he said, offering me a sip. "No freaky light shows this time." The last time Dylan had been with me at a crossing, the brilliant white light had overwhelmed his senses. It was like a million auras coming at him all at once. Dr. A, said he could train his mind to remain calm and that would stop the headaches. I hoped Dylan could get through it okay. Despite his cocky nature, he was a really good guy and actually did want to help, even though it made him physically ill to do so.

A sudden breeze picked up the trash and leaves that were strewn about, making them dance over the patchwork of dirt and grass. And then I felt it. The itch on the back of my legs that warned me a dead girl was approaching.

A flash of intense light erupted across the darkened sky. Dylan pressed the cold water bottle to his forehead, probably to soothe his headache. Under his breath I heard him mumble about a freaky aura.

At first I couldn't make her out, but little by little she materialized out of the fog. She looked older than me, maybe college age?

"Is that the girl?" I asked Dr. Anthony. Sure, he'd shown me a newspaper photo, but seeing the ghost in front of your eyes was always different from seeing a picture of someone when they were alive.

"Yes," he said. "Her name is Morgan. Morgan Waters."

Although I hadn't had a vision of her death, the strong impression of daisies resurfaced. I swear I could smell the sweet, fresh scent.

Morgan made her way over to us in a weird sort of half-floating-half-walking way, crossing the Sacramento

River. Moonlight shone all around, lighting up the freeway behind her.

The water bottle fell from Dylan's grasp, but he made no effort to pick it up. He stared at the spirit, and then rubbed his eyes.

"Man," he complained, wincing.

Morgan staggered, weaving back and forth. She held her hands in front of her in a vain attempt not to fall. Other than her weird movements, she didn't have the usual "deathly" look with blown-out brains, burns or guts trailing behind her.

She pushed aside some strands of long ratty blonde hair that kept falling in her face. She was wearing a tight black T-shirt with the Grateful Dead logo on it. Ironic, considering her current state. The closer she got, the more potent the aroma was of sickly sweet perfume and rotting flesh. *Ugh.* Yup, death did not smell pretty.

"Why am I hurr? W-who urr you?" Her words slurred together. A flash of a metal tongue piercing told me why. "Oh, pruuutty." She bent down by the cross I'd finished for her.

"Stephanie," Dr. Anthony whispered. He gestured toward the girl, who was touching the tiny daises. Since I didn't know her name, I hadn't written it out.

"Oh, right." I took a step closer. "It's Morgan, right?"

She lifted her head and stared at me. Her eyes widened in surprise. "How do you know my name?"

"Well, that is your name, right?"

"Just tell her why we're here." Dylan whipped back around. He pressed his fingers to his temples.

I frowned, signaling him with my hand to stop, but he persisted in being a mega tool.

"You're dead," Dylan yelled, his voice cracking from either the cold or agony the aura happened to be causing. "Just walk to the light or something."

Morgan rose up, staring back at me.

"What? No, you can't be serious. I can't be," she gulped, "dead." She swayed in place, her bottom lip quivering. "You're lying."

"Can't you help her?" Dylan asked.

"I'm sorry to say he's right," I whispered. "You're dead."

Morgan's eyes bulged. "No, no, no," she said. "I just had a few shots and maybe a few beers. They said it would be fun." She stared back at us. "Am I really . . . like . . . dead?"

"Yes. You are," I whispered.

Dr. Anthony stepped in, "Do you remember what happened last?"

Morgan put her hand in front of her face, waving it around. Then her eyes widened. "No, it's all a blur and I've been so cold."

She turned to me, as if I had the answers, but I had nothing. I reached out and tried to touch her. My hand slid through her ghostly form, and a freakin' cold chill shot through my body. I stepped back when the vision hit.

A fraternity party off Sac State campus. Lots of older guys outside of the fraternity house, holding plastic cups and checking out the girls. There were a number of college-aged girls, including Morgan. At the side, I thought I saw Emily Jones with some other girls. Then a bunch of people rushed into the house.

The scene quickly changed to Morgan close to a really cute college guy. Tall, dark hair, and an amazing build. He leaned in close, whispering something. His hand went up her arm, settling close to her face.

Then, the same guy dropped something into her cup.

The images quickly ran into others, first she was unconscious, then the dark-haired guy was on top of her, raping her. I wanted to push him off her and screamed in protest.

Morgan pulled away and the visions left.

"Do you know the name of the guy at the party?" I asked again, wanting at least to give her some justice.

"No, I don't remember."

I glanced back at Dr. Anthony.

"I swear I saw Emily at that party," I said.

"Wait, Emily Jones was at the same place where she," Dylan pointed over at Morgan, "was killed?"

If that were true, then maybe the same guy that killed Morgan might have done the same thing to Emily.

A light suddenly appeared around us and intensified. I had to shield my eyes. Dylan stumbled back, searching for his dropped water bottle. Once he found it, he pressed the bottle close to his face. He then turned away, but not before I caught a glimpse of his contorted face.

A supernatural glow coated the freeway, the off ramp, and the hill. The white light pulsated. A sense of peace engulfed me. At that moment, I knew everything would be okay. I could help Morgan go to the Other Side, and the Dr. could help bring justice to her murder with his contacts at the police department.

"What is that?" Morgan asked. One thing about the dead, they could just pop up anywhere. Morgan had run off toward the trail, but the bright light must have drawn her back. Goosebumps rose on the back of my neck.

With great effort, I turned to face her.

"I think you know," I whispered.

"Yes." Her features transformed. No longer "dead-looking" and the smelly aroma dissipated once she saw the castle she changed and was surrounded by light—the light was all around her, too, and she looked beautiful and peaceful.

"It's going to be all right now. You're going to be okay. I promise." My voice cracked with emotion as I pointed to a medieval-like castle that floated in mid-air before it settled down on the freeway. *Wow, seriously?* The castle looked like it belonged at Disneyland. Everyone's version of heaven or paradise was different.

Apparently for Morgan, this castle held happy memories for her.

Hibiscus, daisies, and Lilly of the Valley flowers carpeted what, only moments before, had been the dusty, dirty freeway. A solo hummingbird buzzed close to my ear, before zooming off into the castle. The scent of the flowers tickled my nose.

"Right. Wow, trippy." Morgan's eyes widened as she strolled to the castle. When she got to the entrance, she turned and waved, and then in a flash of light she was gone along with the castle.

The warmth of a summer breeze floated around me and I could still smell the flowers. I closed my eyes and smiled, savoring the wonderful feeling for a while longer.

Dylan lowered the water bottle. "Talk about clueless. I still don't get that they don't realize they're . . . "

"Dead?" I finished. "You can say it."-

"As long as the girls make the transition to the light, everything is all right. Stephanie's ability to use telepathy, or be able to see what had occurred with Morgan, will be a big help in bringing her justice. Tomorrow, I'll look into leads on that fraternity party and who might have been there. I'll also see if Emily Jones might have attended." Dr. Anthony picked up the burlap bag that had contained the cross. "Ready to call it a night?

"Yeah, you can say that." I snuck a peek at my watch. Two a.m. "Hey, I might even get some shut-eye time, after all."

CHAPTER 12

Thank goodness the next day went by without any more drama. Rescues, aka crossing over the dead, always drained me. It seems like after the light vanishes so does my energy. Each time I did a Rescue I could sleep for days. Hard to do since my Rescues usually happened on school nights. The practice of Rescuing doesn't follow school schedules.

And last night's Rescue erased any fears I'd had that I'd lost my ability. Even though I didn't have the usual dream beforehand, I'd helped Morgan go to the light. Yes, Dr. Anthony had helped too. Plus, what did he call it? Telepathy? I thought that only psychics were able to do that. It felt kind of strange to have something in common with them.

I didn't want to chance calling Cura for a ride as she still couldn't legally drive friends for a few more months. Stupid California law. Plus, we weren't really talking. As I dragged my butt to school, I vowed not to make the same mistake I did yesterday, forgetting my much-needed caffeine boost. I stopped at Starbucks and ordered a mocha iced Frappuccino with extra whip cream and chocolate sprinkles. I took a sip and waited for the sugary concoction to work its magic.

But the sugar rush quickly evaporated once I got to campus. Almost everyone I passed in the hallway seemed intent whispering, sharing cell phone photos, and checking their Instagram and Snapchat.

I scrounged inside my purse for my cell and pulled up Snapchat to see what I might be missing.

The smiling face of Emily Jones pierced through my earlier Rescue euphoria, giving me a virtual kick in the butt. Time was ticking down to help Emily, but so far she hadn't come to me, although I could have sworn I saw her at that frat party. The same one where that Morgan girl had gone to and later had died. I switched my cell off.

You really should 'fess up and let Dr. Anthony know about the meeting back at the abandoned sorority house. That's where all of the recent craziness, like Emily appearing to Hillary occurred. But that would mean telling him about Mom and the others and the whole initiation thingy and the worst part...

Although I hated the thought, deep down I just knew in order to get Emily to cross over, I had to work with Hillary.

I shivered, and took another sip of my drink, although given the way things were already headed today, I would need one of those Unicorn Fraps to get me through.

Everywhere I went I saw posters of Emily in her Sutter High Cheer uniform. Her big smile and vibrant face seemed obscene given that she was dead.

Flyers with info about joining a search team for Emily were being passed out by other members of the cheerleading squad. Hillary, though, was missing from the group. A sour taste replaced the chocolate goodness in my mouth. I threw the rest of my mocha Frappuccino into the nearby trash can.

I kept my head down, ignoring the crowds in the hallways. Although I didn't talk to anyone, keeping to myself, I could hear all the gossip circulating around. They all thought Emily was missing. But I knew differently. I knew she was dead and I couldn't say anything to anyone about it because secrecy was part of the unwritten Rescuer Code (as if there was such a thing), and because they'd either think I was crazy or think I had something to do with her death. That's what the cops did to Rescuers like me.

"We need to talk," Cura's voice startled me. My books fell from my arms with a loud crash. My essay on the Spanish American War fluttered to the floor. I reached out, trying unsuccessfully to catch all the sheets. A few blew down the hallway. Unlike some other teachers, who let you scan and email the essays, Mr. Eipper was totally old school and wanted a printed copy of our assignments. *Damn.* I should have remembered to staple my essay. I crouched down picking up the papers that had fallen. Cura crouched down next to me. She handed me a few sheets I'd missed.

"Here."

"Thanks."

I took the offered papers, shuffling them in my binder, which looked like some mentality challenged kid had tried to organize it. I then shoved the binder back in my locker and closed it.

"Seriously," Cura said, more urgent this time. "We need to talk."

"Not here, okay?"

"Fine with me. At the Burger King then?"

Well, since my first class was Gym, I didn't feel too guilty about missing it. As long as I made it back for History class so I could turn in my paper. "Sure."

One of our favorite places to go after school was the local Burger King. Usually we just chatted and dished the 411, but given all the recent drama, I didn't think we'd be talking about the usual teen girl stuff today.

For one thing, never in a bazillion years did Cura cut class, which she was doing right now. A sliver of hope shot through me. Could her anger toward me be thawing? Or maybe she wanted some advice about her new supernatural powers? Either way, I was happy to have the chance to talk.

We walked into the Burger King, which was pretty

empty after the breakfast rush. Cura ordered a straight black coffee without her usual dose of sugar and cream. I should have taken that as a sign. I ordered a medium Dr. Pepper. We went to our usual booth, straight to the back, close to the soda stand. "Well, are you going to tell me or am I going to have to get it from somewhere else?" she asked, between sips of her coffee.

Buying some time, I glanced out the window. A huge SUV was in the drive-through lane. Some soccer-mom type was picking up her order. I wondered what it must be like to be "normal" and not have to deal with the dead all the time.

"Well?" she asked.

I turned back to Cura. "What do you want me to say?"

"That our Moms and Hillary are wrong?"

I pumped the straw up and down in my soda, causing some of the brown liquid to fizz over the side. I refrained from sucking it up.

"What are they saying?" I couldn't resist the snark. "I mean, besides me being one of the damned?"

I waited, hoping she'd disagree, but she didn't.

I sighed.

Cura frowned and then rested back against the vinyl booth. "That's not what I mean."

"What do you mean exactly?"

"They're saying we weren't supposed to see or hear anything at the sorority house, other than the spells we had to recite. Hillary actually said she saw Emily Jones, and she was dead!" Her eyes looked worried.

I knew I should tell her. Cura was my best friend, even if we were at odds at the moment.

But how do I even begin to tell Cura the "truth" of what I do?

"Yes, she's dead," I half muttered.

Cura's eyes widened. "Why are you saying that?"

"Because it's true."

Cura's frown deepened, so I explained: "I know because," I took a deep breath, "I help dead girls cross over to the Other Side."

Silence.

Cura looked at me wide-eyed. "Ohmigod, just hearing you say that is so freaky. Even though I should be used to it by now."

I shrugged. "Yeah, it's not exactly your average part-time job, but I've come to realize how important it is."

Cura's shoulders slumped. "So, if she's dead, you-you can help her, then?"

"Yes, but it's complicated . . ."

"What do you mean?"

I took a sip of my soda. "The Rescuer Code says the dead girl has to appear to me. Usually I have dreams where she shows me where she was killed."

"Wow, this sounds like something out of a horror movie. You actually have, like, rules on what you can or can't do?"

"Something like that."

Cura took another sip of her coffee.

"I'm surprised you're not telling me I'm nuts."

Cura smiled. Could it be she was finally warming up to me now? "Hey, remember, I grew up with this stuff. My mom is into all this New Age stuff. So, I've always been open-minded about it. To be honest, I'm just disappointed you didn't think I'd believe you. Why did you wait so long?"

"Because . . . well, it was hard for me to accept it myself, at first. And my mom freaked out about it when I first told her about my so-called ability." I leaned in close and whispered. "My dad doesn't even know, or my brother. My mom wants to keep it a secret for my own good, but I know she's hiding something."

"Do you think your mother might have done a spell on your dad?"

I shuddered. "I hope not, but then again, after that one initiation thing? Who knows?"

"Yeah, right."

"So, you can imagine how worried I was about letting anyone know. And with Dylan, well, I didn't really have a choice. We were dating and I couldn't exactly lie about where I was going at night. Not to mention he can see auras, so it was only natural that I tell him." I played with my straw as I continued. "Besides, I was worried that I'd lose you as a friend . . . that you'd think I was a freak, or something."

"Well, I won't." Cura smiled at me. "Friends forever, right?"

My heart swelled. I was such an idiot for not telling Cura sooner.

"Anyway," Cura whispered, "not saying I'm an expert or anything, but what happened at that old sorority house gave me the chills big time."

"What exactly happened to you?" I asked.

She slid down in her seat, the vinyl squeaking under her.

"I hear voices," she whispered. "I swear I hear people around me. Then I turn around and no one is there."

"Yeah, tell me about it."

Cura gaped at me. "Is this what you go through? Because if it is, man, I don't know how you deal."

Boy, talk about an understatement.

Cura stared at me, waiting, it seemed, for me to spill.

I took another sip of my drink, then let out a big sigh.
"Yeah, it's weird and creepy when you describe it, and it's not something I advertise, that's for sure. Look, I know I haven't been honest with you about all of this. I can't tell you how sorry I am."

Cura placed her hand over mine. Warmth surged, erasing the earlier chillness.

"Well, I haven't exactly been very supportive either."

My eyes teared up. I sniffled.

"Thanks."

"Let's promise we won't keep secrets anymore, okay?"

"Promise."

I settled back in the booth.

"I just know that after our little 'initiation' that's when I started to put two and two together," Cura said.

I stared at her, not understanding.

Cura leaned over, propping her elbows on the table.

"The dead girl at the sorority house," she whispered, looking at me. "I mean, I didn't see her or anything. I heard her, though. She whispered in my ear. But it sounded like a hundred people talking all at once— different kinds of voices and I couldn't really make out what they were saying, but I heard the name Emily. Then when my mom showed me the news article, I knew that it must have been Emily trying to talk to me, I guess, or someone, some ghost trying to tell me about Emily."

"Oh," I said, musing over the strangeness of it all. I could see and hear the dead, but Cura could only hear them and Hillary could only see them. Was that because their "powers" weren't fully developed or did they have extra strong hearing and visual perception that I didn't have? Or did it only happen after our mothers decided to play around with the Other Side? Did their spells back in college unleash more than my aunt burning down the sorority house? I would have to ponder it another time, or perhaps ask Dr. A, if I ever worked up the guts to go against Mom's wishes and tell him.

"It's totally nuts," Cura said, giving her head a little shake. "I tried talking about it to my mom but she only gets all sad and changes the subject, which isn't helping the situation."

"Yeah, tell me about that. My mother is the queen of denial."

Cura leaned over and grabbed a handful of sugar packets. She ripped open one packet after another, pouring the sugar into her coffee. I shook my head, since her coffee was probably tepid by now.

"I kinda of figured since I'm part of this club of yours, I may as well know more about it, right?"

Relief washed over me. I knew this took a lot for Cura to admit. Maybe I could actually talk about this stuff with her and maybe it would help both of us deal with whatever came along. Plus, she could help with Emily.

I took a deep breath. "Okay, but I've got to get to class. I have to hand in my history paper. Meet me at six p.m. in front of the office building at 1400 Watt Boulevard. You know, across from that new Starbucks in the Grove Center?"

Cura's gaze didn't leave mine. "And you'll tell me everything?" she asked.

"If you really want the scoop, meet me there. But I'm warning ya. Only come if you're open to learning some freaky stuff."

"And hearing a dead girl in the middle of a condemned building isn't freaky enough?"

I chuckled. "That doesn't even begin to define freaky."

CHAPTER 13

Cura deserved answers, something I'd wished I'd had when I first realized I had these "special powers," back when my friend Allison appeared to me and pleaded for my help. Only back then my "confession" to my mom landed me in the psych ward, complete with a daily cocktail of anti-psychotic drugs. What's worse is she frickin' knew I didn't need to be there. She could have told Dad the "truth,". Deep down, I guess I still hadn't forgiven her for that. I wouldn't wish that on anyone, including Hillary. I was glad I could be there for Cura, but I couldn't help but wish I'd had someone to help me.

The rest of the morning was pretty much okay. I turned in my history paper. I had managed to cobble together a pretty decent paper in between seeing dead girls and dealing with my personal drama. After history class, I stepped outside to call the good doctor. No surprise he answered on the first ring. I knew he was a bonafide counselor, but I wondered about that secret side to him--if there was some kind of underground international secret society that he worked with, like a spy agency for the dead or something.

"Hey, bringing someone around sixish. Just calling to prepare ya and all," I rushed through, "I mean, didn't want you to be surprised."

"I'll be waiting," he said calmly.

Nothing else. It was eerie, like he already knew. Maybe he did. After all, the doc was one mysterious dude. A supernatural power had healed him after he was stabbed in the chest at the abandoned coffee house in our battle with demon Mark, last year. After everything I've been through in the past few years, I've come to expect the unexpected.

* * *

The slight tremor in my hands made it hard to steer the car into the parking lot. I glanced around, worried that Cura wouldn't show up. I resisted the urge to pop into the Starbucks across the street to grab a raspberry mocha Frappuccino, not wanting to break my one frap-a-day rule. I let out a snort of laughter. Here I was worried about how much caffeine-loaded calories to have in one day, when I had bigger things to worry about. Like who, out of the people in my life, would develop supernatural powers next. Or who would be the next girl I had to help cross over.

I turned the car around and parked it. And waited. Five minutes went by. No Jetta. Ten minutes. Okay, maybe, she changed her mind, but it still stung. I swallowed back my tears. Did I seriously think Cura would suddenly want to embrace this wonderful world of the supernatural? I should have just kept my mouth shut.

I decided to go home. I'd call the doc later. I pulled out of the empty parking lot and that was when I saw her. Cura, standing on the sidewalk on the other side of the building. She glanced down, checking her cellphone. Her eyes looked kind of sad. She looked up and saw me. Then a smile lit her face. She waved as I drove up and parked on the street.

"Hey, I was worried you wouldn't show," I said, getting out of the car.

Cura blew a strand of hair out of her face. She'd straightened it. Cura had naturally curly hair that tended to go a bit wild, if she didn't "tame it into submission."

"Are you kidding? No way would I miss this." She grinned.

I smiled back but my stomach was tied up in pretzel knots. How long would her optimism last?

"Ok, let's go."

We walked into the almost empty office building, past the cool-looking lobby fountain. It was a "wall" made of lush-green plants, moss, sea shells, flowers, and glass pots of colorful sand. The water trickled down the wall into a pool surrounded by marble steps where people could sit and enjoy a peaceful moment. I loved stopping there every time I visited Dr. A. There were still a few people milling about, and the security guard was at the front desk, but after five p.m. most people high-tail home. I didn't blame them. Although I was happy to finally be sharing this part of my life with Cura, I was super nervous, too. The lobby directory listed all the professionals in the building and what floors and suites they were in. A lot of psychiatrists, psychologists, and counselor types.

Cura narrowed her eyes and turned back to me.

"We're going to see a shrink?"

"Uh, not really."

"Okaaaaaay." She didn't say anything else as she followed me to the elevator. When we got off on the thirteenth floor and stood in front of the office door, I checked out Cura's reaction.

"You've got to be kidding, right?" she asked. "Light Bringers? Is this some kind of cult thingy 'cuz I'm not into that." Then she let out a long sigh. "But then again after our mother's little wacked paranormal thingy? Maybe we are?"

I didn't know what to say to that, so I turned the door knob, "No, but it is something that will—let's just say—enlighten you."

Jeez, did I just say that? Talk about clichés.

"Yeah, right," she snorted.

Typical Dr. Anthony hadn't noticed us as he probably was knee deep in researching something or other. He sat behind his huge mahogany desk, bent over his computer. Cura gave him a look, then glanced at me. "Cute," she mouthed. "For an old dude."

I raised my eyebrows and turned back to Dr. A, trying to see what Cura was seeing. He was wearing an X-Files t-shirt and faded blue jeans. He seemed to have a never-ending supply of t-shirts from sci-fi TV shows and movies. With his thick, brown hair that was always slightly messy and his wire-rimmed spectacles, I guess he was cute in a 'nerdy' kind of way but he was my dad's age. *Ewww.* "Jeez, Cura," I giggled.

Dr. Anthony's head popped up. "Stephanie," he said, then pushed back from his chair, and limped toward us.

Cura eyeballed his leg, then stared back at me.

I shrugged. "Old injury?" I whispered, unable to volunteer any more info, not knowing that story.

Dr. Anthony put his hand out, "Good to meet you," he said, then directed his attention back to me.

"This is Cura," I offered.

Cura shook his offered hand.

"Let's cut to the chase," she said in her usual Cura-like manner. "I'm sure Stephanie has shared what's been going on with me. Can you tell me why it happened?"

Dr. Anthony glanced at me with his eyebrows raised and a look in his eyes that said, *aha, I knew you were keeping something from me.*

"Dr. A, Cura is curious because something happened a few days ago and now she can hear dead people." I supplied, still feeling somewhat awkward at my discovery that she found Dr. A cute.

"Why don't we all have a seat," he suggested as he walked back to his desk and motioned to the two chairs facing it. This must all seem strange to you." He sat down, acting all nonchalant like a typical doctor type, but I knew from the intense look in his eyes that he was intrigued by the fact that Cura could hear the dead.

"Uh, yeah." Cura said, continuing as we settled ourselves into the comfy chairs, "Especially after that weirdness at the abandoned sorority house, which I'm sure Stephanie told you about." She glanced my way.

Trying to buy myself some time, I lifted the candy jar lid and rooted around for some Tootsie Rolls.

"Really?" Dr. Anthony turned his gaze to me. "No, this is the first I've heard of it . . ." And his eyebrows shot up again. "Stephanie?"

I squirmed in my chair, offered Cura a Tootsie Roll, and when she shook her head, I popped it into my mouth. I held up a finger while I chewed. Smiled and chewed.

No one commented.

I swallowed the gooey confection and debated whether to reach for another Tootsie Roll, then thought better of it.

I flung my hands up in the air in protest. "I kind of didn't volunteer that info. Not that I wasn't going to. The timing just didn't seem right."

"You didn't tell him?" Cura hissed. "Just great. Why am I not surprised?"

I slumped down in the chair, wishing I had grabbed another Tootsie Roll.

"Mom uh, I mean our mothers, took us to this meeting at their old sorority house right off the American River a few days ago," I finally volunteered. As if I had any choice.

"The condemned one?" he asked.

"Yeah, that one," Cura said, "Can you believe it's still standing? You'd think the city would have razed it to the ground by now." Cura nudged me to continue.

"So, our moms all got together—including our classmate Hillary's mom—to set up a 'cleansing' ritual. They all knew each other in college, so that's why they chose the sorority house." I glanced at Cura. "To make sure Cura and Hillary didn't end up like . . ." I cleared my throat. Well, you know . . . like me."

Dr. A nodded sagely.

"While we were there, something kinda went wrong and we kind of saw a dead girl, who we think might be a girl who used to live here. Emily Jones," Cura supplied. "I heard voices and think it might have been her, but since I never hung with her and all, I'm not sure."

Dr. Anthony steepled his hands, tapping them under his chin, as he observed us. I felt like a lab rat in an experiment that had gone horribly wrong. I squirmed in my chair, waiting for him to call me out, demand why I hadn't informed him of all of this.

Still, he said nothing.

Boy, did I wish I had stopped off at the Starbucks, at least, I'd have some caffeine to fortify me. That Tootsie Roll sugar boost was fading fast. "Um—I think Hillary shares our ability too."

Dr. Anthony's eyes widened.

"Hillary?" he asked, his voice soft but steel strong.

"The other girl at our moms' get together," I reminded him.

"This brings a new element into the picture," he said. "Though I shouldn't be surprised."

Cura and I exchanged looks, then I faced Dr. Anthony.

"What do you mean, you're not surprised?" I asked.

He blew out a breath then said, "The sorority house you girls visited for that little meeting? Those girls, or in this case, your mothers, had their own agendas."

"Right," I added. "Messing with the Other Side."

"Wait," Cura said. "You mean, our mothers did the same stuff that Steph does?"

"No," Dr. Anthony replied. "A young woman named Karen Harris, had the gift. The others followed along."

His face reddened at the mention of my aunt's name. A sudden thought flashed through my mind. "Did you know my aunt?" I asked.

Dr. Anthony leaned back in his chair and blew out a breath. "You could say that."

Holy moly! Dr. A had known Aunt Karen? I looked at Dr. A, who looked back at me with his raised eyebrows. Jeez, he was giving me that *I know more than you think I know* look.

Cura's face went white as she must have finally put two and two together. "So, whatever our moms dabbled in with Steph's Aunt Karen caused all of this?"

"Yes, you could say that as well." Dr. A leaned forward once more, laced his hands on the desk, and regarded Cura with a sympathetic look on his face.

She let out a long sigh. "And our moms knew about all this supernatural stuff and hid that from us?"

"Yup," I said, then frowned. One huge piece of the puzzle was still missing. A crucial part. "But if I had the ability, and none of the others did, why did all of them insist on the ceremony?" That was the big mystery that Mom refused to reveal to me.

Dr. Anthony's gaze never left mine. "Your mothers knew both Cura and Hillary were going to develop the powers sooner rather than later . . . One thing I've learned in my parapsychology studies, is that it's not that easy to turn a paranormal ability off at will. Not without causing some consequences."

"Wow," Cura said. "Just like . . . wow." Her fingers gripped the arms of the chair. "I think I'm going to be sick."

Dr. Anthony offered her a bottle of water. She shook her head. Instead she reached into the candy jar and scooped out a handful of chocolates.

"Though this does kind of explains things." She rammed a couple of Tootsie rolls in her mouth. So much for being sick. Her mouth moved with each chew of the chocolate candies. It took her a moment to regain her composure.

"I guess hearing the voices isn't really that bad." She

turned to me. "I mean it's better than the alternative. That I'm going crazy."

Relief splashed down on me like a cool shower on a hot summer day. I wanted to jump up and down and do back flips, that is, if I knew how to do one. Finally, after all this time there was someone I knew and liked—besides Dylan that is—who understood what I was going through.

"What do you know about my Aunt Karen?" I asked, turning back to Dr. A because, somehow, I just knew if anyone knew the whole story, it would be him.

"I'm surprised your mother—" he stopped then seemed to reconsider, "No, I can see why she wouldn't want you to know."

"Well, I'm not." Painful memories of her trying to get me committed to a psych ward resurfaced. What made it even more painful was she that she flippin' knew I could see the dead because of what she and Aunt Karen had done back in college. That hurt most of all. It was like she had tried to get rid of me—to get rid of her own shame.

Dr. Anthony motioned to the computer screen.

"I can tell you, but it will better if we look it up," he said.

Serious? As if I hadn't. But then, again, he would know exactly where to look and what to look for.

Cura and I walked over to the other side of his desk and looked over his shoulder as he went onto a web site about different kinds of toilet paper. Weird. He typed in a password and then a black screen popped up that said SOUL RESCUERS. Cura and I looked at each other, our mouths open. A secret website hidden in plain sight? Wow. His fingers flew over the keyboard. Up popped Sacramento Sorority House Tragedy, 1990.

"What do you girls know about the fire at the former sorority house?" Dr. Anthony turned to look at me. A chill shot through me that had nothing to do with the dead.

"Only what my mom told me. Aunt Karen hated being unpopular. She thought using the whole medium thing might get her into the sorority and it worked. She became popular, the girls asked her to join the group, but then she wanted to do more." I glanced at Cura, who was listening intently. "She wanted to manipulate the Other Side so she could go over there. Why would anyone want to do something that idiotic?"

"Power? Who knows," he said. "It's true that your aunt was born with a paranormal ability, but she got caught up in something dark. Sometimes people don't realize that having a supernatural talent comes with heavy responsibility. And requires guidance by someone with more experience. Karen, did have a guide, but she thought she didn't need one."

"Were you her guide?" I asked.

Dr. Anthony sighed. "It's more complicated than that. I was an apprentice in the Light Bringers Society. Your aunt and I shared the same guide, Dr. Wendel . . ."

"What happened to Dr. Wendel?" Cura asked.

"She is no longer with us." Dr. A, cleared his throat and turned back to his computer.

I gave Cura the universal "neck slash" sign and a look in my eyes for good measure telling her not to go there. I was dying to know about this Dr. Wendel, but I'd known Dr. A long enough to know when he didn't want to talk about something. And he sure didn't want to talk about Dr. Wendel.

"We—I did try to help your aunt before she did that first summoning ceremony at the sorority house. She was banished after that."

"Banished? From what exactly?" I asked, although deep down I knew.

"From Light Bringers. Yes, your aunt worked with us, for a time. But after the fiasco at the sorority house, she was banished."

I settled back, taking this all in. So, my aunt had a big part in all of this. No wonder Hillary's mother hated me so much.

Dr. Anthony stood up and went into an adjoining room behind a wall of frosted glass. Sounds of creaky drawers and papers shuffling floated back to us. Finally, we heard a "Eureka!" Cura glanced at me and I shrugged. He came back out holding a huge manila folder and handed it to me. I opened the folder, which contained a bunch of newspaper articles. The one on top was dated 1990. It was about the sorority house fire.

Cura moved in closer, pointing at the news clipping. "Wait, are those our moms?"

Sure enough, it was a photo of the younger versions of our mothers. All of Mom's sorority was in the picture—complete with big hair dos and colorful, long dresses. They were all smiling and standing, arm-in-arm, in front of the sorority house. It must have been taken before that terrible day.

Unsolved mystery behind sorority house fire.

A photo of the smoldering remains of the sorority house appeared next to the picture of our moms.

Dr. Anthony pushed his glasses back up his nose. "The official investigation revealed that the girls had decided to do a secret pledge," he gave me a leveled gaze, "and accidently left a candle burning after the ceremony."

"Well, we know there was more to it than that," Cura said, exchanging looks with me. "If it went so horribly wrong the first time why did our moms try again with us?

"I don't know." I shook my head. "My mom said they were trying to help us, but they screwed it up . . . again." Inside, I fumed. How could our mothers, take that risk again? Did they seriously think that because they screwed up big time, that they could do another lame spell and make everything be all sunshine?

"Right." Cura slumped down in her chair. "Now we're all freaks."

"Come on, Cura," I said trying to cheer her up. "We're not freaks. Yes, I can see dead girls, and yes, I help them cross over, but I don't mess with anything evil or bad." Well, maybe that one time, remembering my dance with Mark. Hot new guy Mark, who had some kind of power over me. Only at that time I didn't know he was an actual demon disguised as a human.

"I'm still confused." I looked at Dr. A, who was cleaning his glasses. "Why was my mother so insistent that I not tell you about that initiation they tried at the burned-down sorority house?"

"I assume your mother must have told the others about Mark," Dr. A replied. They must have gotten scared about a portal being opened between our worlds. They must have thought it had to do with your Aunt Karen. A demon can't just show up out of nowhere. There has to be a portal for that demon to get through. Anyone who plays with a spell or tries to contact the Other Side, without good knowledge or reason, opens themselves up to the possibility of cracking open a portal, which no doubt happened because of your aunt.

"But why did it take so long for a demon to appear?" Cura asked

"Demons have their own timelines; we're talking about another dimension, here. Sometimes a portal will go unnoticed until some other supernatural activity draws attention to it . . ." Dr. A, glanced at me with a sympathetic look in his eyes. "In this case, Stephanie's ability to rescue the dead."

"Holy crappola," Cura exclaimed. "It explains why Mark just up and 'disappeared' and no one knew what happened to him."

Not much had happened after Mark had "left." Sure, rumors circulated at school and, of course, a few stares and whispers were directed my way as the resident school weird girl. No secret I'd hung with him for a little while. I never said anything other than he'd left town— not really a lie—and left it at that. But there had been no police investigation. Well, how could the cops investigate a person who hadn't really existed in the first place?

The image of finding his leather jacket and the pile of ashes made me shudder.

At least now I had some answers about why our mothers had been so insistent on trying a spell on us. In their attempt to stop a repeat of what Karen had unleashed, their spell had only made things worse. They ended up unleashing the dormant powers in Hillary and Cura.

"Okay, Dr. Anthony. Now that we know all of this, we can help Emily Jones. We just need to get Hillary to join us." I dreaded confronting her again, but I knew we had to do this, or Emily's ghost would keep wandering the halls of our high school forever . . .

CHAPTER 14

The next day at school I found myself bouncing along to my locker, rejuvenated and actually feeling good.

I know, a first, huh?

I thought that Cura would spaz out after our little meeting with Dr. Anthony. I mean, Dylan had freaked when he first found out about my ability to help the dead cross over to the Other Side. And, after the last crossing, I'm still not sure where he stood exactly. He hadn't seemed too thrilled about being part of it.

But the opposite happened. After we met with Dr. A, Cura and I went across the street to the Starbucks and each ordered a Frappuccino with extra whip cream. We talked about all sorts of stuff, a lot about what I do with Dr. Anthony but also other stuff like school, upcoming term papers, and what kind of part-time jobs we were hoping to get in the summer. It was nice. Really nice. I had my best friend back. I could kick myself for not opening up to her sooner? We could have avoided a lot of pain.

"You should do that more often." Dylan strolled up to me, a half-smile emphasizing his wickedly cute dimple. He was wearing a half-zipped hoodie over a Boston Bruins t-shirt—his favorite NHL hockey team. Snug skinny jeans and high tops completed his outfit. Yup, he was definitely looking hot.

Dylan's smile grew bigger. Ohmigosh, could he tell what I was thinking by my aura?

I looked down, my hair covering the blush, I could feel heating up my face.

I took a quick sneak. "What did you say?"

"Your smile. It looks good on you."

I could feel myself blushing even more.

"Oh, been meaning to ask you something," Dylan said. He shoved his hands in his pockets, and leaned against the locker.

My heart skipped a beat. Did he want to take me up on that rain check from the other day?

"You and the doc aren't doing another Rescue thingie anytime soon, right? I'm still trying to get over the last one."

I felt like a deflated balloon. We had to work together to help Emily cross over, but if he didn't want to, would that mess things up? His decision would most likely impact our relationship. But that was a chance I was willing to take.

"Well, is he?" he asked.

"Not sure," I replied. "But you have Dr. A's number. You can text him too, you know."

He stretched his arms overhead. The outline of his muscles caught my attention. Funny sensations pulled at me. I really wanted to touch him, but I needed to ponder another huge problem. After the meeting with Dr. A, I realized I needed to tell Dylan that my aunt had caused the death of his aunt. I doubt that his mom had told him the truth. Dylan was such an honest and upfront kind of guy, that if he'd known the truth, he would have told me by now. What a mess.

"You don't need to get so defensive," Dylan said.

I opened my mouth ready to fire out a sarcastic retort, but at that moment, Hillary marched toward us. Only a couple of her wannabes trailed behind her. Not the usual crew. Ashley, though, stayed glued to Hillary's side. She didn't have the same smug, arrogant look of the others. I noticed her glancing in Dylan's direction and what was worse, I noticed him glancing back. A little too long, if you asked me.

Yes, I was kind of pissed at him at the moment, but he was still *my* boyfriend. She had no right to look at him like that. *He's mine. Back off.* I wanted to shout at her.

I nudged Dylan, extra hard.

"What?" he asked, finally breaking eye contact with the other girl.

A sly smile crept up Ashley's face as she looked back down to read whatever text she'd received on her cell.

Hillary stopped right in front of us. "You," she pointed her French manicured nail at my chest. "We need to talk. Now."

Here was my chance to convince her, but I was still reeling from the whole flirty eye-contact exchange between my boyfriend and Ashley.

"Whatever," I said. "I recall the last time we spoke, you said you had nothing to say to a . . ." I tapped my chin, " . . . a loser?"

Hillary blew a loose curl out of her face. "I don't have time to argue with you. We need to talk. It's important."

Dylan glanced at me, his eyes questioning.

"Starbucks. Now."

Then she twirled on her heels and left.

Dylan shook his head. "What's going on with you two?"

"There's no *us two* about any of this."

The rest of Hillary's group stayed behind to gawk at me. A few had been snapping photos of our exchange with their smartphones.

"What's your problem?" I asked them.

I didn't know why this really pissed me off, but it did. Maybe because of the whole karma thing and, even though Hillary had been a bitch to me, that didn't mean I had to sink to her level.

Ashley smiled at Dylan before hobbling after Hillary on her impossibly high heels.

Dylan grinned at her retreating back.

I smacked him. Hard.

"Why did you do that?" He rubbed his shoulder. "Jesus, Steph."

I rolled my eyes and stormed off. I didn't have time for this. Any of it.

* * *

Sitting with my nemesis at one of those small bistro tables on uncomfortable chairs at the local Starbucks wasn't my idea of fun. Heck, being around her was on my Top 10 of things *not* to do before I graduated from Sutter High.

But I needed her help, especially since Emily's ghost had approached her and not me. That had to mean something.

None of her so-called groupies were with us. I fidgeted with my iced mocha latte, pushing the straw in and out. In and out.

"Jeez, stop that," she hissed. Hillary hunched over her own iced coffee, her eyes scanning the place. Her leg tapped a nervous beat.

"You worried someone might see us together?" I asked, glancing around.

Hillary leveled a menacing glare my way for what seemed like forever but was probably only a few seconds. She sighed loudly. "Whatever."

I waited for her to start. When she didn't, I said, "I know you can see Emily Jones."

"I swear if you tell anyone else I'm seeing a ghost, I'll make your life miserable."

As if she could make it any worse.

I wanted to throw the coffee in her face, but I decided to be civil. "My lips are sealed." I made a motion across my lips, zipping them.

Hillary's shoulders sagged. "I can't deal with all of this." She bowed her head over her coffee and then took a sip. "So, it's true then? Emily's . . . dead?"

"Yes."

"And how exactly do you know that?" I knew what she meant, but I wanted her to say it.

Another Hillary glare. I met her gaze, refusing to back down.

She looked away.

I waited.

She leaned in closer. A whiff of Happy cologne and peppermint gum mixed with coffee hit me. "So, I'm like you now."

"Yes," I said.

Her hand flung out, latching onto mine with one mean grip. Jeez, where did that come from?

"Christ, why me? Why is she bothering me?"

"Ok, chill." I unhooked her killer grip.

She didn't protest.

She settled back in her seat.-"I don't know how to stop her from bothering me."

Here was my chance. I just prayed she'd listen and not blow me off.

"Hillary, I might be able to help you there."

She cocked her head. "Seriously? You can stop her?"

A million thoughts swirled in my mind. Now would be the perfect time to tell her about Dr. Anthony, but I had to take this slowly. If our past history was any indication she'd just throw it in my face.

"I think you know what I do, right? If not, I'm sure your mother told you."

Hillary snorted. "Come on, it's not exactly a secret what you can do."

Right. After the sorority fiasco with our moms, I'm surprised the whole flippin' town didn't know about my little ability.

I shrugged. "Yes, I see the dead. Not only that, I help them cross over to the Other Side."

"What does this have to do with Emily bothering me? Shouldn't she be in your face?"

"That's where I might be able to help. I do crossings, but the dead usually show up in a vision and let me know where they were killed. The fact that she reached out to you and not me, means she feels a connection to you, maybe because you were friends. But if you and I work together we can get her to cross over and she won't be dropping by again. Okay?

I had to give Hillary credit. She hadn't thrown her coffee at me or stormed off yet.

"So, will you help me?" I asked.

She sighed. "Fine, whatever," she said. "I'll do it, but don't think you have something over me, because if I go down I'll drag your sorry ass down with me."

"I wouldn't dream of it."

With that, Hillary marched out of the Starbucks.

I waited until I finished my mocha and then got up. After I threw my empty cup in the trash can and exited, I tried to figure out how I'd get all of us together in order to do the crossing without it going horribly wrong.

CHAPTER 15

After my meeting with Hillary, I entertained the idea of ditching the rest of the day until I remembered that chances were good Mom would be home and I didn't want to deal with her right now. Mom decided to take early retirement a couple of years back after they closed the elementary school where she taught. Plus, she admitted she hated all the meetings and prep work that came with being a first-grade teacher. And she wanted to be there for me throughout my high school years, something she wasn't able to do for my older brother Ricky, who was now in college. Plus she loved being able to have time to work out and go to yoga class. On the flip side, her retirement meant that she was usually on my case more often than not.

After class, I convinced Cura to go with me to the school library to do some research on Emily Jones. Armed with past issues of the year book as well as old issues of the school paper, we picked two, side-by-side carrels to peruse them.

"Aren't you going to fill me in on Rescuing duties?" Cura leaned over and whispered, followed by a snap of her fruity scented bubble gum.

Probably not a good place to chat about being a Rescuer since we could be busted for talking by hundred-year-old Mrs. Holly, not to mention we were already getting dirty looks thrown our way by nerdy students who were studying.

"Later," I whispered. "After this. Promise."

Cura slouched down in her chair.

"I kind of was looking forward to doing the whole kickass thing." She sighed.

I tried to silence her with one of those "looks."

I flipped through a back issue of the school paper and found an article featuring an interview with Hillary and Emily Jones about the school cheer squad. They talked about how close the team was and how they'd bonded over the season. I showed Cura the article, which only confirmed the reason why Emily would reach out to Hillary.

"I talked to Hillary," I whispered back. "I really think she should be included in the crossing."

"Makes sense," Cura agreed with another snap of her gum.

"Ssh!" Mrs. Holly scowled in our direction. Her 1950s style glasses, which would look retro on anyone else, only reaffirmed her ancient dinosaur status around here. She thrust her glasses back up, giving us that don't-make-me-go-over-there glare. "Ladies, keep it down," she barked, while shelving books nearby. "Or take the discussion outside."

"Jeez, you'd think this was a library or something." Cura rolled her eyes. "I'd much rather do the Scooby Doo gang thing anyway."

"Even if that means Hillary is part of the group?"

"Yeah, even then."

I took a deep breath.

Doubt resurfaced. It didn't exactly go well the last time Hillary and I were together at a sleep-over at her place, last Halloween. After I saw a woman's ghost in Hillary's bathroom mirror, I made a colossal mess of things in my haste to get out of her room. I not only spilled diet Coke and popcorn everywhere but broke the bathroom mirror. Even after I had done a bazillion chores to help pay for the damage, Hillary never forgave me.

I looked away. "I know, she said she would help, but how do I know she won't use this as a way to get back at me for the sorority mess. You know she blames me for that."

"Well, you have me on your side. If she gives you any crap, I'll lay into her."

Cura was definitely spunky even though she barely stood at five feet and that was with her Doc Martens. But it did feel good to have her back on my side. "Thanks!"

Mrs. Holly walked up to us and with a grand swoosh of her arm, pointed to the door.

Gathering our things, we left. Once outside, Cura's phone pinged.

"Who is it?" I asked.

"Oh, just my mom. Said it's some kind of emergency." Cura rolled her eyes. "More like she needs a babysitter for the Terrible Fives."

Cura's name for her five-year old, twin brothers Seth and Carter who always seemed to be wreaking havoc, including coloring on the walls with Cura's expensive Sephora makeup.

I was lucky I didn't have any younger brothers. My older brother Ricky was "perfect" of course. He got accepted to med school for next year, but this year, he was working for a humanitarian aid agency in Bangladesh.

Ricky was as clueless as Dad when it came to my Rescue work. Or if he knew, he never let on. He was never a fan of my "obsession" with decorating crosses, but he did stand up for me whenever Mom got on my case. Yeah, I did kind of miss him.

After Cura left, I found a quiet corner on one of the school benches and finished reading my English assignment. Figures our latest book just happened to be *Frankenstein*. I wonder what Mary Shelly would think of my ability to help the dead?

Afterwards, I walked the short distance to my house.

All the while, I kept reminding myself that I had to call Hillary as time was ticking down. I figured Emily had less than 24 hours to cross over or else she'd be stuck in her ghostly form forever. I wouldn't wish that fate on anyone. Dr. Anthony told me that sometimes ghosts wanted to stay here and not go to the Other Side, thinking it would be just like it was when they were alive. But that wasn't the case. They ended up in limbo. Or they might turn into a dark spirit over time, becoming more and more angry. And worst of all, they ran the risk of being used by demons. It made me shudder to think of poor Emily Jones being exposed to those dangers when we could help her get to the light and cross over.

Once home, I grabbed a diet Cherry Coke from the refrigerator and a bag of chips before heading up to my room. I settled down on the edge of my bed and cracked open the Coke. I took a few chugs, the carbonation tickling my nose.

"Okay, here goes nothing," I said out loud and dialed Hillary's number.

It rang once. Twice.

"Yeah, who's this?" Hillary's familiar 'tude came through loud and clear.

I closed my eyes, drawing strength from deep inside.

"Hillary, this is Stephanie," I rushed. "You still want to help with Emily? I need to know now."

Her voice became muffled. "Wait a minute."

I heard a door shut and then Hillary said, "I said I would. Where do you want to meet because it can't be here."

"Of course not," I countered. "You wouldn't want it to get out that I was at your house."

"Whatever," Hillary retorted, using her signature comeback word. "So where? And it better not take too long."

I gave her Dr. Anthony's address.

"Where's this?"

"The office building is across the street from the new Starbucks off Arden Way. Dr. A's office is on the thirteenth floor. There's a sign on the door that says, Light Bringer's Support Services. I'll call Dr. A to let him know we're coming."

"Omigod, wait, you have a ghost psych dude that helps?"

"Something like that. Just be there at five. You can do that, right?" Then a thought popped into my head. "Do you have something of Emily's? Or do you know of something that she liked?"

"Okay, I don't know how that's going to help."

"Trust me, it will. You should also wear something that isn't brand new. I'll need your help painting some designs on a cross."

"Okay, whatever, let's just get this over with."

With that, I heard a click.

Now I just had to pray she'd actually show up. Emily Jones' fate rested in Hillary's hands.

CHAPTER 16

After I called Cura, to let her in on our plans, and then a quick call to Dr. Anthony, I finished the rest of my homework. Or tried to. I kept trying to visualize if I could figure out where Emily had been murdered. I knew it had to be related to that frat party at the cheer camp since I had seen Emily in the background of the vision that Morgan had shown me just before she crossed over. I really wanted to call the police to report the murder, but right now my main objective had to be crossing Emily over. I'd leave the police stuff to Dr. Anthony, who had connections with them.

Around four thirty, Cura picked me up and we proceeded to Dr. Anthony's.

"So how did you get out of babysitting?" I asked, remembering the frantic phone call from her mom.

"Oh, I told Mom I had somewhere I needed to be. She got someone else from our church to fill in."

"I'm glad, as I really need you with me right now." Did I mention how much I loved Cura.

"No way I'd miss this. So, she actually said she'd do it?" Cura asked.

"Yep, let's see if she follows through."

We pulled up to the office building and made our way to Dr. A's office.

Hillary, who'd already arrived stood up, but not before she shoved one of Dr. Anthony's parapsychology journals under a People magazine that lay opened on a small table. "Took you two long enough."

Dr. Anthony looked up from his computer. "I just called Dylan. He should be here soon."

Hillary frowned. "Don't tell me. He's a part of this, too?"

"Something like that," I said.

She snorted. "Why should I be surprised? Mom did say his family was one tool short of a tool shed."

I took a step forward, wanting to wipe the smirk off her face.

Cura grasped my shoulder. "She's not worth it."

"Ladies, we don't need to bring negative energy into this room," Dr. A stepped in smoothly. "If we're going to help Emily cross over, we will all need to clear our minds of any negative emotions. The dead are sensitive to dark energy and might be scared off. We can't chance that."

I sighed. "You're right, as usual." Man, I hated saying that.

"Sure, Dr. Anthony. Anything to help Emily," Hillary said flashing a smirk my way.

"Let's get started," Dr. Anthony said, motioning us to the table. "Place the talisman here."

I laid it down.

Hillary's eyebrows rose. "You weren't kidding about the whole decorating a cross thing."

"Well, I can't exactly do that as I don't know her. Dr. Anthony, you did fill her in on why we need her?"

He nodded. "I told her, but it helps if you show her what you do with the talismans."

Hillary stroked the cross. "Wow, you make these?"

"Yes."

"Pretty impressive, though you know they do sell things like this at most of those Christian stores, right?"

Dr. Anthony cleared his throat.

Cura rolled her eyes.

I ignored her snide comment. "Did you bring what I asked?"

Hillary walked over to the chair where she'd left her bag and pulled out a pretty sweater with a bright floral design of large, pink, lavender, and coral peonies.

"Will this work?" Hillary handed it to me.

I fingered the soft material, noticing the Nordstrom tag.

"She left it behind after a cheer meet last year and I put it in my locker to return it to her, but I forgot about it with all the hubbub with her parents and her deciding to move to Florida. Hillary shrugged. "We weren't besties, or anything, but she was a friend."

"Maybe that's why she reached out to you?" Cura offered. "The sweater was the only personal item of hers left in the school and it was in your locker."

I smiled at Cura and nodded my head in approval. She was a fast learner.

"Should we let her parents know?" Hillary asked. "Should we call the police?

I was surprised that Hillary cared enough to ask that. Maybe she was starting to get it. "Dr. Anthony can take care of the police thing." I glanced over at him, and he nodded. "Our part is different, but still important." I pointed at the plain wooden cross. "We have to decorate this cross."

"How will decorating it help Emily cross over?" Cura asked.

"It matters because it acknowledges her," Dr. Anthony said. "It lets her know that her life mattered and by planting the cross down at the site of her death, it will open a path for her 'life force' or 'spirit' to cross over to the Other Side."

"Mom calls it 'chi,'" Cura said.

Dr. Anthony nodded in agreement.

"Seriously? That stuff is actually true?" Hillary asked.

"How can you doubt it after everything we've seen?" Cura countered.

To that Hillary only shook her head, muttering under her breath.

I placed my hand over hers. For once she didn't flinch. "We can help Emily, but only if we work together."

CHAPTER 17

Once Dylan showed up, we all worked together. Hillary ended up designing the peonies on the cross. Who knew she had artistic talent? I'd certainly never seen her in the art room at school.

"I think we need to add in some birds," Hillary blurted out.

Boy that popped out of nowhere. I glanced at Hillary. "How about Robins and Blue Jays?" I suggested.

She nodded and gave a little shrug. I began to sketch them onto the cross. It seems Emily loved wildlife, too.

After Dylan and Cura finished drying the talisman with a couple of hair dryers, Dr. A. motioned to Hillary from his desk. He just finished printing up a map of the area around the university.

"Emily seems to be reaching out to you. Did she, by chance, share anything with you? Like a particular place? It could help us find her body is."

Hillary grimaced. "Ew, they actually do that? That would traumatize me forever."

"I take that as a no?" he asked.

"If we don't have a location, then how will we be able to cross her over," I asked. I'd hoped that after the bird suggestion that Hillary might be able to help us pinpoint a location. Unless Dr. Anthony got a hunch like he did with Morgan, the only thing we had was that she'd been at that frat party. But there was a lot of ground to cover on the university campus.

"Wait!" Cura asked, "I don't see ghosts or anything, but does it count if you hear something?"

That got all our attention.

Dr. Anthony motioned to a chair next to his desk. "You did say you thought she was trying to talk to you. Can you remember any of the words?"

Cura's eyes widened. "You know, I thought it was strange and all. It was like a bunch of whispers. You know, like when you walk into a coffee shop and you can hear this buzz of conversation.

"Close your eyes," Dr. A said. "And take some deep, slow breaths."

Cura sat down and closed her eyes. We all stood around her waiting. All you could hear was breathing. Strange, even Hillary had become quiet. It's like we all wanted Cura to remember . . .

Cura's eyes flew open. "Dumpster!"

Dumpster.

I thought back to the other day at school when the contents of the trash can were thrown everywhere by some paranormal force. Was this Emily's way of trying to communicate where her body had been dumped?

Dylan finally piped up. "There must be a trillion dumpsters in the city."

"Morgan's body was left in the woods outside of the university." I said. "And wasn't her killer at the frat house?"

"Right," Cura said. "Maybe Emily's body is in a dumpster on campus."

"But she's been dead for how long?" Dylan asked. "More than a few days. Wouldn't it stink big time? And wouldn't the garbage guys have picked up the garbage by now?" They would have seen the body and it would have been reported."

"Or maybe whoever drugged her might have dragged her body somewhere close to a dumpster." I hit my hand on the table. "That could be anywhere."

We'll go to the area where Morgan was killed, Dr. Anthony suggested. "Maybe Emily will reach out to Hillary, maybe it's close enough to where her body is that she will be able to show you." Dr. A, glanced at me. "If you and Hillary work together, you'll be able to figure it out."

"Glad you have that much faith in my ability," I said. There were only a few hours left before Emily would be lost to us forever. We had to act now.

"Let's just do this," Hillary said. "Maybe then this nightmare will be over."

For once, I was in full agreement with Hillary.

*　　*　　*

Dr. A drove Dylan, while Cura and I went with Hillary. On the drive over, I filled Hillary in on who Morgan was and how her death might be connected to Emily's. I thought she'd totally freak out, but instead, a steely look flashed in her eyes.

"After we help Emily, let's get those bastards who killed her," she said, her hands tightly grasping the steering wheel of her car.

I exchanged glances with Cura, who was sitting in the back seat. One thing about Hillary, she might be nasty and mean, but if she considered you a friend, she had your back.

Once we arrived at the same spot where we helped Morgan cross over, we parked and got out. Right on schedule, the fog began rolling in. I just hoped that Emily would show up. Dylan helped Dr. Anthony with his large duffle bag. I was glad Cura was with us too. She'd seemed a bit uncertain of her role but now, after she found that her ability to hear might be helpful, she seemed more confident.

I carried Emily's talisman and stood close to where Morgan had appeared to us a few days ago.

Hillary stood close by and for once wasn't glued to her cell. "Okay, Emily, we're here," she said out loud.

"Uh, it doesn't quite work that way," I said.

Hillary only shrugged. "Well, you don't know unless you try. And your way hasn't worked with Emily so far."

I bit back a retort as I didn't want to mess this Rescue up but man, just when I thought that Hillary was, maybe-sort-of-okay, she acts all Hillary-esque again.

Dr. A handed Dylan a small cooler bag filled with frozen water bottles. I thought that was very thoughtful of the good doc. Dylan thanked him and took out a bottle.

"What's with the water bottle?" Hillary asked. Does this paranormal stuff make you thirsty?

"You don't wanna know," he responded. "Trust me, I'd almost rather see a ghost."

I turned to him, my eyebrows raised.

"Okay, scratch that," he amended.

I glanced down at my watch. No one really wore watches anymore. Most kids just used their phones or if they were sporty, they wore one of those gizmos that could measure heart rate and calories burned. Call me old-fashioned, but I liked the retro one I'd found at the local thrift shop. It looked like something out of an *Indiana Jones* movie. The actual watch face was large with roman numerals on a faded golden backing and the strap was made of soft, Nubuk leather. And unlike an electronic gadget or a phone, proved reliable out in the boonies, like where we were now.

With each passing minute my anxiety level rose. There was less than an hour left and we still didn't know where Emily's body might be.

Then the familiar itch behind my legs began and, for the first time ever, I was actually relieved to feel that annoying tingling.

"I think she might be here," I said, nudging Hillary. "Why don't you call out to her?"

"I thought you said that didn't work?"

"Forget that," I said, louder this time. "Just call out to her, okay?"

Hillary glanced over at Dr. Anthony who nodded. "She's connected to you. Talk to her," he said.

Cura clasped her hands over her ears. "I think she's really close."

We all looked toward the freeway and waited.

"Emily, are you out there?" Hillary shouted. "We want to help you . . ."

Nothing. It was eerily quiet. I glanced at Dr. A, and he looked as anxious as I felt.

Then Hillary's eyes widened and a smile slowly lit up her face. She began to clap and jump up and down shouting, "Hey, hey! Ho, ho! We've got spirit. Ready to go! Hey, hey! Ho, ho! We've got spirit. Ready. Set. Go! S. P. I. R. I. T. We've got spirit. Ready. 1, 2, 3! Go team! She finished by doing a cartwheel and landed on her feet shouting up and down. I looked at Cura, who's mouth was hanging open. I shrugged. Hey, at this point what did we have to lose.

The fog grew thicker and denser, but only around the freeway and river. When a sudden burst of light flooded the area around us Dylan groaned and pressed one of his water bottles to his forehead.

"Hill?" Emily staggered out of the fog. "Why are we here?" Her ripped clothing and bruised body showed evidence of something more than just being drugged.

"You tell me," she said. I had to give Hillary credit, she didn't break a sweat but looked as confident as ever. The only give-away was the tremble of her bottom lip.

"I don't know. Should I?" she said, rubbing her bare arms. "It's so cold. Why is it so cold? You're supposed to do a back flip at the end of that cheer.

"Yeah, well, I improvised . . . Besides you were always better at the back flips."

Emily smiled, looking less confused. "I-I tried to talk to you at school, but you ignored me. Why?"

Hillary scuffed her shoe and looked down. "Well, I had no idea what to say to a dead girl."

"What?" Emily asked her eyes clouded with confusion. "What are you talking about?"

I quickly stepped in front of Hillary. She did great, but she still had a lot to learn about being sensitive.

"Who are you?" Emily asked, her attention now on me.

"Someone who can help you, but can you answer a few questions?" I reached out and Emily stared down at my hand. "Please, you need to let me touch your hand."

Emily looked over at Hillary, uncertainty in her eyes.

"Why does she have to touch her?" Hillary asked in a stage whisper over her shoulder to Dr. Anthony. Since he was our mentor, I waited for him to fill Hillary in.

"Because the connection will help Stephanie witness not only the murder but the site where it occurred. Only then can we use the talisman to help her cross over."

I took advantage of Emily's hesitation and reached out. My hand went right through her and I felt an immediate chill go through me.

Right then the vision hit.

Emily being asked to go to the frat party after the cheer meet. Hanging out with a group of college kids including Morgan, who had introduced her to a number of the frat guys.

Being left alone with a faceless older guy. Drinking. Lots and lots of drinking. A queasy feeling and then darkness.

I started to pull away when another chill hit harder this time.

Some of the guys, including the faceless one, taking Emily into one of the upstairs rooms.

Clothes tearing, struggling, muffled screams.

Then a claustrophobic feeling crashed down on me.

An old blanket was thrown over her.

Hands lifted her. Carried her away in the dead of night.

I witnessed the guys throwing her in a dumpster right off the college campus. A few of them threw old trash and empty beer bottles over her.

The vision quickly left.

"I'm so, so sorry," I said softly to her. Tears streaming down my face.

My connection with Emily had triggered her own self-awareness. She nodded, her eyes filled with pain and sadness. I'd learned that just acknowledging their suffering helped the dead a great deal. And helped a murder victim begin her healing process.

"What did they do to her?" Hillary asked.

"Something really bad." I swiped at my eyes. Even though I hadn't known Emily when she was alive, I'd felt the same pain and horror she'd experienced in her last moments of life. "Dr. Anthony, promise they'll arrest those guys," I said over my shoulder as I tried to compose myself.

"Yes, I'll call right after we know the site," he said, "Where is it?"

"The dumpster outside of campus. Can we get there in time?" I glanced back down at my watch. Less than thirty minutes.

Emily observed all this with confusion and sadness.

"Em," Hillary turned to her and said softly, "I know it must be so hard for you. But you've got to go back to that dumpster. We'll meet you there. Only then can we help you. I promise you we'll help you."

Emily nodded and disappeared in the fog.

Dr. Anthony signaled me over. I grabbed the talisman and hurried to his car.

"I'll follow," Hillary said, getting in her car with the others.

Thank goodness the campus wasn't too far. Dr. Anthony sped down the freeway, going over ninety miles an hour. I prayed no police officer would pull us over. Seriously, what excuse could we use? "Sorry officer, but we have a spirit emergency."

No, I don't think that would go over too well.

Dr. Anthony skidded to a stop. We jumped out, leaving the car doors open. Only one thing mattered. Helping Emily.

I didn't have to look far for her. Emily wavered in and out next to the dumpster.

"I can't believe it," she cried, tears streaming down her face. "They threw me in here?"

I looked for a grassy spot next to the dumpster and when I found it, I slammed the talisman down.

The ground underneath shook, and I fell on my rear.

Cura and Hillary hung on to each other. Dylan, came up to me and helped me up. I could tell he was in a lot of pain. We needed to figure out how to stop him from getting these headaches during a rescue, but that would have to wait until another time.

Then everything shifted. Bright beams of light flooded the area where we stood. It felt cleansing. Like it was washing away the evil of that night. Emily's eyes widened and she began to walk toward a golden light that was shining down. I could see a figure standing in the light's glow, an older woman. She reached her arms out to Emily who gasped. "Granny!" The light surrounded Emily, now, her feet left the ground and it was like she floated toward the old woman.

Hillary broke away from Cura, running to catch up to Emily.

"Emily wait!"

Emily turned around, still floating, but she was transformed. She was dressed in a pretty floral print dress and her hair was brushed and tumbled down around her shoulders.

I swear those guys will pay for what they did to you," Hillary said. "You have my word."

Emily smiled and reached out her hand to touch Hillary's shoulder. "You know, it wouldn't have mattered if you'd stayed with me that last night at cheer camp. I still would have gone to that party. So, don't blame yourself. Okay?"

What? I stared at Hillary who quickly looked away.

No wonder she'd been freaking out so much. I mean, I could see how that would be a given for anyone who had never witnessed a ghost, but to actually feel like it was your fault that a friend died?

So much for thinking she was a total hardass.

Hillary nodded at her friend, tears streaming down her face. "Are you going to be okay?"

"Yes, and you will too." Emily smiled once more, and turning away, walked toward the old woman who embraced her tightly. They laughed happily as the light surrounded them. It grew brighter and brighter and then shot up into the sky like a rocket.

Then darkness reappeared.

The sound of quiet weeping filled the area. I walked over to Hillary and hugged her. For once she didn't push me away. Cura joined us.

Right then I thought, I could get used to this whole Scooby Gang thing.

CHAPTER 18

So much for togetherness.

If I had thought helping Emily cross over would change Hillary, I was dead wrong. Pardon the pun. The next day at school, Hillary was her usual snarky Miss Diva self and either ignored me or threw snooty looks my way in the halls.

Whatevs. I was just relieved that we'd finally helped Emily cross over. I knew it would be only a matter of time before it would hit the papers about Emily's body being found and the frat guys being arrested. They were responsible for the death of both girls. Morgan had managed to get away but had died where we'd found her near the highway, meanwhile Emily had been thrown into a dumpster. I wondered if the killers had just been too drunk or too stoned to care. I guess the court would decide that.

Despite the sadness of it all, I was happy that it had brought Cura and me closer together. We were besties again and I vowed never to keep anything from her again. As for Dylan, well he was kinda hot and cold, so I wasn't sure whether it was the after-effects of his headaches from two back-to-back Rescues or just that things were getting weird between us. He'd stopped by my locker to chat between classes and Ashley walked by with Hillary and gave him a flirty smile. He blushed and smiled back. I just about lost it, but I didn't want to make a scene. There had been far too many of those lately. I wondered if Hillary had confided in Ashley about what had happened, but judging from how Hillary and Ashley giggled together, I doubted it.

Dylan and Cura and I had had lunch together and it felt like old times. That, at least, had been fun and kept me in a good mood for the rest of the day. When I got home from school, I noticed an expensive red Beemer convertible in our drive way. Odd. I walked past it, taking a quick glimpse inside. Pristine, minus any wrappers, or anything to give me a hint of who it might belong too.

I opened the front door and could hear Mom talking with someone. Strange, considering she never had people over this time of day.

Mom's shrill voice grew louder and louder. I made my way to the living room, curiosity laced with anxiety guiding my steps. For once, I was dying to know the source of Mom's anger. At least this time, it wasn't me.

"Why did you decide to show up now? You don't belong here." Mom sounded super angry and frustrated. She then glanced over my way and froze. Another woman sat on the sofa. Something about her felt familiar. She gazed intently in my direction.

"Is this your daughter?" the woman asked.

"Weren't you going to your friend's?" Mom asked, her forced smile not fooling me at all. She totally dissed the woman, not only by not answering her question but by sitting as far away from her as possible. Mom's back was so stiff I knew anything could set her off.

I shrugged, too curious about who this woman might be to worry about Mom's wrath. "Do I know you?" I asked the woman.

Her raspy laugh filled the awkward moment. Mom glared daggers at her.

"No, but I'd like for that to change," she said, patting the space next to her. "Why don't you join us?"

Resignation settled over my mother's features.

I settled down next to the woman. Tension hung in the room like a heavy cloud. Whoever this mysterious woman was, she was making Mom beyond upset.

"Didn't your mother tell you about me?" she asked, glancing over at Mom, who was busy straightening out the *In Style* magazines on the coffee table.

"No, she didn't," I said, sneaking a glance at Mom. "Was she supposed to?"

Mom dropped a magazine, finally staring at me. Worry flashed across her face before she let out a long sigh.

"This is my sister Karen," she said. "She decided to drop, by, but she'll be leaving soon."

Wow! I couldn't believe it. Aunt Karen out of the blue. After so many years. Why now? As my head ping-ponged from one sister to the other, I could see the similarities—they shared the same cupid's bow mouth and green eyes.

"Now, why would I leave so soon," Karen said, her deep raspy voice sending a chill through me. "Especially when I finally get to meet my gorgeous niece."

I turned to my mother, waiting for a better explanation. Something was off big-time.

"We're family," Karen added when Mom didn't say more. "Family is forever, no matter what transpired in the past."

Surprised, I stared back at Mom.

"You mean, after that spell you did years ago at Mom's sorority house?" I asked, inching away from Aunt Karen.

"What did you tell her?" Aunt Karen asked.

"Nothing that wasn't true. You should be ashamed to even be showing your face here."

"I can't believe you still blame me for that. The police said it was an accident," Aunt Karen countered, brushing aside the fire and deaths as if they were of no consequence.

"Wait, I'm confused," I said, "Didn't you do a spell and it burned down the sorority house?"

Aunt Karen let out an exaggerated sigh. "Yes, but I

wasn't the only one there. Right, sister? No one forced you to join the circle."

Mom squirmed and dug her fingers into one of the plump, fuchsia cushions, almost cutting right through the colorful fabric.

I didn't need Dylan's ability right now to know a humongous red aura pulsed around Mom. Mad? That was a total understatement.

"Mom?" I wanted to know her part in her sister's accusation.

"I only did it because you swore it would work. Your friends at that—" Mom waved her hands aside, "—para-something club promised it would help strengthen our ability to help the dead. I was stupid enough to believe you. Never again."

"You're still the same as you always were," Aunt Karen said. "Miss Perfect, who never did anything wrong and never took the blame for any of her mistakes."

"We agreed," Mom changed the subject, "it was best if we just went our separate ways." She gave her sister a pointed glare.

I knew I should be on Mom's side, but if what Mom just revealed was true, then her involvement with the Other Side, hadn't just been to help her sister fit in. She had actually been keen on it. But then, after what happened at the sorority house, she dropped it like last year's leggings. Maybe Mom was a bit jealous that I shared the same gift with her sister. Or, maybe she was scared that I would end up screwing up like Karen did. It seemed like Mom had been ready to lay blame on me for something I'd never done and had no intention of doing. But the fact that Karen and I shared the same gift? Maybe Karen could help me figure out what had gone wrong at the Sorority House Fiasco 2.0 . . . Or right . . . Considering I wouldn't have been able to cross Emily over without Hillary and Cura's help, and they wouldn't have been able to help me if our mothers hadn't done that spell and triggered their own abilities.

"Mom, maybe she can help me," I finally said.

"Stephanie Samantha Stewart." Uh oh. Mom used the three-name warning. She was pissed. But I didn't back down.

Aunt Karen only chuckled. "Not one to beat around the bush, are you?" She opened her bag, pulling out a pack of Mores and a silver lighter, with what looked like her name engraved on it.

"Really," Mom said. "Can you, at least, do that outside?"

"Jeez, Mom," I said, rolling my eyes. "It's not as if you don't indulge." Mom thought no one knew, but it was common knowledge that from time-to-time she sneaks a smoke in the garage and then covers it up with vanilla-scented spray. She throws the butts away, but the smell still lingers.

"Oh, right." Aunt Karen didn't argue and dropped her pack of cigarettes back in her bag. "Another thing you frown on."

I snuck a glance at my mother, who sat with her arms folded and her eyes narrowed.

Aunt Karen threw her head back and laughed at Mom's discomfort.

Mom said nothing, but continued her death glare.

Karen snorted.

"Come on, Jean, don't be such a child. Anyway, I think someone needs some guidance right now. And who better than me?"

Mom jumped up, clenching her fists at her sides. Her whole body seemed as tightly wound as a coiled metal spring.

"You have a hell of a lot of nerve coming to my house, acting as if you've done nothing wrong, and then to think I'd even consider you helping my daughter with your spells?"

Aunt Karen's lips tightened and instead she turned and looked back at me.

"What do you want to know?" Aunt Karen asked.

"There was a fire at the sorority house and two girls went missing in the fire and their bodies were never recovered," I said. I pulled at a loose thread on one of the pillows. "They said it was an accident. It was, right? An accident?"

I wanted to add that I knew they did a spell that went wrong but I wanted to see what Aunt Karen had to say.

Mom folded her arms over her chest, her lips had tightened to a thin line.

"Yeah, right, an accident," Aunt Karen said. She fumbled back inside her purse and grabbed a cigarette, ignoring Mom's earlier request. She lit up and took a long drag. I grabbed a small decorative plate and handed it to my aunt, to catch the ashes before they fell on the table or carpet or couch. That would really piss Mom off.

Aside from her attitude toward Mom, there was something else about Aunt Karen that I couldn't figure out yet. Whenever she looked at me, I felt kind of strange. Like she was trying to reach out to me somehow. Was it because we shared the same gift? Did Mom tell her about me or had she just figured it out on her own?

Mom, on the other hand, looked like a cat ready to pounce on a mouse.

Aunt Karen's eyebrows lifted. Her eyes crinkled in amusement. "Don't get your panties in a bind, Jean." She turned back to me, her voice sounding disappointed. "That's all you know about that night?"

The smoky air made me want to gag, but my mother's sister fascinated me in a morbid kind of way.

"I also heard that you guys did some kind of spell and said a chant?"

I didn't want to mention that it probably attracted a dark paranormal entity.

Aunt Karen snickered. "Yeah, you could say that."

"You know exactly what happened," Mom interceded. "You released something—some kind of evil, that caused the death of our friends."

Aunt Karen shrugged and took another drag of her cigarette.

"You have a hell of a lot of nerve waltzing back into our lives." Mom spat out. "What about your promise? Did you forget that?"

Promise?

Aunt Karen took another long drag of her cigarette. The smoke circled around her head like a hazy cloud of secrets and lies.

"You can't expect me to stay away after I heard about what had happened again, back at our old sorority house."

"Did you release some bad dude?" I whispered, afraid that if I didn't ask now, I'd never get the chance to ask again.

Mom gasped while Aunt Karen pinned me with her green eyes, so much like Mom's. "What do you know about that?"

"Enough," my mother hissed.

"Jeez, Mom. It's not exactly a secret about Mark and me. And if there are other demons out there, can't this help me stay on the look-out?"

"It won't happen again. End of story," Mom replied.

During this whole time Aunt Karen watched our exchange with amusement. "Tell me more about this Mark, Stephanie."

I frowned. "I think you know the type. A tall, good looking guy with an annoying little habit of being a mega-lying demon" Had Karen gotten herself mixed up with a demon too?

She took another puff of her cigarette. A vicious smile touched her lips giving her a viper-like expression.

"You could say that about any man," Aunt Karen purred. "They say one thing and do another."

"You need to go. Now," Mom declared.

"Well, if you're going to be that way." Aunt Karen reached into her Versace handbag and pulled out a card. "Stephanie, here's my card. Call me if you want the truth."

I snatched the card and shoved it inside my hoodie pocket.

Mom frowned at me. For a moment, it looked like she wanted to snatch the card out of my pocket. Then the doorbell rang.

Saved by the bell.

Mom rushed to the door and flung it open. Dylan stood on the front porch.

"Uh, Hi, Mrs. Stewart...is Stephanie home?"

Aunt Karen stepped up beside Mom before she could reply to Dylan. "Do I know you?" Karen asked, in her smoky voice.

"Uh, I don't think so," Dylan replied, his eyes, skittering away from my aunt.

I pushed my way between Mom and Aunt Karen. "I'm here," I said, pleading with my eyes for him to stay.

Dylan shoved his hands into his pockets, avoiding eye contact with me as well as Mom and Aunt Karen. He shuffled backwards a few feet.

My aunt gave him a cat-like grin. "My mistake. You look like someone I used to know."

"Don't you have somewhere you need to go?" Mom asked.

"Right," Aunt Karen said.

Dylan stepped farther to the side. His bangs covered his expression, but his body language practically screamed tense.

"Ooh, but he is cute," Aunt Karen said, giving him a once over.

The tips of Dylan's ears turned red.

Mom glared at Aunt Karen, her hands on her hips. "Aren't you leaving?" she repeated, louder this time.

"Hey, I'll come back later," Dylan said, still not looking at any of us.

"No, don't go." I stepped outside on the porch and laced my arm into Dylan's. Only then did he give me a sidelong glance that said I-can't-stand-her-aura.

I moved in closer to Dylan as Aunt Karen stopped in front of us.

"I hope you take me up on my offer," she said in her raspy voice. As she passed us, her fingers lightly touched Dylan's shoulder. "Take care of her."

Dylan flinched.

She gave us a little wave then got into her Beemer and drove off like a speed demon. No pun intended.

Dylan gave me a what-was-that-all-about look. "Weird, much?"

"Uh, tell me about it," I whispered. I glanced back at Mom still standing in the doorway. Her face flushed with anger. I thought for sure she was going to yell at me.

Suddenly her features crumpled. Bowing her head, muffled sobs racked her body. With each sob, her body trembled.

Feeling like a piece of crap, I stepped away from Dylan and hesitantly took a step forward, not really knowing what to do. "Mom? Mommy?"

She lifted her head and wiped her now raccoon-smudged eyes with the back of her hand. "Why didn't she just leave good enough alone?"

"Uh, I'm going. I'll call you later, Steph, okay?" Dylan turned on his heel and walked away.

I frowned at Dylan and turned back to my mother. I'd have to talk to him later. One fire to put out at a time.

"I get why you might be upset that she just showed up out of the blue, but she *is* your sister. You guys were close once."

"That was a very long time ago . . . I wished she'd just stayed away, like she promised," she whispered. "It would have been better for everyone."

I didn't know what to say.

"I'm just protecting you. I'm a good mother."

"Mom, I never said you weren't."

"Just don't call her. Promise me." Her eyes pleaded.

"Sure, if that'll make you happy." The whole time I crossed my fingers in my pocket and avoided her eyes.

She didn't say anything. The grandfather clock in the foyer, bonged the hour. I couldn't help but feel like something bad was going to happen and I needed to know the truth before it did.

"Got to finish my paper." I raced past her, hoping she couldn't see the guilt in my eyes. I hated lying. I'd lied to Cura about my abilities, I was still lying to Dad. And now I had to lie to Mom about reaching out to Aunt Karen. I hated lies. They always lead to trouble.

Once back in my room, I fingered the business card in my pocket. I had to know. I pulled the card out.

Secret Treasures

Okay, talk about cliché. Bright-colored swirls outlined the words on the card.

I went over to my laptop and Googled the name.

A website of a fashion boutique in North Highlands popped up, along with a couple of social media site links. Judging by the designer purse she was carrying it had to be for a more elite clientele.

I snatched up my cell off the table, scattering some of my Spanish notes in the process.

An overwhelming urge to call Dylan hit. I know he'd felt and seen something around my aunt. I knew it couldn't have been good because of how he'd acted around her. Instead I texted him: *What did u c?*

Dylan replied right away: *Don't want to talk about it, k?*

I flopped down on my bed and frowned. *Sorry about that.*

Another text from Dylan: *Will talk l8r*

I stared at his lame response and almost threw my phone across my bed.

I grabbed my iPod off the dresser drawer, settled back against the bed headboard, and let Cone's latest album transport me away.

My stomach was in pretzel knots again. They always say there are two sides to every story. I couldn't help but wonder what Aunt Karen's take would be on all of this. Why hadn't she been invited to the initiation last weekend? Or was she specifically told not to come?

This only made me more determined to find out why. I promised Cura I'd be upfront with her and I would. What better place than to start with this latest development.

I grabbed my phone, texting her: *U never guess what just happened. Text me. Steph*

I snatched the half-empty bag of Cheetos off my computer table and popped one of the puffs of artificial cheesy goodness into my mouth. I let it melt on my tongue as I pondered the day's events.

What's up

I wiped my fingers on my pants, smearing the orange powder, then typed: *U will never believe who just showed up*

Who?

My aunt Karen.

Wait? Really?

A long pause, then I typed: *Can I come over?*

Sure

Grabbing the extra set of car keys, I dashed back down the staircase.

Mom hadn't moved from the porch. She glanced down at the keys and didn't object.

"Where are you going?" she asked.

"Cura's. Okay?"

Mom stared at me for a few moments. Worry lines etched around her eyes. I didn't have time for this. I only knew one thing: I had to get out, now.

"Just be careful, honey."

I nodded and got into my mom's car.

CHAPTER 19

"Watch out for the terrors."

Cura opened the door, motioning behind her. Her twin brothers were wrestling on the ground. They were identical and, at first glance, hard to distinguish. I knew, though. Carter, the oldest by two minutes—a fact he was very proud to own—had a heart-shaped birthmark on his left ankle. Seth hated to be dressed like (his words) a Carter-clone. And when push came to shove, Seth didn't back down. Like right now.

"Why is she here?" Seth gasped, in between tumbles.

"Probably girly stuff," Carter replied, then tackled Seth again. Both boys rolled on the floor, now oblivious to us. I couldn't help but smile.

"Wait a minute," Cura said. "Let me get my mom before we go to my room."

Cura went down the hallway, leaving me with her rambunctious brothers. Seeing the twins reminded me how much I missed my big brother. Sure, we fought, but it would have been good to have him around for times like these.

Cura's mother trailed right behind my friend. I caught a glimpse of a crystal necklace under Mrs. Stratton's red open-sleeve tunic. Cura's mother had always been nice to me, but today her smile seemed forced. I couldn't help but think she blamed me for that night at the sorority house.

"Nice to see you Stephanie. Can I get you anything?"

"No, I'm fine," I said.

"Let me know if you need anything."

"Hey, you two, don't break anything," Cura said in passing, as if her brothers actually listened. We had to maneuver around them to avoid getting hit, or worse.

The twins rolled on the floor, ignoring us.

We walked down the hallway and made a quick left. She opened her door and it still took me off-guard whenever I saw her room. I swear the British had re-invaded. Her walls were covered with London posters along with images of David Beckham, Prince Harry, and the Spice Girls. A Lego interpretation of Big Ben under the British flag added the finishing touch.

"So, your aunt just decided to pay a little visit?" She plopped down on the huge Tardis in the middle of the bed's coverlet and patted a space next to her. "Tell me everything."

I pushed aside some of her classic vinyl Brit rock and New Wave record jackets that were scattered on the bed. A huge fan of British music, Cura had to be the only person I knew who actually had vinyl records.

"I don't get it. Why did she decide to show up now?" I asked.

"Do you think we might have set off a supernatural trigger when we helped Emily? If your aunt messed with something dark, like the doc suggested, do you think she might have sensed all of us coming together when we did the crossing?"

Cura had a point. Aunt Karen was connected to me through blood and our unique "gift." When she cast that spell twenty years ago, at the sorority house, perhaps it had left a sort of "spell residue" that remained and was re-ignited when our moms tried their little experiment.

"I don't know. Maybe? All I know is there was something off with her."

"What do you mean by off?"

"Well for one thing, Mom kept mentioning how Aunt

Karen broke a promise. I know it has to do with more than her promising to stay away.

"That kind of makes sense. She burned the sorority house down. Who knows what else she's capable of?"

"But it gets even more creepy. She gave me her business card and told me if I wanted to know more about my gift to give her a call. Right in front of Mom. I know it freaked Mom out. She doesn't want me to get in touch with Aunt Karen." I handed Cura the card.

Cura looked it over. "Secret Treasures?" She snorted. "Talk about corny."

"Did your mom ever mention this place?"

"Nope. Yours?"

"No. If anything, she couldn't wait to throw her ass out the door."

"Wow, talk about a dysfunctional family reunion." Cura handed the card back to me. She got up and walked to her dresser, reaching into a bowl she came up with two mini chocolate bars.

"Here." She lobbed a dark chocolate one over to me. I snatched it. "I think I need one of these right now."

"I know, right?"

"So, what's going on with all these secrets? Confusion clouded Cura's face.

"I don't know." I shrugged.

Cura's eyes widened. "Omigod, do you think our mothers made a pact not to say anything to the cops about it?" She unwrapped another mini chocolate, and popped into her mouth.

"Probably. If they had told the cops what really happened, Aunt Karen would most likely have gone to prison."

"What about our moms?" Cura asked. "She might have dragged them down, too, because they were involved."

I blew out a breath. "I know we're wading into dangerous territory here. But I have to find out the truth. You with me?"

Cura gave a firm nod. "Ooh, does this mean it's official?"

When I frowned, she rushed on, her voice going a mile a minute. "I'm part of your Rescuer's club now, right?"

"I guess," I said, remembering how she wanted to know everything. At the time, I'd been hesitant and to be truthful. I was still a tad bit leery about letting her be involved. But if I wanted her to trust me again, I had to be honest. *Even if that meant she might be a target?* an unwelcome thought intruded. I just hoped it wouldn't come to that.

Cura sat back, a pensive look settling on her features. "Call Dr. Anthony. He needs to know your aunt is back in town."

I know I should, but he had a history with my aunt. And even though I was itching to find out what that was all about, I also knew that Dr. A was very secretive about a lot of stuff. What if he shut down my investigation? On the other hand, Mom was Miss Organization. She'd practically color-coded my drawings and Ricky's art stuff from when we were little kids. If anyone had something on Aunt Karen, it would be my mother. She'd been openly hostile toward her during their little visit. And if what Cura had suggested was true, then maybe Mom had kept something from that fire as insurance . . . "First, let me check out what my mother might have on her sister. She keeps everything."

"Do you need me to come, too?"

I really appreciated Cura offering to help, but I needed to do this by myself. Plus, if we were caught, I didn't want to have to explain to my parents why both of us just happened to be rummaging in the attic. I knew Mom had one of her yoga classes in a few and Dad had to work late.

That's okay, I can do this. If I need your help, I'll text you," I added, more to give myself the confidence I needed right now.

CHAPTER 20

I rushed back home, knowing that nothing short of a major catastrophe could keep Mom from her yoga class. I only had a small window of time in order to follow my hunch about that fateful night.

Neither of the family cars were in the driveway. *Phew.* I was safe. I opened the door, all the while my heart raced, and I dropped my house key. I picked it up and put it on the keychain gallery next to the door. As I made my way to my parent's room, I rushed up the staircase, clutching the banister so I wouldn't trip.

Sneaking around in Mom's things was so first grade, but I really didn't have any choice in the matter. I rummaged through her drawers, knowing I didn't have much time. Frilly underwear and bras filled her top drawer. Okay, this was just wrong. I tried not to think about the reasons why my mom would need sexy lingerie. Ew!

Hmmm. I took another quick peek at the time. Four forty-five. I know I only had about a half hour more before she got home.

I tried to think where I would hide something I didn't want others to see.

Nothing in her bedroom. I shouldn't have been surprised because why would she keep stuff where Dad might find it?

Dang, now I had to check the attic. I just hoped there wasn't any creepy crawlers up there.

I closed her door, first making a final scan just to be sure everything looked the way it had before I went all Nancy Drew.

I walked to the far end of the hallway, past Ricky's room, and looked up. A cord hung down from the ceiling. I gave it a yank, releasing a set of stairs, as well as some dust that filtered down on me. I sneezed. My eyes watered, too, but I didn't have time to worry about this.

I climbed up, crouching down once inside. The ceiling sloped down, making a tight fit. A metal cord dangled from the sloping ceiling. I yanked the cord, which released a sepia glow that only added to the creepy, unused feel of the place. I had to laugh considering how I helped the dead all the time, yet I walked around my house trying not to think of the creepiness just a few feet above my head.

As my eyes adjusted to the dim light, I saw a plastic contraption, passing for a bookshelf, leaning precipitously to the side. A thick layer of dust coated everything. Some old tattered books lined the shelves. Poetry, non-fiction books on old religions, a battered copy of the Bible, and some old photo albums.

Looking around, I noticed a ratty blanket in the far corner. Curious, I went over and yanked at the moth-eaten blanket, uncovering a box. I sneezed a few times from the dust I'd unleashed and opened the box to find an old college notebook.

I flipped through the pages. A musty scent, along with more dust tickled my nose, making me sneeze again.

An old *Sacramento Bee* news clipping fluttered to the floor. I picked it up.

Sacramento State's Upcoming Stars
Fall 1990

The picture in the newspaper showed a group of girls smiling at the camera. They were wearing fancy dresses made from shiny material and hideous shoulder pads. One of the girls looked like a younger version of Mom. Wow, she was so pretty.

Another girl had her head tucked into Mom's shoulder. Brown hair cascaded down in ungodly big spiral curls. I'd only seen my aunt once but knew this had to be her. They both looked alike.

I kept poking through the box, lifting out a couple of old college interior design text books. Even though Mom had been an elementary school teacher, she had thought about switching majors to interior design. At the bottom of the box was something wrapped in an old gray cloth. I lifted the object out of the box and unwrapped it.

A small, plain wooden cross.

Not like the ones I decorate. This one had some writing that looked like an ancient language etched on it. Strange. Small enough to hold in my hand, the cross looked like something Dr. Anthony might have in his cabinet of grisly rescue tools.

I started to put the cross back, but something made me decide to hold onto it. Maybe I could show it to Dr. A. If anyone could figure out what was written on the cross, it was him.

Creak.

Holy crap. Mom was back. I fumbled with the cross and shoved it in my pocket. Throwing the books back into the box, I hastily covered it back up with the old blanket and pushed it back into the corner, inadvertently kicking up more dust. I sneezed and covered my mouth, worried my mom could hear.

I scrambled back to the opening, and climbed down the rickety metal stairs. My foot missed a step, and I almost went airborne. I clung to the metal bar, trying to get my bearings. My heart did a crazy drum solo.

I took a couple of deep breaths, trying to settle down.

I landed on the carpet with a soft thump. I cringed, hoping Mom hadn't heard me. I released the catch to the attic stairs and pushed the metal rungs back up, shutting the entrance once more.

Brushing off my jeans, I scrambled to my room, hoping to find a hiding place for the cross that would evade my mom's x-ray vision. I took off my dusty shirt and threw it in my dirty clothes bin, praying Mom wouldn't see it. I had a feeling that whatever was written on that cross was important. Big time important.

CHAPTER 21

The next day, I stumbled through my morning classes in a daze, almost missing the last warning bell for third period, and cursing myself for not grabbing more than a Pop-Tart to tide me over until lunch.

Mr. Nelson had a practice of locking the classroom door. And if you were late? Too bad. Lucky for me, he hadn't showed up yet.

I struggled to the back of the room, armed with my flippin' heavy Algebra textbook, and notebook. I collapsed in my chair and munched on the strawberry Pop-Tart. It had gone cold, but at this point it was a boost of sweet energy I was hoping for. I hadn't slept well the night before. Between the sorority house fire mystery, Aunt Karen popping back into our lives, Dylan drama, dead girl rescues, and an old wooden cross that my mom was hiding in the attic, I'd barely had enough time to do homework, let alone eat breakfast or get any sleep.

Right at my heels, Cura entered the room and smiled in my direction.

"Ready for later?" I asked, reminding her about our plans to call my aunt this afternoon. I was kind of worried she'd bail.

"Sure," she said.

"I ended up going through the attic and found something." I opened the side of my backpack and peeled back the gray cloth.

Cura leaned over.

"That looks like a baby cross, like the kind you'd hang over a crib. And what are those weird symbols?"

I shrugged and wrapped the cross back up, shoving it back into my backpack. "Don't know, but I have this feeling my aunt might."

Cura's eyes widened. "Okay, the creep factor just went up. Shouldn't we talk to Dr. A first? I thought we were going to do that—you know—ask him about your aunt?

"Yeah, I know. But Dr. A is kind of over-protective and secretive." Like my mother, I thought. Why is it that grown-ups always loved lecturing kids about every subject under the sun, from why it's important to eat a balanced breakfast to why you need to do volunteer work before applying for college, but when it came to talking about important stuff, they were always hush-hush.

Cura nodded. "Okay, but keep me in the loop."

Mr. Nelson strolled in, his large battered briefcase in one hand, a super-sized coffee in the other, and a glazed chocolate donut in his mouth.

My stomach growled and I wished I'd grabbed two Pop-Tarts, but too late for that.

He looked up at the huge clock right when the last bell rang. Then he smiled.

I squirmed in my seat. So did everyone else.

"Well, I hope you all spent as much time on your algebra homework as you do texting, because today we're having a pop quiz," he said.

A collective moan, including mine, echoed in the room.

He cracked open his briefcase. Gray patches were worn through the vinyl. He took out a newspaper, then stack of papers underneath it. No doubt the pop quiz.

Cura gave me a worried look and slumped down in her seat.

He lay the newspaper on the desk and heaved a deep sigh.

"So tragic about Emily Jones." Mr. Nelson cleared his throat and then took a sip of coffee. "I just read about the police finding her body in a dumpster on the Sacramento State Campus."

A few students began whispering about Emily, speculating about the college boys who'd been arrested in connection with her death.

Cura and I glanced at each other, knowing full well Dr. A had been working with the police to catch the killers. This was the same group of boys who had given Morgan the narcotics that had led to her death, as well.

Mr. Nelson passed out the quizzes. He cleared his throat again and said, "If you kids ever have any problems at home, you know you can come to one of us, right? One of your teachers or your guidance counselor. We're here to help."

I guess he wasn't such a bad guy after all. I almost wished I could tell him that Emily was at peace. Instead I slumped down in my seat, dreading the quiz, which I knew I would blow. Too bad I couldn't Rescue myself from pop quizzes and term papers.

CHAPTER 22

Needless to say, I blew that quiz. Big time.

Note to self: Yes, your Rescuing is important, but unless you want to repeat eleventh grade again some serious studying needs to be your top priority.

I winced, realizing how much that thought sounded like my mother. *Ugh.* Once I got to the school cafeteria, I grabbed the first available table. Cura trailed behind, her shoulders slumped.

"You know what? Screw that test," Cura said and sat down next to me. She rummaged inside her bag, pulling out two protein bars and handed me one. "See? I'm prepared for any crisis, which right now is finding out what your aunt might know."

I unwrapped the chocolate-peanut-butter bar and took a small bite. The thing about most protein bars is that while they look like chocolate bars, they sure don't taste like them.

"Do you see any ghosts?" She dropped her voice, glancing around.

"No, it's good. For now."

"Whew. I don't hear anything either. That's a good sign, right?"

It still blew me away that Cura could now hear the dead.

"You sure you're okay?"

"Sure, although you'd think one of those dead people could at least whisper the answers to the quiz."

I chuckled, wishing I'd thought of that myself.

Her face scrunched up. "But at least I don't see them like you do. Now, that would totally be messed up," she said around a mouthful of protein bar.

"You get used to it." I shrugged.

"Let's call her now!" Cura suddenly said, all random like. "You know, let's call your aunt."

I hesitated.

"Well?" she asked again. "Why not? We're looking for answers and she might be able to give them to us."

I pulled my cell from my bag, but hesitated. This had been my plan from the start, so why was I feeling the proverbial cold feet?

"Well?" Cura repeated, more insistent.

Suddenly, Dylan appeared, as if out of nowhere.

"Hey, you never texted back last night," Dylan said, a sting to his voice.

Between visiting Cura and my Nancy Drew sleuthing, I'd forgotten. I'd never forgotten to text him back before. I wondered if it was everything that was going on or whether it was his hot/cold attitude that had begun to drive a wedge into our relationship. He stood by our table, shifting his backpack to his other shoulder.

He didn't wait for an invite, but plopped himself down next to us.

"Should we tell him?" Cura asked.

"Tell me what?"

Cura motioned to my backpack.

I gave her the "don't go there" look as I didn't really want to share this with him yet, because I just knew he'd try to talk me out of calling my aunt. I didn't want that.

Dylan snorted. "Does she also know about that chick at your house yesterday?"

Cura snorted. "That was no chick. That was her aunt."

Dylan stared long and hard at me, and then ran his hand through his hair.

"No way. Your Aunt Karen? No wonder she seemed

so familiar." He dropped his hand and moved closer. "Have you told the doc she's back in town?"

"No, not yet," I said.

Cura nudged me hard.

"I will after I call my aunt."

"You sure that's such a smart idea?" Dylan asked. "There's something creepy about your aunt. She had a wicked aura around her."

"Jesus, Dylan," Cura hissed. "Why don't you say it louder?"

A few people mingled around, not paying much attention, but I still felt wary of being overheard. I couldn't help but worry that if word got out about our abilities, we'd be carted off to the closest looney farm.

"Well, Mom isn't being up front with me about everything, so I have no choice."

Dylan raised his eyebrows at that.

"She left a card and told me to call if I wanted to talk."

"After her mom threw her out," Cura added.

"Yeah, I was at your house when your aunt showed up, remember?" Dylan said. "You know two girls died in that fire at the sorority house twenty years ago. Hillary's aunt and my aunt. Did you stop to think about that? Your mom's sister killed my mom's sister and Hillary's mom's sister.

Yes, I knew this. Boy, did I know. But my gut told me to follow through with this. "You don't get it," I finally said. "She knows something that might help us."

"Maybe if you'd texted," he said and left it at that.

I'd been meaning to do that, but didn't mostly because I knew how he'd been lately with all of my so-called "responsibilities" and this latest development, I knew, wouldn't smooth over our relationship issues.

"Sorry if I didn't get around to that," I said again, then I lowered my voice. "But you haven't exactly been around lately, either."

"Whoa, time out," Cura said. She put one hand on each of us. "Let's just call your aunt. If Dylan's right, then we'll bag her and go straight to the good doc. Agree?"

Typical Cura, I knew she was only trying to defuse the awkwardness

"Do whatever," Dylan said, grabbing his backpack.. "Don't tell me I didn't warn you."

I bit back a nasty retort. Let him take his tantrum. I didn't need him before and I sure didn't need him now. I had Cura and Dr. Anthony on my side.

"Fine, whatever," I said, zipping up my bag.

Dylan walked backwards, his hands up in protest. "When you decide you need help, call me."

"What was that all about?" Cura asked. "Wait, forget I asked." She opened her purse, rummaging through it. She pulled out some Chewlistic bubble gum. "Want some?" When I shook my head, she tossed a slice of the neon pink gum in her mouth. The over-kill sugary scent made me want to gag.

"So, you know I don't exactly get what Dylan's ghostly ability is," Cura said between pops.

I motioned for her to come closer. "He sees auras of people," I whispered. "I just hate it when he gets all preachy about it like he just did about what he saw around my aunt." I shook my head. "Seriously? A wicked aura? What the heck does that mean?"

Cura's face wrinkled in confusion. "Auras? Are those like those new age thingies my mom's into?"

Cura's mother, though she'd belonged to the same sorority as Hillary's mom and my mother, didn't fit the image of a sorority gal. Her Stevie Nicks hair and clothes, her taste in that meditation-type music that featured gongs and pan flutes, and her love of New Age things like crystals was different from the other moms. But that didn't mean she was a paranormal junkie. Nope. The moms had obviously squashed their experimentation from when they were in college. "No, it's like a colored halo that Dylan can see and feel around people that usually tells him what kind of person they are—or if they're in a pissy mood or a happy mood."

"Wow, serious?" Cura smacked her gum. "Man, is this whole town on some kind of supernatural fault line or what?"

"I'm starting to think it is."

"It's not as if Dylan doesn't know about you seeing dead chicks and all. So why did he just throw a huge hissy fit?"

"Good question." Once again, I could feel tears threatening to erupt at any moment. Something I didn't need right now because I knew once they came, I wouldn't be able to stop crying.

"Hmm." Cura smacked her gum again. "So, you see the dead. I hear them. Hillary sees them, too. And Dylan sees halo thingies."

I nodded. "Yeah, something like that."

I placed my hand over Cura's. "You know, let's just cut class and grab some real food." I motioned to the half-eaten protein bar. "Then we can call my aunt."

Cura frowned for a moment then brightened up.

"Sure, after that sucky quiz and Dylan's 'tude, I need an In N Out cheeseburger with animal-style sauce."

I laughed. "Sure, why not. What do you say? My treat?"

Cura smiled. "Sounds good to me."

We gathered up our stuff and made our way out to the parking lot. I needed a brief break from all of this high school drama. As we walked to Cura's car, I mused over what I'd say to my aunt and how I'd bring up the mini cross. Deep down, I knew Dylan was right and I should contact Dr. Anthony first. I hated when he was right. I pushed the guilt aside, for now, though it lingered in the background.

CHAPTER 23

Thank goodness, the last period of the day! I couldn't wait to go home and put today behind me. I hadn't run into Dylan again. That didn't stop the growing apprehension that we were headed for a break-up. A sick feeling gurgled in my stomach that had nothing to do with my fast-food lunch with Cura.

I hurried down the hallway to my least favorite class: biology. At least I'd convinced Mom I didn't need the AP, advance placement, version. Unlike some students, including Dylan, I didn't think the world would end if I didn't carry a full crap load of AP classes.

An overpowering, slightly sweet disinfectant smell floated up to me, causing me to almost lose my lunch right there. Maybe it hadn't been such a good idea to grab that double cheeseburger and side of fries.

I scanned the room for the offensive scent and almost dropped my books.

Holy shit. In all the craziness of the last few months, I'd kind of overlooked one part of my science curriculum. I knew about the genetics and other stuff, but I hadn't really read—more like skimmed over—this week's lesson.

I had to dissect dead things. Not people, thank God for that, but insects and even frogs. As the telltale itch slowly made its way behind my legs, that could only mean one thing.

I'd never seen the ghosts of animals or any creepy thing, so I'd just assumed I would never get a paranormal visit. Wrong.

I stared at the half dried out carcass of a frog. Next to it lay the instruments we needed to dissect it. I swallowed back the bile. I checked around me, seeing if a ghost might have popped in. You'd think by now I'd be used to seeing dead things.

Why hadn't I signed that waiver thing to get out of dissecting bugs and, in this case, frogs? Too late now.

To the side of my table a fuzziness shimmered just at the periphery of my vision. No, cross that out. More like a room filled of fuzzy jumping things. Sure enough, the ghosts of the frogs were everywhere; over the tables, under the desks, one even settled on top of Mr. Studd's balding head.

Ribbit.

The ghost-frog got comfy on Mr. Studd's head, fixing a creepy stare down at me. Its beady eyes blinked once while emitting one loud humongous filmy bubble. It grew and grew until it popped.

I winced but, of course, only I had witnessed it.

Mr. Studd reached to scratch his head and the ghost-frog slimed over to the other side.

That cheeseburger and fries started to come up.

"You okay, Miss Stewart?" Mr. Studd asked, the amphibian apparition shadowing his movements. The ghost-frog's beady eyes blinked out a froggy Morse code. Omg, was it trying to communicate with me? It was hard enough to help dead people, but frogs too? No, this was way too much.

"Uh, I need to go to the bathroom," I said, barely holding back the undigested cheeseburger from hurling out of my mouth.

"What's wrong, Stephie?" Jason, the star quarterback asked. "Too chicken to cut up the froggie?" He dangled a dead frog by its long legs. I still hadn't forgotten his part in egging on Hillary at lunch a while back, when she got up on the cafeteria table and started the infamous, "Itchy Stephie" chant.

Now I knew I'd be sick.

"Why don't you go to the office...?" Mr. Studd offered, searching for the yellow office passes on his desk.

I didn't stop to hear anymore. I ran out, down the hallway, passed the Nurse's office into the girls' washroom where I proceeded to deliver the cheeseburger into the toilet.

CHAPTER 24

An intense sugar craving almost always hit after seeing a ghost. I guess that included the amphibian kind. Lovely.

That little experience with the dead froggies helped me get out of last class and home early. I texted mom on my way home. She bought it, although I expect it had more to do with her being distracted by her surprise, unwanted reunion with Aunt Karen from the day before.

Careful not to set off the Mom alarm, I tiptoed into the kitchen, opened the pantry doors and snatched a bag of Sun Ships, a diet Cherry Coke, and a pack of trail mix with real chocolate bits and none of the crappy carob stuff that Mom tried to pass off as being the "healthy" choice. Mom was in her exercise room/office, chatting with someone on the phone. I couldn't help but wonder if the news of her sister's return had gotten out.

I shut the pantry doors and, awkwardly holding onto my junk food stash, tiptoed out of the kitchen and back to the stairs leading up to my room.

"Honey, can I speak with you for a minute?" Mom asked, popping her head out of the office.

I gripped the bag of chips closer, almost losing the trail mix.

Maybe if I act like I can't hear her, she'll leave me alone.

Silently I made my way upstairs.

Creak.

"Aren't you supposed to be sick?"

I whipped around, nearly dropping the bag of Sun Chips.

"Uh, I'm feeling a little better now.

Even I didn't buy that lame excuse. I shifted in place, waiting for her to blow a fuse and go off about how I needed to take school more seriously.

She let out a heavy sigh. "We need to talk about my sister, Karen."

"Uh, now? Can't it wait?"

"Yes, now."

"You know, I'm still feeling a little woozy." I wobbled, but that only got me an eye-roll from Mom.

"Your junk food fix can wait," she said.

"Okay, whatever."

Defeated, I followed her back to the living room. The over-clean scent of lemon cleaner made me sneeze. If I didn't know any better, I'd swear she'd tried to disinfect our house after Aunt Karen's visit.

Mom sat on the couch, patted the cushion next to her. For a moment, I feared she'd found out I'd snuck into the attic. But if she did, I'm sure she would have confronted me about that by now. So far, though, she only seemed anxious.

I placed most of the junk food on the glass coffee table, but kept the bag of Sun Chips.

"Want one?"

She shook her head. "About yesterday. Well, I think I should explain something," she said.

I waited, hoping she'd come clean about Aunt Karen. When she didn't, I asked: "Do you know why she just showed up?"

"No, but I have to warn you that you need to be careful. I know she's my sister, but I worry that she might not be here just to be social. Trouble follows her."

"Wow, Mom, that's kind of harsh."

"Remember when I told you she was the one who messed with the paranormal and did spells?"

"Yes, that's old news. Her spell sparked a fire at

your sorority house and two people died. Hillary's aunt and Dylan's aunt."

Mom sighed. "That's an understatement."

"But if you were all involved in the ceremony and in the spell-casting, why single her out for blame? Why can't you try to forgive her? It was a mistake. A tragic mistake, but still a mistake."

"Easier said than done." Mom's fingers did that dancing thing on her lap, meaning she craved a cigarette.

"Do the other moms know Karen's back in town?"

"Not yet. Please don't tell anyone. Let me handle this."

Well, too late for that, but I didn't want to remind Mom that Dylan had seen her and I'd just shared the info with Cura. For sure I wouldn't share that Cura and I were going to call her. No, right now it was best to just agree with whatever Mom said. Later, when it got out that I did contact Karen, then I'd deal with the consequences.

"Okay, Mom."

"I thought, I really thought," Mom muttered, "she would have learned her lesson and stayed away from here. I don't know what she means to accomplish by showing her face now."

"Seriously? You really thought she'd never just show up?"

Mom stared at me in disbelief. "Yes. Exactly."

"Maybe she thought, after all this time, she could start over. It's not as if the internet was around then. It's not like her name is out there, calling her an arsonist."

"You're wrong there. I know. So, do your friends' mothers. Dylan's mother knows and still holds what Karen did over us. Why else do you think she goes out of her way to avoid us? And with you dating her son? I'm sure that didn't go over too well."

Talk about understatement of the year.

"But Mom, people can change."

"Not Karen."

"You don't know that. You haven't seen her in forever."

Mom stared at me. I could see a ton of sadness and regret in her eyes. "I don't want to chance it. Either way, it's best she stays away."

"Mom, I get what you're saying. I really do." I placed the half-eaten bag of Sun Chips on the table. "And in a weird way, I get why you guys tried to do that spell with us. You didn't want us to go through what you did."

"No, I didn't." She shook her head. "None of us did. But look at what happened. Cura can hear the dead and Hillary can see the dead. What we tried to do backfired. Again."

"And you're worried that some dark force was unleashed?"

Mom nodded. "That's why I didn't argue about doing the initiation the other night. I really thought it might redeem us."

"Wait, if it wasn't your idea, then whose was it?"

"Lisa's," she said.

I jerked back. "Why am I not surprised?"

"Yes," Mom's voice broke. "She lost her sister and after rumors got out about you seeing the dead., she worried that her daughter might get the same ability. We were all there. If it happened to my daughter, she was afraid it could happen to hers, too. Karen changed that night. It was almost as if she became another person. I don't know if it was because she knew she'd caused a lot of harm, but there was a darkness about her." She looked up, wiped her eyes. "I don't know what to do to make this right. Maybe you should tell Dr. Anthony…?"

"No," I jumped away as if I'd touched fire. "Let's not chance it. Who knows what might happen? Maybe something even worse."

"Honey, I know that you were able to see that poor

girl who appeared during the ceremony we tried to do at the sorority house a few weeks ago—"

"Mom, it's okay," I interrupted her. "I crossed Emily over. You don't have to worry."

"You did?"

I nodded. "Yes, I did."

I knew I should share that Cura, Hillary, and Dylan helped, but I was reluctant to continue the conversation. Just at that moment the phone rang. Saved by the bell, again.

CHAPTER 25

Dinner rolled around. The thought of sitting and engaging in small talk didn't appeal to me. Still, Mom insisted on the family sitting down for dinner in the dining room. No way out of this.

Good news, though. I think Mom had finally been somewhat honest with me on why she'd taken me to the initiation. I knew I should leave it at that, but I still wanted to talk to Karen. I couldn't help it. I guess, knowing that she and I shared the same abilities made me curious. It made me want to find out more about her. Mom didn't have to know.

I twirled the spaghetti around my fork, not hungry but not wanting to ask to be excused as that would get Mom on my case.

"So," Dad cleared his throat, "why haven't we seen Dylan around lately?"

"He was here the other day, though he didn't stay long." My fork slid, leaving a red mess on the tablecloth. My gut told me that Dylan had been avoiding me for a very good reason. I just didn't want to say what I feared, that he would break up with me. Maybe if I didn't, then he wouldn't?

"Oh, sorry I missed him," Dad said, concern in his voice. "He's the decent one out of that whole bunch."

"Dad!"

"Well, it's true."

"Dad, why don't you like the Van Burens? They didn't do anything to you."

Mom and Dad shared one of those looks.

"It's nothing like that," Dad said, "That family just has issues."

"And what family doesn't?" I retorted.

"Touché," he said. "You got me there."

"I think it might be for the best if Dylan doesn't come over as much anymore," Mom said smoothly. "Stephanie needs to concentrate on other things, like getting her grades up. This is her junior year, after all. The one that the colleges look at."

"Oh, just let her be a kid. What's wrong with that?" Dad winked at me. "She has time to bring her grades up."

Thank you, Dad.

"Tell that to the colleges she applies to."

Gee Mom, maybe I could add my special abilities to my application: Dear UCLA, my extra-curricular activities include helping murdered girls cross over into the great beyond. I almost snorted with laughter.

"Speaking of which, did you know Mom's sister showed up just the other day."

Mom glared in my direction, clenching the tablecloth.

"Really?" Dad asked, looking at Mom. "Karen's in town? I thought she broke off from the family over a feud?"

"It's no big deal." Mom shrugged, though her lips tightened. "She was passing through and thought she'd stop by."

Dad frowned.

"Didn't she mention something about getting together with you and your sorority sisters? Maybe at your old sorority house?" I asked, knowing I should stop, but unable to. Sometimes Mom pushed my buttons, especially when it involved lying to Dad.

Dad stopped mid-bite. "Why would she want to do that? You don't mean that burnt out sorority house by

[191]

the bridge? I don't know why the officials haven't razed that eye sore yet."

Mom picked up the dish of grated Parmesan and sprinkled some onto her plate. "More cheese? I just love parmesan . . ."

"Yeah, what's up with that?" I asked. "Why is that creepy place still standing?"

Dad took another bite of his dinner. "Apparently some people," he said, giving Mom one of those looks, "still feel it's important and want it to stay. Heaven knows why."

"It is an important part of our town's history. It's a heritage building. You just can't just destroy that," Mom retorted.

"Well, that fire destroyed any of its landmark beauty," Dad said. "Now, it's just a hazard. Besides I heard some crazies have been sneaking in and doing God-knows-what."

If he only knew the half of it, I thought.

Mom cleared her throat and stood up. She smoothed out her perfectly pressed pants while zinging me with one of those *don't-think-we-won't-discuss-this-later* looks.

"I have red velvet cake for dessert." Then she added. "Help me, honey?"

I gulped. Not a question. More a demand.

"Uh, you know I really need to do something for school. I promised Cura I'd meet up with her."

"Since when do you turn down dessert?" Dad asked.

"Can I be excused?" I said. I slipped my sweaty hands in my pants pockets. I knew if I stayed around, Mom would give it to me in the kitchen. No thanks.

Dad didn't even blink.

"Sure. Your mother and I need to talk in any case."

Uh, oh. Apparently, I'd opened an old wound. Part of me felt guilty for doing that to Mom, but I didn't want to stick around for her angry tirade.

I didn't give Dad a chance to change his mind. I darted out of the dining room and up the stairs to my room. Right when I closed the door, the familiar ping went off from my cell. I rummaged around in my bag, pulled it out, seeing a text from Cura.

Hey, did you get a text from Hill?

No? Why? I replied.

She wants us to meet at her place.

I hesitated to answer, not sure what to do. The argument in the dining room grew louder. That alone forced my decision. Well, that and it was a Friday night, meaning homework could wait. Even hanging out at Hillary's had to be better than sticking around here.

Sure.

Good! Meet you there

Not knowing what to expect I kinda knew black would be the key color. I searched through my closet until I found a pair of black jeans. I threw on a black pullover t-shirt and a black hoodie. After I dressed, I took two steps down the stairs.

The muffled sounds of my parents echoed up to me.

"...You didn't think it important to tell me this?"

"...I didn't think it was the right time..."

"...damn it, Jean, when is it ever the right time with you?

I flinched, feeling bad that I'd opened a can of worms. So many secrets in this family, and I, for one, hated them. But I had more important things to deal with right now.

CHAPTER 26

I drove out to Hillary's house and parked my car on the street, behind the familiar red Jetta. Relief hit as I knew I wouldn't be alone to face Hillary. I strolled down the sidewalk, side-stepping some trash. Weird that there was trash on the sidewalk, knowing how anal Hillary's mom was. I hesitated for a moment, debating if I should turn around and go home.

No, Cura would rag on me if I didn't go in and stand with her. Besides, I should probably let Hillary know I was going to contact my aunt. The three of us were in this together, since we'd all been affected by the events at the sorority house twenty years ago and then, again, just a few weeks ago.

The door was open so I walked inside.

Semi-darkness greeted me. Candles of all shapes were clustered together on a long rectangular table and a few larger ones were on a smaller table beside a couch. A chill went through me. If I didn't know better, I'd think I stumbled into a ceremony. I searched for Cura.

"Hey, so you did show up," Hillary's voice whispered in my ear. "Didn't think you would if I texted, so I asked Cura to invite you."

I jumped. "Jeez, don't do that."

Now that my eyes were adjusting, I could make out the ghoulish look to the house. Sepia light flickered over Hillary's face.

"Don't you know Halloween is in October?" I asked.

She only snorted. "Remember all those candles our

mothers had back at that sorority house? Well, I did my own research and found out all about the significance of candles in spell-casting ceremonies. Who knew you can't just use any candle, either? Beeswax ones are the best. Plus, color is important too." She motioned to the red and purple candles. "These are for power and strength."

"Wow, you're really into this," I said. I had to give Hillary credit. She'd done her research.

"I thought it best to get into the mood, if you get my drift." She chuckled, as if telling a joke.

Last time I was here was actually at Halloween, and she'd suckered me into playing a lame game of Bloody Mary, which turned into a disaster.

"Hillary, I get that you're into all this now, but this is not the way to go about doing the kind of work we do," I finally said. At that moment, all thoughts of sharing my aunt's visit vanished. Who knew what she'd get up to if she knew Aunt Karen had been in town.

She only smiled.

Cura stepped out of the shadows. She rubbed her bare arms, frowning.

"So that's why you have all the candles? You're planning on doing another ceremony?" Cura asked.

"Why of course," Hillary said. I stared in disbelief. She'd totally lost it.

At least my legs weren't itching, meaning no ghosts were here...yet.

"Okay, whatever you say," I said, playing along with her. I gave the area another once-over. The candles cast creepy shadows on the walls, but without my trademark itch, I knew this was probably only a case of nerves playing tricks on me.

Hillary placed her hand on my arm. I resisted the urge to push her away. The shadows flickered over her face. "Let's all go into the kitchen," Hillary said as turned and walked ahead of them.

"Is it just me or is she certifiable?" Cura asked.

"Let's just humor her," I said.

"Give the word and I'm so out of here," Cura whispered.

I nodded. She didn't have to tell me twice, though deep down I knew if Hillary had totally lost it, I'd have to intervene and get her some help from Dr. A.

"So, what's keeping you two?" Hillary called out from the kitchen. "We don't have all night."

Cura seized my hand, tight. "I'm staying close to you. I don't trust her."

We walked into the kitchen and I did a double take. Wow, Hillary didn't skimp on the candles.

Another bunch of beeswax candles were in the kitchen, too. Red, purple, and even a black one, were arranged on the granite countertop. Hmm, I'd have to ask her the importance of the black candle, though I kind of had a feeling it might not bode well. I spied a silver bowl of water with what looked like rose petals floating on the top. This must be her half-hearted attempt at recreating the failed initiation.

"Hillary, are you sure you know what you're doing?" I asked.

She shrugged. "Of course I do. How hard is it to do a spell thingie?" When we didn't say anything, she went on, "There's like a bazillion spells online. I didn't remember the exact one my mother used, so I chose a simple one to try out."

"No way," Cura said. "You shouldn't be messing with something you don't understand."

Hillary huffed. "I think I totally understand that I can see the dead. After I helped Emily cross over, I thought I'd be weirded out, but instead I felt so alive."

I gaped at her. I didn't know what I expected her to say about the Rescue, but that sure wasn't it.

"What?" she said, "Don't tell me you don't feel the same way each time you send a ghost on their way."

The spirits come to us. We don't go chasing them." I motioned to the candles. "I don't do spells or anything like this. It doesn't work that way."

"What do you mean? It did with our mothers?" she protested. "Why not us?"

"I don't feel comfortable doing this," Cura finally said.

I nodded. "I don't, either."

Hillary looked all offended. "You're just mad you didn't think of this first."

I let out a loud sigh. "Like I said before, it doesn't work that way. Anyway, don't you think your mom might be mad if she knew what you were doing?"

"I don't care. She's the one who started this. Not my fault that I actually like this new ability of mine."

Even in the semi-darkness, I swear I saw Cura blanch. "Uh, I agree. This so isn't a good idea," Cura added, inching closer to my side. "I'm leaving. She's wacked."

Hillary frowned. "No, you're both going to stay here. Especially you." She pointed to me. "Now that I've officially joined the Ms. Ghost Whisperer Club, I want to see the dead on my terms." She turned to Cura, "I thought you'd want this, too."

"Okay, now I know you're nuts," Cura said, scanning around for an exit. She tugged on my sleeve. "Let's get out of here."

I agreed with Cura, but something kept me rooted to the spot.

"Hillary, where's your mother?" I asked again.

"Forget her. She'd only talk us out of this or worse."

"You know, this time I would agree with her," I said.

Hillary's eyes widened then narrowed. "Don't tell me that. We have to stick together."

"Like when you kind of knew I could see Allison's ghost? I didn't see you sticking with me then."

"Whatever. That was in the past." She shrugged. "You know she told me you might say that."

"What are you babbling about? Who told you?" Cura asked.

"Why your aunt of course," Hillary giggled. "She told me lots of things, including this." She motioned to the candle arrangement.

My mouth opened, then closed. So Karen had made more than one visit.

"What's wrong? Sucks to find out you're not so 'special,'" Hillary made air quotes, "after all, huh?"

She turned back to Cura, who hovered close to the door. "We can do this without Stephie."

Cura only shook her head. "If she's not included, then I'm not staying around, either."

I took that opportunity to make my way over to Cura's side, "Let's get out of here."

Right then the kitchen lights flashed on.

"What is going on here?"

The sudden brightness blinded me for a second, then Hillary's mother glared at us, folding her arms across her chest. Her shoes tapped an ominous beat on the ceramic floor. I thought for sure that one of her sky-high heels would break off.

"You're supposed to be at some function," Hillary said, finally regaining her composure. Anger laced her words.

Hillary's mother directed her anger not at her daughter but, rather, at me. She pointed her acrylic French manicured nail in my direction.

"You need to leave," she hissed. "Now."

She didn't have to tell me twice. I swung around, making for the exit, but the next comment stopped me in my tracks.

Hillary's mother didn't back down, her nostrils flaring. "Why is your aunt Karen back in town?"

"You know?" I whispered, taken back.

She huffed. "Word gets around. Trust me, nothing good comes when that woman is around. And you just proved my point with this ridiculous display of candles."

"Hey, I called Steph over," Hillary held her ground, her bottom lip quivering. "Why do you ruin everything?"

Hillary's mother's face crumpled. "Honey, I can't believe you're saying that. Her aunt started all of this."

Hillary's smile grew. "So, what's wrong with that? Maybe she had the right idea."

Mrs. Swanson's face reddened. "That aunt of hers killed my sister!"

"You don't know that," Hillary said. "Didn't you say it was a terrible accident? Anyway, it happened long ago. Why are you holding that against her?"

"You don't know what you're saying," her mother said, her eyes filling with tears and her lips trembling.

I knew I should say something, but I still couldn't get over the fact that my aunt had visited Hillary and, judging by the candles, shared some spells with her, too. I didn't buy, for one moment, that she'd "searched" the internet for a random spell.

"I'm sorry you're not too happy that your silly spell didn't work the way you wanted," Hillary finally said. "But you know what? I'm happy that it backfired on all of you. It's like I now have a super power."

Silence.

Mother and daughter didn't budge.

I finally spoke up. "Cura and I are just going to leave now."

Mrs. Swanson whipped around to face me. Her eyes narrowed. "I don't blame my daughter for this foolishness. But you, on the other hand? I told her to stay away from you as nothing good would come of it."

Hillary snorted. "Yeah, right. Why should she have all the fun with the dead?"

Mrs. Swanson swung back around, pointing her long

acrylic nail at Hillary. "You will have nothing to do with that aunt of hers. Do I make myself clear?"

Hillary folded her arms, glaring back. "You can't tell me what to do."

"Oh, yes, I can."

Hillary regained her usual frosty composure, ignoring her mother. "Steph needs to be here," Hillary said, anger in her voice. "That's all I know and care about right now. Somehow, we're," she pointed to Cura and me, "all a part of this now. We need to work together to help the dead. Why stop there? I, I mean, we could do big things with this ability. Hollywood here we come!"."

Surprised, I stared at Hillary. Forget the whole Hollywood mention. We'd had our moments. Okay, we totally didn't care for each other, but for her to just make that admission to her mother? That took some serious backbone.

Hillary started walking toward me when Mrs. Swanson clamped her hand down hard on her shoulder. "Stephanie, you need to leave."

She didn't have to say anything more. I'd had enough anyway.

Before Cura and I got out the door, I turned back around. A few of the candles had burnt down to their stubs, leaving a sulfur taint to the otherwise perfect surroundings.

I couldn't help myself. Sure, I wasn't too happy that now others knew about my ability to help the dead, but on the other hand . . ."You know, I only came here because Hillary asked. Don't you think I want to be normal?"

"Even though normal is highly over-rated," Cura said, a twinkle in her eye.

"And because of you and our mothers," I glared at Mrs. Swanson, "decided to play with fire twenty years ago and then, again, a few weeks ago, I have to accept what I am and so do Cura and Hillary. So, thank you, Mrs. Swanson, for being so curious about the paranormal that you and your friends allowed yourselves to unleash something you couldn't contain. Something that would change your daughter and us for the rest of our lives.

Mrs. Swanson's mouth dropped open.

Hillary nodded in agreement with me and crossed her arms. Wow, that was a first.

That old familiar feeling, of not being good enough, resettled on my shoulders. I wished I could shrug it off, but this only reminded me that it had never left. I should be used to it by now.

Hillary's mom was a hypocrite, and maybe my mom was, too. They had started this whole thing for their own selfish reasons and now they were trying to lay all the blame on us and Aunt Karen. Aunt Karen had been younger than them. She'd just wanted to fit in. Maybe if they had been more accepting of her in the first place, she wouldn't have gone to the extreme in her spell-casting.

"You know, maybe you and our moms asked for it. What did you expect when you messed with the Other Side? Santa Claus?"

I didn't wait for her parting comment, but turned and left with Cura right behind me.

CHAPTER 27

"You rock." Cura gave me a big hug and we said our good-byes and got into our separate cars. At least I could count on Cura, and strangely enough, I was touched by Hillary's support back there.

Still, I'd had enough of all of this. Mrs. Swanson actually had the nerve to blame me for Hillary's lame attempt to conjure up a spell. I banged my fist on the steering wheel. Plus, why did my aunt pay a visit to Hillary? What was she up to? Was she trying to make amends or was she making trouble?

I turned the ignition on and sped away.

Back home, I snuck back upstairs to my room. I didn't want to deal with my parents. Dad's frantic pounding on his computer keyboard meant he was working late in the home office he shared with Mom. As I walked to my room, I noticed my parents' bedroom door was closed and the light off. I guess Mom was feeling drained, too. She must have gone to bed early after her fight with Dad.

I plopped down on my bed, musing over the latest turn of events. I hadn't gotten any closer to finding out what all this meant . . .

My cell buzzed.

I covered my head with a pillow. Hopefully it would stop but, no, it persisted.

Sighing, I reached for it.

Was that trippy or what?

I stared at the screen, tempted to say how Hillary's

newfound passion for the paranormal, kind of freaked me out. But nah, Cura didn't need to hear this.

Then before I could respond, Cura added: *Why didn't she tell us your aunt visited her?*

I texted back: *Who knows? Everything is upside down. Still shocked Hillary stood up for me to her mom.*

I could almost hear my friend's chuckle. Then she texted: *You still calling your aunt?*

Cura's question reminded me what I'd been putting off. I placed my cell on my end table, crossing over to the other side of my bedroom. My backpack lay amidst a growing collection of dirty clothes. I unzipped and rummaged through it until I found the now tattered card.

My cell binged again. I ignored it, fumbling with the card in my hand.

Once I went down this path, there was no turning back. But not doing anything led nowhere. I walked back to the table, picking up my cell.

U there?

I stared again at the card. *Yes. Tomorrow. Will get back to u.*

No sooner did I reply, when another text from Cura raced across the screen. *Okay. Be careful!*

CHAPTER 28

Waking up early on Saturday morning, determination pushed me to dress and get this over with. Now I had to follow through before I chickened out. Again. I went downstairs to the kitchen. The yummy smell of blueberry pancakes and real maple syrup wrapped a comforting arm around me. I loved the weekends since Mom went overboard on the whole motherly thing with cooking. During the school week, I was usually in a hurry to get to classes, so Pop-Tarts and granola bars were my usual breakfast fare. Weekends were special. I embraced the feeling like a comfy blanket. I so needed this right now.

At the kitchen table, Dad sat reading the *Sacramento Bee* Sports section. He was wearing his favorite Axl Rose t-shirt and sweatpants, his regular Saturday morning uniform. In his earlier years, Dad had gone to his share of heavy metal concerts and even played a mean electric guitar in a garage band with some friends. He was actually quite good.

Mom flipped a fresh pancake over the griddle. On the table were a stack of still hot, fluffy pancakes. The warm, blueberry aroma drew me in. I plopped down across from Dad and helped myself to a few.

No mention of last night's argument. No accusations. I felt as if I walked on brittle glass and if not careful, I'd crack through. So typical. Mom and Dad were always overly polite to each other after they had a fight. Like they were casual work acquaintances or something. Avoidance was our last name.

Dad looked over his reading glasses. "So, you had a fun night?"

How much did they know? I worried if Mrs. Swanson had ratted me out, but knew she and Mom weren't exactly on friendly terms after the sorority fiasco. That thought, of course, reminded me of what I needed to do. If Mom knew I was going behind her back to contact Karen, she would flip higher than the pancake she was tossing on the griddle. Dad wouldn't be pleased, either.

I swirled a slice of pancake into the gooey goodness of the maple syrup and popped it into my mouth. "I guess," I said chewing.

Mom stopped after flipping the pancakes, giving me a sideways glance. "It's nice that you girls are still getting together." She walked over, adding more pancakes to the dwindling pile on the table. She pushed back a strand of loose hair off her face. Even this early in the morning, Mom looked perfect. A pair of pressed designer jeans and a button-down shirt were peeking from underneath a red checkered apron. The only thing that broke that image were a pair of fluffy pink slippers.

"Yeah, right," I muttered between bites. "Real fun."

"You should do it more often," she said, and waited for a comment. When I didn't reply, she only sighed and went back to the griddle.

What happened to the whole, *you-need-to-get-your-grades-up* speech? I swear I never could understand my mother.

Dad shook the paper and flipped to the next page. "So, what constitutes a fun night now?"

What I wanted to say: *Going to a place where a former friend, who is now a dead chick magnet, tries to have a little fun with her new gift by lighting a gazillion candles in her house followed by her mother kicking you out of the house after trashing your aunt. Yeah, my idea of fun.*

Kim Baccellia

Instead I said: "You know, we watched some chick flicks and ordered pizza. No big." I took another bite of pancake, forcing myself to chew, then swallow. Suddenly, the sweet taste of the syrup was too overpowering. I hated lying, but couldn't tell the truth. Not with Dad right there. Mom didn't want him to know about any of this. My abilities. My helping the dead cross over. Everything with Aunt Karen and the sorority sisters. Dad was completely in the dark, and that made the fluffy pancakes turn into a stone inside my stomach.

"Sounds like fun, pumpkin," Dad said. "Glad you're hanging out with friends."

Inside I cringed. I knew Dad was only trying to make small talk, but how could I tell him that I wished I could just do normal things like hang at a friend's house and have pizza? I hated lying. No longer did the whole loner thing feel so right. It felt . . .well . . . lonely.

I took a quick sip of orange juice. "Gotta run."

"On Saturday?" Dad asked. "Since when are you so anxious to do anything on a weekend?"

I took another sip of the orange juice.

"I've really got to work on this paper..."

I didn't lie but I didn't tell the whole truth either. No harm.

Mom put her hand over Dad's. "Let her go. I'm sure she will let us know if there's something she needs to go over. Right?"

Now Dad looked confused. "Stephanie, is there something you need to talk about?"

"Jesus, I just have to do a paper, okay?"

"Well, I'm just worried about you. When the police called us after they found you at that abandoned coffee house a few months ago . . . I just don't want you to think you can't talk to us about anything that you're going through. You know that, don't you?" Dad asked.

I glanced at Mom, who was suddenly busy cleaning up. There was so much I wish I could talk about. But

Mom wanted me to keep quiet about everything. I had no choice. I couldn't talk about it with Dad, and Mom hated talking about it, so I was stuck lying and I hated it.

"Yeah, sure Dad." I smiled and gave him a quick side hug. I went to the fridge and grabbed a can of Diet Cherry Coke. No, make that two. I needed the extra caffeine.

"Remember your promise," Dad said, not backing down, "No secrets."

I don't know how Mom did it. But this lying business was really getting to me. Instead, of telling him what I really wanted to, I got out of there fast. "I know Dad. Love ya," I said and made a hasty exit.

CHAPTER 29

I had to get away from it all. The secrets and lies were all too much. Snatching the car keys off the key holder, I jumped into Mom's car. The cold morning air bristled around me.

I sent a quick text to Cura that I hadn't forgotten about calling my aunt and would get back to her later. Tossing my cell back in my purse, I glanced across the street and stopped. Panic seized me. Figures Dylan would be out. Now would be a good time to ask him why he'd been avoiding me, but to be honest I hadn't been exactly trying to talk to him either.

Dylan was loading his surfboard onto the roof of his truck. He crisscrossed the board with thick bungee cords on the cab, giving them an extra tug. All sense of time stopped and I wished that I could go back to before all the crazy stuff had hit the wall. I sighed. Why couldn't I just give up helping the dead? Although he didn't say it, I knew my ability had created a wedge between us.

When Dylan yelled out, I lowered the window.

"Hey," he shouted, giving his surfboard one last tug. "Where you going?"

Now would be the time to fill him in about Hillary's little performance. But instead, I said: "Library. Got to do some research on the Spanish American War."

Dylan looked away, rocking back and forth on his heels. Even from here I could sense his pent-up energy. "So you finally decided to start it?" he asked, looking back at me. "You know it's due next Friday."

No mention of the last few days. No apology. Nothing. I stiffened.

"Well, it's not going to write itself." I shrugged, trying to act all indifferent while inside my heart was breaking in two.

I had to take another tactic or I'd start to cry, which would only make things worse. "Going to hit the next big wave?" I asked, forcing a smile on my face. "Isn't it too cold?"

"That's what a wetsuit's for."

I grinned, picturing what he looked like in his wetsuit. Amazing no doubt. "Right!" I said.

Dylan smiled.

I swear a small part of me died right there. I struggled with the desire to jump out of the car, run across the street, throw my arms around his neck, and do the whole cheesy romance thing. I wanted— No, I needed his strength.

Dylan's fingers brushed through his hair. Nervous energy crackled off him. "You know, I really think we should take some time off," he finally said. "I need time to regroup. And the whole Rescuing thing? Well, I just can't deal with it right now."

All of sudden, my mouth felt like someone had shoved a pack of cotton balls inside. I kind of knew this was coming, but to actually hear him say he wanted out, really hurt. Still, I had my pride. I gulped. "Sure, I think it's for the best."

He cracked a half grin. "Whew, I thought that would go worse . . . So no hard feelings?" he asked. "You know, about the other day?"

I knew Dylan hadn't been that comfortable with my gift of helping dead girls and knew his way of escaping was going off to Half Moon Bay. "No, we're good," I said, while inside I screamed otherwise.

"Cool," Dylan said, shoving his hands into his pants. "We're still friends?"

Ouch. I knew it was coming, but that didn't stop the sting and, omigod, did it burn something fierce. "Yeah, of course," I said, looking away and trying to not let him know what I really wanted—him. I knew that if I stayed there a minute longer I'd burst into tears.

"Great," he said, although this time his smile wavered. He gave the bungee cords another tug, before opening his truck door and climbing inside.

I sat like a doofus in my car, wishing and hoping he'd act like the hero in those romance movies when the guy realizes how dumb he's been and chases after the girl he loves.

No, instead, he leaned out the window and said, "Later." Then he sped out of his driveway.

I waited until his stupid truck faded from view then I let my guard down. The damn burst and I couldn't stop the tears from pouring down my face.

I turned the ignition and drove away, angrily wiping my tears. I had to be strong. If anything, I had bigger things to worry about like figuring out what my aunt was up to and why she was bringing Hillary into it.

No, I needed to be my own hero and no one, not even Dylan, could save me.

I had to save myself.

CHAPTER 30

I actually did drive to the library. I figured I could make the call from there, that way I wouldn't be totally lying to my parents.

Once there, I pulled out the card before I chickened out.

Here goes nada.

She answered on the first ring.

"I didn't think you'd call," she said in her raspy voice, before I could even say anything.

"Can we talk," I asked. "I have a lot of questions."

"Fine, let's meet at my house…"

"…no," I cut her off. "A neutral place like a coffee house. I'm bringing a friend too."

"Oh?"

"Yes, her mom is one of your sorority sisters."

"Oh, yes," she answered. "I'd love to meet her."

After we agreed on the Starbucks close to Sutter High, I hung up, I felt, even more confused if that made sense.

I texted Cura about meeting Aunt Karen.

She texted back with: *We need to visit Doc A first*

I hesitated. I knew Cura was right.

I texted: *Fine.*

* * *

No surprise, Cura had beaten me to Dr. Anthony's office. I should be angry that it had been her this time around calling him. I mean, it was my job after all. Add some guilt that reared its ugly head into the mix, calling me out on avoiding this whole situation. I felt like a kid caught snatching a cupcake meant for a church bake sale.

Cura was sitting on one of the benches that surrounded the nature wall fountain in the lobby of Dr. A's office building.

"Hey," I said as I plopped down beside her. She gave me a smile.

"I love this fountain," she said, "I could sit here all day and watch the water trickle down through the plants and flowers."

"Me too," I said as we sat for a few moments gazing at the peaceful fountain. I couldn't help but wonder about Dr. A and his Light Bringers' group. I knew that Dr. A knew some pretty powerful people and had access to pretty secretive and mysterious info, but he only told me stuff on a need-to-know basis. Visions of Matrix-type dudes all dressed in black with black sunglasses danced in my head. The only glimpse I had into Dr. A's "real underworld" was when he'd gotten stabbed in behind the coffee house, a few months ago, when everything with my "demon" boyfriend went down. I thought for sure Dr. A would die right in front of my eyes, and then all of a sudden, this bright shaft of light shot down from the sky right into his wound, wrapped around the knife and yanked it out. Then the light began crisscrossing the gaping hole in what looked like laser stitches. Not something I could share with Cura, I didn't want to freak her out.

We got up and rode the elevator to the thirteenth floor where Dr. A was busy tapping on his keyboard. Who knew what he was working on.

"Hey Dr. A, what are the Light Bringers anyway?" Cura blurted out. Got to leave it to my bestie. She gets right to the heart of the matter.

Cura and I both sat down as Dr. Anthony leaned

back in his chair, pushed his glasses up his nose, and looked as though he were weighing his words very carefully.

"We're part of a broader network of people from psychologists, to clergy-people, to scientists, to army personnel, law enforcement, even the secret service. And we work with people like you, Cura and Steph, who can commune with the Other Side. We offer support for what you do as gatekeepers between our dimension and the next. We do this for the greater good of human kind. Part of what I do as a parapsychologist is to document these paranormal experiences and make sure the information is circulated to the right people."

"Wait, so you documented our Rescues?" All this time I thought no-one knew about what I did. Apparently not.

"Well, I document the paranormal experiences mostly of children and teens. What you do, though, is very unique and only a very few people are privy to the Rescues that you're involved in."

"So, you're like a ghostly Giles for Stephanie?" Cura asked, referring to the cult classic *Buffy the Vampire Slayer, a* TV series we binge-watched one summer. Although Dr. A was much younger and cuter than Giles.

Okay, got to stop going there.

Dr. Anthony cracked a grin, as though he'd heard it all before. "Yes, kind of like that."

But that still didn't explain the supernatural experience I'd witnessed back at the coffee house. I started to ask about that when Cura smiled, continuing with her questioning. "That's cool, but what about demons and stuff?"

Icy fingers clutched at my insides, reminding me how close to the truth Cura was with my recent experience with Mark, and finding out he had in fact been one of the undead. *Ew*, just the memory of kissing him made me want to Purell my mouth.

Dr. Anthony glanced at me and said in a smooth tone, "I doubt you girls came by here just to talk about my work. Is there something pressing you want to discuss?"

I leaned in, ignoring the candy jar, although I swear those Tootsie Rolls called my name. "Someone from our mother's past just showed up. We thought you should know."

"Who showed up?" He asked.

"My mother's sister, Karen." I replied.

Dr. Anthony's face blanched. "Karen Harris?"

"I know you mentioned you knew her, but I have a feeling it was more than that. Am I right?" I asked.

Cura nudged me, motioning to Dr. A's hand. It trembled.

"Yes," he said, visually shaken. "Yes, we knew each other."

"How exactly?" I asked. Then it dawned on me. Mom had mentioned that her sister had a boyfriend she'd met through some underground paranormal group. Could it be possible he was that person?

"Wait," Cura leaned in and grabbed a bunch of Tootsie rolls. She handed me a few. So much for keeping away from the sweets.

Cura unwrapped a roll and popped it into her mouth. "So, let me see if I heard you right." She said around a mouthful of the chewy chocolate. "You and Stephanie's aunt have a history?"

"You were her boyfriend, weren't you?" I asked.

"Wow, really?" Cura unwrapped another candy and shoved it into her mouth.

"We dated for a while," Dr. Anthony said, his eyes looking down at his desk. "But nothing came out of it."

"My aunt and you went on some crossings together, didn't you?" I sat back, the candy forgotten. "Were you her mentor back then? Isn't that, like, a conflict of interest?"

Cura coughed. "Good one. Can't date the person you help out on crossings. Or can you? Date them that is?"

Dr. Anthony's ears reddened.

"It wasn't like that. She showed interest in the paranormal and claimed that she could see the dead. I worked with her, guiding her, but she seemed to be more interested in the darker aspects of the paranormal. And then, after the tragedy at your mothers' sorority house, she was banished from the Light Bringers. I haven't seen or heard from her since."

"So seriously, you two were a thing?" I still couldn't get over this picture. My mentor dated my aunt, until she went all psycho and caused a fire that killed two young women.

"You said she's back in town?" he asked, sounding more in control. "I need to let the Light Bringers know this."

Cura glanced sideways at me, mouthing, *Are you going to tell him?*

"My aunt didn't just visit me but Hillary, too. Do you know why she'd do that?"

Dr. A scratched his chin, as if contemplating this new twist. "Karen was always impulsive." He looked at Cura, "Did she visit you too?"

My friend shook her head. "Nope."

I butted in, knowing if I waited too long I'd lose my nerve. "I want to talk to her. If anything, I want to know why she went to Hillary. Something isn't right."

Cura snorted. "That's the understatement of the century. Don't you think your aunt put Hillary up to that little ceremony back at her house? And what was with those gazillion candles?"

Yes, something definitely was off. Hillary had originally hated the whole idea of seeing the dead and suddenly now had a change of heart?

"Another reason why we should meet. At least that way I might be able to find out the real reason why she's back. I figured since she was family and all, she'd talk to me and if you're her ex," Dr. Anthony squirmed at that reference, "then I doubt she'd be open with you."

"Well, if you ask me, I think she's dangerous, which is why I suggested to Steph that we speak to you first Dr. A," Cura said crossing her arms. "You agree, don't you?"

Dr. Anthony nodded. "The better reason why the Light Bringers need to handle this. You don't know what your aunt might still be capable of," he said, and then reached for his landline phone.

"Let me talk to her and I promise I won't do anything stupid. Please?"

My mentor leaned back against the chair and did his annoying habit of tapping his fingers together. His way of stalling. Or musing over a way to stop me. "I should call her first," Dr. Anthony said, his voice flint hard.

"No!" I protested, leaning forward in my chair. "She's my aunt. And we do share similar abilities. If you confront her she might just pick up and disappear again. And that might make her even more dangerous." I really needed him to trust me on this because I wanted to find out everything about Karen and Mom. "Please, Dr. A. I promise, if anything goes wrong I'll text you right away."

Dr. A blew out a breath. And put the phone back in its cradle.

I almost sighed in relief.

"Wait, what about me? I'm part of this now. So I'm going with you." Cura sat back, waiting for me to tell her otherwise.

"Okay, but we have to be very careful." I didn't want to drag my friend into this but, on the other hand, I didn't want to hide anything else from her. I looked back at Dr. Anthony. He frowned and I thought for sure he'd demand both Cura and I drop this whole idea of meeting up with my aunt. So, his next comment surprised me.

"First we need to come up with a plan to stop your aunt if she's still tampering with the dark side."

"Like what? Don't tell me that same lame chant our mothers said because it didn't work," Cura said.

"No, not a spell but rather a talisman," Dr. A got up and walked over to the cabinet in the corner. He did a weird tapping with his fingers on the wood that sounded like some kind of Morse code. The wood panel opened like something out of an *Indiana Jones* movie. Cura and I looked at each other, our eyes wide. Dr. A removed a battered old wooden box from the secret shelf. He placed the box on the desk and opened it. It was empty. But then he did another tapping thing inside the empty box and out popped a hidden drawer. Inside was a small polished cross.

My eyes almost bugged out of my head. It looked just like the cross I'd found in Mom's stash in the attic.

"Wow, Mom has one almost exactly like that one."

I still had the cross wrapped up in the same gray cloth, at the back of my closet.

Dr. A nodded. "These are rare and one of them was stolen from me years ago." He looked up at me. "Just before the fire at the sorority house."

"Apparently, if it's the same thing." I picked up the mini cross. Turning it over, I traced with my finger the strange symbols on the surface. "Yes, it's the same."

I handed the cross back and took out my cell. I scrolled through a number of photos. "See? Is this it?"

Okay, maybe not the smartest thing to do, but I couldn't resist taking a photo of the mini cross. It wasn't as if Mom went through my cellphone as I never left home without it.

Dr. A took the phone and glanced at the photo. "So that's where it ended up."

Cura had gotten up and joined us. She leaned over, checking out the photo and looking at Dr. Anthony's. "Yeah, same one."

I wondered why my mom had the cross. Did she steal it from Dr. A, or did Aunt Karen steal it?

"So, I decorate crosses and my mother had an old mini-cross with ancient writing on it?" I fingered the etchings. "What does this say? Do you know?"

"It's from an ancient text. The language no longer exists, but basically it's a rune to ward off evil."

"In this case, probably whatever took over my aunt, right? Or something like it?" Just saying this gave me the chills.

Cura continued to stare at the cross. "Does that mean my mom might have one, too?"

Dr. A shook his head. "No, only the one who leads the spell would have one. Karen must have taken it all those years ago, without my knowing, and the cross ended up in your mom's hands.

"So, what do I do with this?"

"If your aunt is foolish enough to try another spell, this might help you."

"But how?"

"It operates in a similar way as your talismans. Only in this case, you smash it down on an object that she is using to summon the power. That could be a bowl or even a mirror."

A memory flashed. At the burned down sorority house, there had been a mirror in the room where our mothers had set up the ceremony. Could that have some significance?

"Be careful, though, if she tries to get you to use blood. Those spells are dangerous and will unleash evil into our world."

"Did you just say blood?" I recoiled at the image of using blood in a chant or spell.

"Omigod, we did fall into a CW TV show, didn't we?" Cura exclaimed.

"But don't do anything without calling me first," Dr. Anthony went on, ignoring Cura's comments.

I nodded.

"Promise. No thinking you can do this on your own. I'm here to help you."

"Okay, I promise."

A coldness splashed down on me with the realization this might not be the smartest idea I'd ever had, but I pushed it aside. I had to do this.

CHAPTER 31

Hillary didn't answer our texts. Since my aunt had already paid her a visit, I figured including her in our meet-up with Karen wouldn't be a biggie. I did, after all, say I would be bringing a friend. One more shouldn't be a problem. While walking back to our cars, Cura kept checking her cell.

"Give her time," I said, while fumbling around in my purse for my car keys. Sure, I acted all calm, but inside a million thoughts collided into one colossal muddle.

"You know, bag her." Cura's sudden change of thought had me glance up. "We're supposed to meet up with your aunt. Let's just go. I'm sure Karen will fill us in on her little discussion with Hillary, and if she doesn't we can bring up that we know she talked to Hillary. She can't hide anything from us."

I dropped my keys on the wet ground. Picking them up, I said, "You sure?"

"Why shouldn't we?" Cura persisted. "Besides, it feels like the good doc was holding back on us." She cocked her head. "There's more to this story, and maybe your aunt can give us some answers, even though she is creepy."

She had a point there. Still, I fidgeted. "Right." Dr. A's mention of a blood spell had taken me off guard. Was that what my aunt had used twenty years ago that led to the fire at the sorority house?

Just at that moment a beep went off on Cura's cell.

"Finally!" Cura smiled at the text and then showed me the message: *Count me in.*

I should be happy Hillary hadn't dissed us, but another emotion resurfaced that was hard to ignore. What had my aunt shared with her that had driven her to want to try her own spell-casting? Then again, she did show back bone standing up for me when her mother trashed me. That had to mean something.

"Since we're meeting her at Starbucks," Cura pointed across the street, "I can grab a yummy drink. Don't tell me you're not thinking the same thing."

Visions of a sweetened caffeine concoction danced in my head. I glanced back at Dr. Anthony's office building, almost expecting him to come running out to stop us. He sure was a mysterious dude, and I vowed, after all this was over, I would ask him exactly what had taken place between my aunt and him.

Cura didn't give me time to waffle. She faced me with her hands on her hips, giving the don't-act-like-a-butt expression complete with a loud snap of her gum.

"You coming?" she said. She didn't wait.

I rushed to catch up with her.

The Starbucks was packed with people just chilling around. The roasted scent of coffee teased us with its comforting aroma. I ordered a tall Americano iced coffee with not two, but three shots of caramel. Cura got her usual iced caramel macchiato with extra whipped cream. I ordered a skinny soy vanilla tall for Hillary. Best to get on her good side.

We hadn't been waiting long when Hillary sat down next to us. I pushed the drink in her direction.

"Glad you two came to your senses," she said, looking at the offered drink. "A skinny vanilla?"

"Of course," I said, while inside rolling my eyes at her snarky comment. Typical Hillary.

"When my Aunt Karen stopped by my house a few days ago, she said she'd answer any questions I might have. So, I told her we'd come over. I figured you'd want to come, too."

Hillary straightened up and smiled. "Hell, yeah."

"So, did my aunt tell you to do that spell at your house the other night?"

Hillary frowned and took another sip of her drink. "Oh, that? No, I just Googled a spell. Figured, why not? Though I hate to admit this, I do think your idea of us three going over to your aunt's is a good one."

Hillary waved her hand. "Duh, of course it would be better if we all showed up at your aunt's house."

"Why are you so interested in all of this? Especially in meeting with Karen," Cura asked.

"Why not?" Hillary shrugged. "I think our mothers just misjudged her. She didn't mean to hurt anyone. She'd only wanted to do a spell to help intensify what they were able to do. Help the dead. It was like their own super power. She didn't think it would backfire."

"OMG! She told you that?" Cura asked.

Hillary nodded. "Yeah, she pretty much did. She feels like she got a bum rap from our moms after the fire.

"But your mother was right," I said, "It was because of her that two sorority sisters died, including your mom's sister."

"It *was* an accident," Hillary protested. "I thought you'd at least stand up for her as she's your family and all."

To be honest, I didn't know what to think. Hillary was defending my aunt? The woman who had caused the death of her own aunt? And this, after she'd stood up to her mom for us? I felt like I was in a bizarro world.

"Let's call Karen now," Cura blurted, ignoring my stare, "She told Stephanie she'd meet us."

"Seriously, I'm surprised you waited this long to contact her. Like you said, she probably could teach us a lot."

Now, I wished we hadn't invited Hillary along. A sick feeling began to churn in my stomach. Would this entire thing blow up in our faces? Hillary was too gung-ho, and that could prove volatile and dangerous.

I opened my purse, and pulled out the now dog-eared business card.

"Did you go to her house already?" I asked.

"No, she showed up when my mom was out showing a house. She didn't stay that long, but only because I figured Mom wouldn't exactly want to see her. You know, baggage and all."

Hillary wasn't exactly the sensitive type, even if she'd never known her mom's sister, she was acting like the fire was just a little mishap.

"Well, are you going to call or what?" Hillary snapped.

I blew out a breath and tapped out the numbers.

My aunt answered after the first ring.

"Stephanie?"

A chill went up my spine at the sound of her raspy smoke-tinged voice. Thank goodness, the three of us would be going together.

"Yes, it's Stephanie. Uh, so are you available to meet up now?" Hillary gave me the thumbs up. "Would it be okay if we came by your place?" Cura made a writing motion with her hand. "Oh, and can we get an address?" I turned my back, but not before catching a classic Hillary rolling her eyes.

"Sure," Karen said. "Got a pen?" I motioned for a pen or pencil and Cura gave me one. I wrote the address on the Starbuck's napkin.

After I hung up, I gave the address to Hillary, who typed it in her smartphone's GPS app.

"Hillary showed us where it was on the map. "Strange. I thought we'd have to drive somewhere outside of Sacramento."

"Maybe it's only a rental," Hillary said. "Or maybe

she only just moved back to Sacramento."

"Or maybe she's been here all along and was just keeping a low profile," Cura chimed in.

I nodded. Still, I decided I'd ask Mom if she knew that her sister lived in town, and if she did know, why had she kept it from me.

We drove over in Cura's car.

My aunt's townhouse was nestled in one of those swanky, gated communities with the fancy manicured grounds, high-powered security cameras, and guards that manned the gates. The whole place reeked of privilege and money. I wondered how she'd done so well. Was the retail biz that lucrative, or was there more to it? It's not like we were poor or anything, but still . . .

"Come on," Hillary said, "Tell me you aren't excited to finally check out what she has to say."

I nodded, though I didn't tell her this outright.

She settled back with a smug smile.

Cura glanced at me. "What do we say?"

"The truth," I replied.

Karen must have let the guard at the security gate know that we were coming, because he waved us right in.

The community was made up of swanky condos and townhomes, suitable for upscale single professionals, well-to-do young marrieds, and rich retirees. We drove the short distance to the address on the card. A row of pristine cookie-cutter townhouses lined both sides of the street, complete with immaculate lawns.

Karen opened the door a few moments after we pressed the bell. It was weird seeing her again. She definitely looked like my mom, but she was way more glam. Her outfit screamed rich, rock-star rebel. Her long, dark hair was swept up in an elaborate updo, showing off a humongous pair of silver hoop earrings. Silver-studded black, leather pants, matching leather jacket with a fitted, sparkly gray t-shirt underneath completed her outfit. Her tanned and line-free face would have made a great "after" pic. Her lips and cheeks had that puffy look that women got when they'd had too many of those injections.

"Stephanie." She opened the door wide, her eyes appraising Cura. Hillary shoved her cell back in her oversized bag. She didn't squirm like I did. Cura evaluated the situation before sliding closer to my side.

My aunt turned to Hillary. "Hillary, I'm glad you're here."

"Yeah, whatever. You going to fill us in on how we can become super powerful or what?" Hillary asked.

I shrunk back, waiting for a nasty come back or something. Instead my aunt threw her head back and laughed. "Boy, you get right to the point, don't you?" She nodded her head as though in approval. "You remind me of your mom ."

Hillary rolled her eyes.

Karen grinned. "Also like your mother." She then motioned us inside. "Where are my manners? Please, Come on in."

She signaled us over to a seating area in the living room. Two fancy beige leather sofas sat facing each other. Large plush pillows with bold purple stripes hugged the ends of the sofas. Modern art adorned the walls, including a huge Andy Warhol-like painting of a woman with spikey blonde hair. I think it was some celebrity. I gaped at the painting, then glanced at Cura who raised her eyebrows and shrugged her shoulders. Aunt Karen's taste was rich and eclectic, that was for sure. I sat down on one of the sofas, its smooth leather welcomed me. I glanced down at the glass coffee table. A pack of cigarettes and an engraved silver lighter lay in wait. The only odd thing was a cheap-looking dollar-store ashtray, which totally stood out like a sore thumb. Maybe she broke her swanky one.

"I didn't know you lived here in Sacramento."

"Oh, this place?" Karen gestured to the surroundings. "I'm only staying here for a little while."

Triumph shone in Hillary's eyes that she'd been right.

Cura, wandered over to the fireplace mantle and picked up a framed photo of Karen with our moms. "So it's true, you did belong to the same sorority as our moms," she said.

Karen laughed again. This time it sounded sarcastic. "Yes, I did. Oh, the memories." She reached over to take a cigarette out of the carton and then lit up. A sweet clove scent wafted in the air.

Cura placed the photo back.

"You sure look good for someone my mom's age," Hillary said.

"Just like your mother," Karen said again. "Hillary, I think you and I will get along just fine." She took another hit and sat down opposite me.

Hillary scowled and remained standing. Cura scooted over to sit down beside me.

I jumped right in, hoping to defuse the tension in the room. "So here we are. You said you could help us, or at least let us know what our mothers aren't telling us about your ability to communicate with the dead."

Karen nodded.

I really wanted to ask why my mother had been so adamant about telling Karen to get out. Yes, I knew she had been behind the fire and the deaths, but I sensed there might be something else. Something even darker. Why else had Dr. Anthony alluded to a blood spell?

Karen lounged back in her chair, observing us. She flicked off some of the ashes of her cigarette in an ornate ash tray, silent at first. Probably mussing over what to say.

"Why weren't you there?" Cura asked. "At the old sorority house when our moms tried the spell?"

"Because they didn't want me to tell you the truth,"

Karen said. "Something your mothers declined to tell any of you. I bet they tried to get rid of your abilities, didn't they? Or they refused to acknowledge them."

Silence filled the room, along with the oversweet scent of cloves and ashes. Karen stared intently at each one of us. Awkward with the appraisal, I squirmed, suddenly wishing I had listened to Dr. Anthony and had him call his Light Bringer friends.

"You got that right," Hillary said bluntly. "Forget them. I want to know how we can do more with our powers. You said you would help us with that."

"Of course. I'm a woman of my word. Why don't we start now?"

Uh oh! My spidey senses were telling me this was not a good idea, after all.

"Uh, maybe we should just talk first?" I asked, suddenly feeling uncomfortable.

"Why talk when I can show you?"

"Cool!" Hillary nodded and sat down next to Karen.

Look, maybe we can do this another time." I stood up and pasted an easy-going smile on my face. "We should be going anyway, right Cura? Hillary?"

Cura's shoulders slumped in relief. "I actually need to get an assignment done. It was great meeting you Karen . . . ."

"Hey, I'm not ready to leave yet. I want to learn more." Hillary glared at us.

No way could I leave her here with Karen. I really needed to check back in with Dr. Anthony. Karen's idea to start training us made me nervous. What if she really was into some dark and dangerous stuff? What if the fire wasn't an accident?

I started walking backwards toward the door. Cura was right beside me.

"Nice meeting you," Cura smiled and waved. Then under her breath she said to me, "We are so out of here."

I nodded.

"You can't leave.." Karen said, with a smile that didn't quite reach her eyes. "I haven't started your first lesson yet." Karen's eyes flashed with anger and for a split-second seemed to turn red. I blinked, thinking it was a trick of the light coming in through the window.

"Let's get out of here," Cura whispered.

Karen lit another cigarette just as Cura reached for the doorknob.

"Ouch," Cura yelled, flinching back. She rubbed her reddened hand. "What the heck?"

At that moment, the familiar itch on the back of my legs flared up like a bad case of eczema. That only meant one thing: the dead were close by.

Karen tsked, slowly stubbing her cigarette out in the ashtray.

"You wanted to know my side of the story." She stood up and crossed her arms over her chest. "And I'm going to tell you. Then you can go home. Until then, shut up and listen." Her voice sounded deeper. Harder.

I tried to open my mouth to argue, but nothing came out. It felt as if an invisible muzzle had clamped down on my mouth, sealing it shut.

The itch now throbbed. Almost unbearable, I rubbed my leg to no avail. I looked around, checking for the presence of a ghost.

"Oh, she's here," Karen said. "But she's being quiet. For now." She glared to the side and I swear the shadow on the far wall quivered.

"Yes, I see her!" Hillary looked triumphantly my way. "Now who's the badass, Ghost Whisperer?"

My body trembled. We'd basically walked into a viper's den. How, could I have been so stupid?

"Now where was I before being rudely—" she glowered at the now terrified Cura, "—interrupted? Oh, yes, that very special day."

She looked at me. "You said you wanted my side of the story. So let me tell you my side." She motioned to

Hillary, "At least one of your friends has an open mind."

"Depends on what you mean by open," I said.

Aunt Karen frowned and then she chuckled. "My bad. You did come here to learn. So, let me share what I know."

What choice did I have? She'd basically locked us in.

I nodded.

"I don't like this, Steph," Cura whispered, grabbing my hand.

I squeezed her hand. I didn't either.

With a flick of Aunt Karen's wrist, the curtains closed and the candles on the mantle lit up.

"Wow!" Hillary walked up to the mantle and ran her fingers over the flame. "That was unbelievable. Can you tell us how you did that?"

Ignoring Hillary, I asked, "Something tells me you didn't learn that from Dr. A, or the Light Bringers."

Karen's eyes flared once more. An eerie red glow. Inhuman. This was bad. Like Mark-the-demon bad.

"You're right. I didn't learn anything from those do-gooders. They have no idea what I can do." She stood up and strolled around us, giving each one of us the once-over. Her gaze drilled through me, the hairs on the back of my neck rose.

Cura's hand tightened around mine.

"Why don't we all sit back down and I'll tell you everything." She motioned us back to the sofas.

When we hesitated she said, "Don't worry, I won't hurt you." She smirked. "Besides, all I ever wanted was for you to know the truth." She emphasized the last word. "But then again, maybe you're all too scared of your mommies?"

That got Hillary's irk.

"Hell no." She stomped over and sat down. "They've been lying to us all these years."

I sighed, figuring we should hear her out. What

choice did we have? She'd basically locked us in her house. "It's okay, Cura," I reassured her, even though I was still worried.

She nodded and we made our way back to the couch.

"Believe it or not, I was an outcast." She directed a forced look of sympathy my way. "You also know that your mothers were all part of the Alpha Phi Sorority. I was desperate to join. But at first, they only laughed at me. I was never 'one of the group.' So I decided to use another way to get in."

"You told them about your ability," I said. "But how did you convince them? I mean, even though I see them, I can't make others see them, too.

Karen smiled. "I tried a few spells. Harmless stuff. Your moms couldn't see any ghosts, but they could sense them. I had the ghosts move objects around and flicker lights. It was a great show."

"And they were so impressed that they invited you to join?" Cura asked.

"Yes, they did. My sister wasn't happy about it. She was jealous."

That surprised me, because Mom had told me she was happy about Karen being accepted into the group. Was Karen lying or was Mom?

"Around that time, I joined a parapsychology group on campus. They were kind of a fringe group, and their goal was to study paranormal phenomena and work with people who had paranormal abilities. Well, I was one of those people, because I could communicate with the dead. So, I joined up." She gave a little chuckle. "They were a bunch of do-gooders and nerd types. But I did learn a lot about what not to do. The dark side of channeling and why we needed to be careful. The thing is, I found all the goody-goody stuff boring. What was the use of having all of these powers, if I couldn't use them?"

"So, you didn't make any friends with anyone in the

group? You just quit?" I asked, knowing full well that Dr. A had admitted they'd dated.

Karen sat back and smiled like a cat. "Well, I did get it on with one of the guys in the group. He was pretty hot and he knew a ton of stuff."

"And you learned everything you could, right?" Hillary nodded and grinned back.

"You got it."

"So, what did you do after you quit the group?" Cura asked.

"I just did my own thing. I'd learned some stuff in the group but, like I said, they were losers, so I started hanging out at a bar off campus. My sister kept nagging me to stop going to that bar. So, all the more reason to keep going. It was a biker bar on the edge of town. There were some hot guys there. One night, I had a spell book with me, and I was leafing through it and the waitress walked up to me and told me she could teach me stuff that wasn't in any book. And she did. Boy, did she ever."

"So, it sounds like you didn't care about hanging out at the sorority anymore if you were always at that bar."

"Yeah, I was having fun. Sowing some wild oats. And it was about time, too. I mean, my wonderful big sister was on the cheer squad for the football team at the college. She was dating the captain of the team. So how could I compete with that? She was perfect."

Karen glanced at me. Her eyes filled with bitterness. Was that what this was really all about? Jealousy? Had she been jealous of Mom? And she wanted to upstage her somehow? "So, you wanted to show up Mom?" I asked. "Was that it?"

"Well, there was more to it than that. But yeah, your mom was so perfect at everything. She had no idea that, from the time I was born, I could talk to the dead. Our parents just thought I was an introvert and weird. They sent me to psychologists and different doctors. Nobody could find anything physically wrong with me. They had no idea what I could do. I had always been ashamed of my powers. I had always tried to keep them hidden. Then your mom started dating that football player, someone I'd had a crush on since high school. I just wanted to show her that I could do something that she could never do in a million years."

And that was it. That was at the root of everything. The reason why Aunt Karen had been so driven to proclaim her powers. Because of Mom.

"Wow, I had no idea your mom was the Queen Bee," Hillary glanced at me. "So, you're just like Karen, then aren't you?"

"Stephanie is her own person." Cura jumped in, defending me. "She has nothing to be ashamed of and no one to impress. What she does is good and honorable. She helps girls who've been murdered, cross over. She is noble. Something you could never understand, Hillary."

Aunt Karen threw her head back and laughed.

"You're more like your mother than you are me. You're too much of a goody-two-shoes to do some of the things I've done."

"Like what?" Hillary leaned in, eagerness lighting her eyes.

"I like your style, Hillary." Aunt Karen winked. "But we'll have to leave that for another time."

"So, you wanted to show up Mom, and you decided to try a new spell," I said bluntly, changing the subject.

"You got it. I'd learned a lot from that witch at the biker bar. She knew stuff that you could never find in some lame book at a university library."

I listened with baited breath, afraid to hear the rest.

"I had everything ready. The candles, the sage to burn off negative energy, and I drew the inverted triangle on the floor . . ."

"What went wrong?" I asked.

"Your mom, interfered. Just as I was saying the

incantations she told me to stop. That what I was doing wasn't right. It was evil. The other girls got involved and soon everyone was yelling at each other. What they didn't realize was that the sacred circle we had created had broken because of the arguing. A dark force entered the sorority that night and someone in that room started the fire. I don't know who did, but soon the entire floor was covered in smoke and flames. I shouted for everyone to run—to get out, but it was too late. You all know what happened . . . "

"You can't paint yourself as the victim here," I said.

"You weren't there. You can't judge me!" Her harsh words made me flinch.

"No one's blaming you," Hillary said. "It was a tragic accident."

Karen's eyes softened and she patted Hillary's hand. "Thank you."

Karen settled back, a faraway look in her eyes. She reached for another cigarette, lit it, and took a slow drag.

"That must have been why our moms tried that lame excuse for a ceremony again," Hillary said. "They were worried about the dark entity and they wanted to stop the ability that Steph has from spreading to us." Hillary stood up and began to pace. "But our moms were all wrong." She pointed at Cura and me, then at herself. Her eyes were wide, her face was pale. "We're not freaks. We have a special gift. A power that can do a lot of good. So, did Karen, but their ignorance got in the way, almost destroyed it. Then they tried to destroy us." She sat back down beside Karen. "You've got to share what you know with us. I don't know about them," she motioned to us, "but I want to learn more."

Karen stared at Hillary for what seemed like a long time. Her eyes blazed with that weird red fire again.

"You girls need to know first that you already had this ability. But it lay dormant. Your moms tried to suppress it.

"They sure did," Hillary said.

"The spells I learned from that witch will intensify your powers."

"Really?" Hillary asked. "Then count me in."

"Good." She whipped her head around to Cura. "What about you, retro doll? Do you want to learn more too?"

Cura winced. "I just want the voices to go away. Can you do that?"

A Cheshire-cat smile crept up Karen's face.

"And what about you, dear niece?" she asked me. "Don't you want to expand your horizons?"

I shrugged, not sharing that Dr. Anthony had already trained me. I still had an ace up my sleeve with the talisman. For now, though, I'd see what she was planning.

"Why do you think I'm here?"

"Right," my aunt said. "Just think of all we can do together."

Cura and I looked at each other. Hillary leaned in closer to Karen. She looked as if she'd won the lottery or something.

"Have you ever wondered what it would be like to actually go there?" she asked out of the blue as if discussing planning a trip to Iceland.

"Seriously?" Hillary piped in. "You can do that if you're not dead? I thought that kind of stuff only happened in the movies."

Karen chuckled. "You can travel over if you know what you're doing."

"You," Karen pointed in my direction, "have some of the tools and knowledge, but that so-called mentor of yours hasn't exactly been truthful."

Ohmigod. So she knew Dr. A was my mentor? What else did she know?

Cura gaped at me.

"I bet his," she made air quotes, "'organization'

didn't tell you that when you slam down your talisman the world splits in two."

When I frowned, she persisted. "You've seen glimpses of that other world. I know you have. But why stop there? Go big or go home I always say."

I hated that she made what I did, helping those girls cross over, sound like a circus magic act. But I'd be lying if I said I didn't want to know where this might lead.

Karen grinned. "I thought so."

"Wait," Cura asked, "You can actually do that? Go to the Other Side without being," she coughed, "uh, dead?"

"Why not?" Karen asked all innocent like.

Silence.

"When I tried it the first time, I was missing a vital element. But I have it now. The missing link," she said, looking at me. "You're more gifted than you could ever know."

Whoa. Mega whoa. I felt as if I'd been gut-punched. Disbelief turned to anger. My mother had discouraged my ability from the start, and even had me go to a real shrink whose answer to seeing the dead involved a drug cocktail, leaving me in near zombie state. And even Dr. A, who was my mentor, had only told me a fraction of the truth. Why?

"What do we need to do?" Hillary asked. "Because whatever it is, count me in."

CHAPTER 32

Needless to say, I didn't get much sleep the following two nights. We swore we wouldn't tell our mothers about our meeting with Karen and we knew she wouldn't call them up and tattle either.

I felt completely torn about everything. Yes, Karen was mom's sister, but her stunt of "locking" us into her house so we would be forced to listen to her was creepy. I'd been taken by surprise when she told us that Mom had been the one to try to stop the ceremony. And our moms knew that we all had this latent ability, but they'd kept it all hush hush, and even tried to erase it from us. But the biggest shocker of all was the two dimensions' theory. Was it true? And if it was, why didn't Dr. A tell me about it?

In addition to my zombie state from lack of sleep, I had a hard time concentrating on my weekend homework, which did not bode well for Monday. Hopefully, none of my teachers would throw any surprise pop quizzes.

Oh, and the cherry on top of the hot mess sundae that is my life, was my break-up with Dylan. And knowing that Miss Ashley was on the move didn't exactly thrill me when Monday morning rolled around. It seemed that wherever he was, Ashley popped up. Making goo-goo eyes at him.

It hurt. Omigod, it hurt bad.

Cura was standing by my locker when Ashley and Dylan walked by, laughing at some secret joke. Her eyes met mine and I read the sympathy there. "His loss," Cura said, smacking her bubblegum.

I shrugged, organizing my books, trying to keep from losing it. "It is what it is. Besides, I have too many important things on my mind anyway. And he wasn't exactly being supportive."

"I just thought," Cura moved in closer, "seeing as he has his own paranormal gift and all, that you two were meant to be."

"Well," I sighed, "I guess some things aren't meant to be."

"Yeah," Cura agreed half-heartedly. Dylan was her friend, too, so our break-up not only affected me but her.

Cura's eyes then widened. She nodded to the corner. "Guess who?"

I didn't need to ask. The sweet scent of Clinque's Happy wafted over to us.

It still felt so surreal to have Hillary stand next to me, let along acknowledge my existence.

Right on cue, Dylan walked past us again, with Ashley at his side. She giggled at something he said. *Again? I mean really? It's not like he's a stand-up comic.* I clenched my fingers into the palm of my hands.

He may as well have stabbed me through the heart.

Hillary then swung back to face us. "Forget them."

I couldn't believe that Hillary was actually on my side about this. Maybe she had a heart under all that Sephora makeup and over-processed blonde hair, after all.

"We've got more important things going on . . . like tonight," she said.

I frowned. "What are you talking about?"

"Karen promised us a lesson after we let her spill her guts about what happened twenty years ago. Let's call her and do this."

"I'm not sure if I'm ready," I protested.

Hillary rolled her eyes. "If anyone's ready, it's you. You're the most experienced out of all three of us."

"Look, it's clear that Dr. A and our moms were trying to stop any of this from happening. And while Karen is a bit of a wild child, she does know a lot."

Cura nodded. "Yeah, I mean she creeped me out at first, but when she told us her side of the story—it kind of made sense."

"Exactly," Hillary said, crossing her arms over her chest. "Besides, this is all about helping dead girls who have been murdered. The more we know, the more we can help them, right?

I blew out a breath. "Okay, okay. But we do this together." I hated to admit it, but maybe Hillary was right. Everyone I trusted had disappointed me or lied to me, so maybe we had been too hard on Karen. Maybe she could actually teach us something. And if nothing else, it would get my mind off Dylan.

Cura clapped her hands. "Yay!"

Hillary added, "We won't have to worry about people getting in our way anymore."

I stared at Hillary in disbelief. "Since when is this a problem for someone like you?"

She gave me one of her infamous once-overs. "Trust me. No one will bother you or any of us again."

CHAPTER 33

After class, we met in the school parking lot next to Cura's car.

"Do you think we should call Dr. Anthony and let him know what's going on?" Cura asked, jingling her car keys. She gave me a sideways glance, waiting for me to agree.

"We don't have to tell him everything," Hillary protested. She turned my way, "But then again, I bet that's your M.O."

I squeezed my hands together. Hillary had only met Dr. Anthony once, but already I could tell she preferred my aunt over him.

"I don't tell him everything."

Hillary swept her long hair to the side, rolling her eyes. "We're teenagers," Hillary added. "We're supposed to question authority. And excuse me if I'm not right, but I bet he wasn't completely upfront about your aunt. At least with Karen, we can learn more than just how to decorate crosses."

Ouch. "Whatever," I snapped back, Hillary's words annoyed the heck out of me. "Let's just call her already."

Hillary smirked, snatching my cell out of my hand and called Karen, who arranged to meet with all of us later in the evening.

Night came faster than I was ready for. Hard enough to wait for the 'rents to settle down. I snuck outside, climbing down the trestle outside my window. I couldn't help but glance at Dylan's house. How many times had I snuck out like this to go visit him? How many times did we talk late into the night, snuggling on his bed? His lights were off, which meant that he'd either gone to bed early or was out.

Already the thick fog had rolled in, making it hard to see much of anything. I stood at the curb, waiting for Cura. I'd worn all black—black jeans, hoodie, and even black, high-top tennis shoes. I pulled my hoodie over my head and felt all spy-like. Before I'd left the house, I'd rewrapped the gray cloth around the small talisman I'd found in the attic, and placed it in my pocket. Just to be safe. I also made sure to grab a larger unadorned cross and placed it on the ground next to me. We might need it.

Cura's Jetta puttered up to me. I grabbed the cross, rushed over, and opened the car door.

"You're dressed like we're going to rob a bank or something," Cura said, giving me a quick glance..

She didn't look that much different, though instead of a hoodie she had on a thick oversized wool sweater. To give her credit, the brownish color did come off as discrete without being too obvious.

"So, you ready for our first lesson with your aunt?" she asked.

"As I'll ever be."

"Good, let's go."

We'd followed the directions Aunt Karen gave us, using the freeway and getting off by the American River. Tall trees blocked out any moonlight. Add the drop in temperature and you had a horror movie in the making.

"I think that's Hillary's car," Cura said, pointing up ahead.

Sure enough, Hillary leaned against her mother's leased Mercedes-Benz. Dressed in black leggings, a black wool tunic, and designer ballet flats, she took a long drag from a cigarette, exhaling a series of perfectly formed smoke rings.

What was with all this smoking? The ability to see the dead, suddenly made you think you were invincible?

Cura drove up to Hillary and parked. I reached into the backseat and grabbed the larger cross. I had a feeling I would need the talisman tonight. I didn't quite trust Karen, aunt or no aunt.

"Took you guys long enough," Hillary said, dropping her cigarette and snuffing it out at our approach. "So, I guess we just wait for Karen?"

I shifted the heavy cross so it leaned against my hip. "I know as much as you do," I said, biting back a snarky retort. As if being a Rescuer included reading minds.

"Ah, you're all here," Karen strolled out of the fog with a raspy chuckle.

I jumped, the talisman almost tumbling out of my arms.

Karen pointed to the talisman, not acting surprised. "Good, you brought one. We don't have much time or we'll miss this opportunity." She walked up the dirt path, toward a forested area.

We trudged behind. A few branches slapped against my body. I held them aside for Cura, but let them fly a when Hillary got close.

"Bitch," Hillary muttered.

I snickered. Childish, I know, but I didn't care.

We got to a clearing in the middle of nowhere. There was something strange about this spot. A thickness in the air . . . I had no dream or vision to guide me, so I wondered if Karen knew if a spirit were nearby.

"Let me guess. We have to wait for a dead girl to show up," Hillary stated. So maybe she was paying attention after all.

"Yes," Karen said, a look of impatience flashing in her eyes. "We wait for the girl in question to come here."

Cura scanned the surroundings and hugged herself. "Omigod, she died somewhere around here," she said, more to herself.

Now that got Hillary's attention. "Killed? No flippin' way. Like right here?"

"She'll appear here because she was murdered here," I replied. "She's attached to this place. It was the last place she was before she died."

Karen nodded at me in approval. She gestured to my cross. "You didn't decorate it?"

I opened my mouth to explain that I couldn't decorate it because I didn't get any visions about the girl, but she interrupted me before I could answer..

"Good," she said then strolled over and snatched the talisman out of my hand.

"Hey," I protested. Too late. A gleam shone in her eyes.

I felt naked without the cross. An uneasiness snaked through me. Was Karen declaring that she was in control?

"Let's see, I think it's right around here . . ." she walked a few paces a clearing in the trees. A cluster of fallen leaves protested under her feet. She lifted the cross high in the air and slammed it down into the ground. Hard.

Right on cue the fog grew heavier and surrounded us.

CRACK!

The world as we knew it shifted, revealing a shadowy "other" place. The fog began to move and ripple, like a wall of water; the kind that you see when you visit a public aquarium. But it wasn't water, it was air. Bright little points of light flickered on the other side of the "wall," like a bunch of fireflies flitting around. It was beautiful. Mysterious. Magical.

Cura gasped.

I came back to my senses and scanned the area, searching for a spirit, but saw nothing. Suddenly, a mighty wind picked up around us and the lights grew brighter as a space opened in the wall. Like a doorway . . .

"Hurry, before it closes," Karen shouted.

"Wait!" I yelled, the flickering lights had surrounded us, swirling around us. One beam of light landed on my skin. It tingled like an electrical zap. I flicked it off.

"C'mon," Karen rasped above the wind. "What are you waiting for? This is what you wanted right? Knowledge? I'm showing you something spectacular. Something that Dr. Anthony would never dare to show you."

Hillary glanced at us, then back at Karen. "I'm in!" She jumped through the vortex-like opening.

Cura stared at me, her eyes wide. "I'll go if you go." Her voice trembled.

I swallowed and glanced at the opening once more, then at Karen, who was looking at me as though she had all the answers to every question in the universe.

I turned back to Cura and reached out for her hand. "Let's do it together," I said, and when she nodded, we jumped through the opening. I could sense, Karen right behind us.

Something happened as we jumped through the opening. The flickering lights multiplied and swirled around us, picking us up and carrying us down a brightly lit path. We were no longer walking. We were floating. Surrounded by beautiful warmth and light.

Then the light force suddenly dropped us to the ground with a thump and promptly scattered.

The glowing warmth left my body. And I was sad it did. It had been the most amazing feeling I'd ever felt.

It wasn't dark here, but it wasn't light either. The sepia-colored sky felt heavy. The air had grown colder. The trees were all misshapen, bent and twisted, with long gnarly branches. There were no leaves. Not on the trees. Not on the ground.

I'd only ever seen glimpses of the Other Side. But the light always looked welcoming and loving. This was more like a Tim Burton version of Heaven. Twisted and cartoonish. Wrong.

Karen paced back and forth, surveying the area. I could have sworn she was cursing under her breath.

Kim Baccellia

Hillary stepped closer to Cura and me. Suddenly her hand clutched mine, hard. Those acrylic nails stung.

Out of the shadows, a girl not much older than us appeared. One side of her face had melted away. Her party dress hang in tatters. Then another girl materialized out of the shadows and stood beside the first girl. Both looked familiar, but I didn't know where I'd met them.

Another blast of icy air whirled around us.

The first girl directed her gaze toward Karen, mouthing something. Her eyes widened and she frantically waved her hands. The howling wind drowned her voice out.

"No!" Karen yelled. "You can't go yet!"

Out of the twisted shadows, an inky thick liquid, slithered out like an otherworldly snake. It moved toward the first spirit, and twisted around her leg. She tripped and fell backward, her mouth open in a scream as it yanked her back. The creature split itself and twisted around the waist of the other girl, pulling her away as well. She turned to us, her eyes desperate. She reached out and her mouth formed the word. *Nooooooooooo* . . . . Then she too, was gone.

"Oh no!" Cura shouted pointing to the opening behind us. "That can't be good."

The doorway we'd jumped through was starting to close. My gut told me we needed to get out or we'd be trapped forever. I didn't wait for my aunt.

The wind grew stronger and stronger.

"Let's get out of here!" I screamed.

"You don't have to tell me twice," Cura said.

Hillary's fingernails tore into my skin. She nodded.

The wind was so strong, I feared it would hold us back. We linked arms and the three of us were able to push through the force of the rushing wind. I had never been much of an athlete, but boy was I running as fast as I could. It wasn't as fun leaving it as was arriving. My blood felt like ice. I could barely move. Barely breathe. I was so cold I thought I would freeze right in that doorway between the two worlds. Even if I'd wanted to look back, to see if Karen was behind us, I physically couldn't. It was all I could do to move forward. As we got closer to the portal, I felt a darkness overwhelm me, like I would never be happy again. Like all my light and love was being sucked out of me. With one final push, we made it through and then there was only blackness.

CHAPTER 34

I opened my eyes and gazed at the night sky. For a
moment I didn't know where I was. And then I
remembered everything in a mad rush of images and
feelings, like we'd gone into sensory overload. But lucky
for us, we'd made it back.

I heard a groan to my left and a grunt to my right. I
glanced at Cura and Hillary. They looked as gob-
smacked as I felt. We slowly stood up and made our way
back to our cars.

"Do you think she made it out?" Cura asked.

"I don't know." I shivered, wrapping my arms
around myself. "I didn't want to hang around to find
out."

"I'm sure she's okay," Hillary shrugged. "She knew
what she was doing. After all she's super experienced at
all this stuff."

"Well, that was the freakiest thing I've ever been
through." Cura blew out a breath. "I don't know what
else to say."

"I do." I said. "We weren't meant to be there . . .
Those girls . . . They looked familiar to me. What we did
was dangerous and we can't ever go there again."

"What are you talking about?" Hillary scoffed. "That
was such a rush."

"A rush?" I turned to her. "We could have gotten
trapped there forever."

"All I know is, your aunt Karen is one powerful
witch."

"We don't even know where she is," Cura chimed in.

"I'm sure she's off somewhere doing something cool." Hillary countered.

"Look, we should talk about this, but not right now." I was bone tired and needed to get home and crawl into bed. "Let's just go home and we can figure this all out tomorrow."

"Fine, I'm outta here anyway." Hillary strutted to her car and got in. "Later girls." She zoomed away.

"Let's go," I said to Cura. "I don't want to be here."

We got into the car and were silent all the way home.

*   *   *

The next day, I was either dozing off or jumping at the slightest sound. I carried the mini cross in my pocket. The rune etchings reassured me. I'd forgotten I had it in my pocket last night. Who knows, maybe it had kept us from becoming trapped there.

"Hey, spacing much?"

Hillary's voice jarred me. Startled, I pulled away from my locker. A few papers flew out in protest.

I bent down, picking up the papers. Thankfully none of the books fell out. Although I hate to admit it, without her posse of wannabes, she seemed less threatening.

"Was that not . . ." she bent down close, whispering in my ear. " . . . the most amazing trip?"

I don't know if Hillary was remembering the same "trip" as I was. Yes, it started out amazing, but then it turned dark and scary. Had she blocked that part out?

Her eyes glowed with something that I wasn't used to seeing on her face: excitement. Hillary never got excited about anything. She was the most sarcastic person I knew.

"I want to try it again?"

I stared at her in disbelief.

"It's too dangerous," I hissed, scanning the hall to

make sure no one could hear us. "Don't you remember how we almost got stuck over there?"

Her smug expression switched to surprise and then settled into annoyance. "So maybe we hit a glitch," Hillary said. "But that's because we didn't know what we were doing. Now we do."

I shook my head.

"Don't tell me you didn't get a rush from it all?"

The crowded hallway did nothing to silence her. I'd hoped she'd get a clue and drop it, but I should have known better.

"It was cool, at first. But it got way too dangerous and creepy, way too fast. We weren't supposed to be there. Didn't you get that from those girls we saw?" I gave one final push to my already closed locker. I tried to walk around her, but she wouldn't budge.

"So, maybe we can help those girls. Maybe they were in the wrong place and we can help them cross over to the right place."

"It's too dangerous, Hillary." I shook my head. "We could get trapped, or worse . . . "

"I want to go back. All of us."

"I'm not doing it," I said.

"You have to. You just have to. And I *have* to." Her eyes widened and I swear she was trembling, a thin line of sweat trickled down her forehead.

I frowned. Something was off with Hillary.

"We have to go back again," she repeated, with an edge in her voice.

I was about to ask her why she was so determined, when I spotted Dylan walking down the hallway with Ashley by his side.

Relief surged through me. Maybe Dylan could help. He could read auras, maybe he could figure out what was off about Hillary. I pushed past Hillary, who tried to block my path.

"Dylan," I yelled.

He scanned the hallway and when his gaze fell on mine, he leaned down and whispered in Ashley's ear. She laughed. Knife-sharp pain sliced through me.

Hillary grabbed my elbow, turning me around to face her. I glanced over my shoulder and watched Dylan and Ashley walking away. The knife twisted a bit more.

"Deny it all you want." Her grip tightened. "But I know you were pissed off with Dr. A not telling you about the portal between the two dimensions. If you don't come, I'll tell your mother you snuck out to see Karen."

I jerked away. "Your mother wouldn't be too happy if I told her what you did, either."

Hillary only smirked. "Don't worry about her. I have that under control."

CHAPTER 35

My gut was telling me this was a big mistake, but I had no choice. Hillary had contacted Karen again and set up another meeting at Karen's house. I couldn't let Hillary go alone. So, I asked Cura if she would come, too, and the three of us went back into the lioness's den.

We sat in the living room of Karen's posh townhouse. She came back from the kitchen swinging a wine bottle in one hand.

"So girls, are you ready for our next adventure?" She placed the wine on the table beside a tray of four wine glasses.

Cura nudged me. "Omigod, is that for us?" she whispered.

My aunt only smiled. "Let's celebrate our first successful endeavor."

"But we didn't do anything," I protested feebly.

Aunt Karen shook her head. "We entered the other dimension. To me, that was success."

She popped the cork and filled each of the crystal-stem glasses. I took the offered glass, staring at the rich crimson liquid. Sweetness tickled my nose. I'd only sampled a little wine during the holidays when Grandma Stewart let me sneak a sip. I didn't like the taste, but I wasn't going to say anything, especially because I didn't want to hear Hillary's sarcastic retort that would surely follow.

"Cheers," Karen said, after each of us had a glass.

After we drank a sip or two, I placed the glass back on the table. Something bothered me.

"So, I guess you had no trouble getting back?" I asked. "When we ran out of there, I didn't see you behind us."

"Oh, don't worry about me," she smirked. "I always find my way back."

Hillary snorted a laugh and took another sip of wine.

"What happened to those girls we saw?" Cura asked, her voice sounded wobbly to my ears.

"We helped them of course." Karen swirled the wine in her glass, inhaled the aroma and took a long slow sip.

"How did we help them exactly?" I challenged. "That black, inky snake came out and yanked them away. Plus, they were trying to tell us to leave. They didn't exactly look happy."

Karen narrowed her eyes at me. She clearly didn't like my thoughts on the matter. "You just don't understand the other dimension and how it works," she replied.

"Yeah, Steph," Hillary chimed in, taking another sip. "We did the impossible just by entering that realm. I'm sure if we go back we'll see them again and be able to talk to them. Find out who they are and what they're doing there."

"But that's not what a Rescue is," I protested, angry that no one seemed to be listening to what I was saying. "Each time I help a girl cross over, I've seen a bright light. And the girl is always at peace. She's always happy. What I saw on the faces of those girls. . ." I winced. "That wasn't happiness."

Hillary rolled her eyes.

Karen picked up the wine bottle and refilled Hillary's glass. Hillary promptly picked up her glass and started sipping again. Cura and I glanced at each other. What was going on here with Hillary and the wine-drinking?

"Stephanie, my dear, sweet niece," Karen said in her raspy voice. "Let's just celebrate the crossing we did.

I'm certain those spirit girls were not our problem. We weren't meant to help them. For all we know, they were just a projection of your own fears."

I opened my mouth, but quickly shut it. I just knew no one would listen to me. My gut screamed to get the heck out of there. Karen wasn't making sense. And Hillary was drinking way too much.

"So, are we going back tonight?" Hillary interrupted, changing the subject. Her eyes gleamed with excitement. She took another longer sip of her wine.

"Honey, we're celebrating," Karen said. "But don't you worry, we'll go back soon."

Hillary settled back with a grumpy look on her face. I shook my head. Boy, she was really into this.

"I still don't get why I'm not having any more dreams," I said, fingering the rough edges of the talisman in my pocket. I didn't tell anyone I had it with me.

Karen waved her hand, dismissing my concern.

"You don't need those dreams anymore. You're part of a team now," she said, "And I'm your guide."

Karen sat back and smiled at us, but her smile didn't exude warmth. If anything, I felt a chill skitter up and down my spine.

Cura and I looked at each other once more. My gut was telling me that Karen was guiding us down a dark path. But if I didn't go along, I couldn't protect Hillary and Cura.

CHAPTER 36

Something felt wrong. An image of a dark room and ropes flickered through my mind. Cura was sitting on a chair, with a rope tied around her waist. Her hands were on her knees, palms up. Blood dripped from her wrists. She screamed.

I woke up in a cold sweat. Panic squeezed my heart and I couldn't breathe. *Omigod.* I remembered the last time this had happened, only that time Dylan had been the one kidnapped and tortured.

We'd driven Hillary home last night. She'd been in no position to drive herself. Cura dropped me off after that and then drove home. It was almost 11 p.m. when I landed in bed, dead tired. My muscles felt all wonky after that wine. Had Karen put something in it? I fell asleep as soon as my head hit the pillow. Then I had the terrible dream.

I jumped out of bed, grabbed my cell from my bedside table, and texted Cura. My fingers fumbled a few times. All the while praying that my subconscious might be wrong this time.

Hey, u there?

Nothing.

Maybe she'd already left for school and was driving and couldn't text back? I rushed to get ready, said a quick good morning to my parents, who were having breakfast. Mom shoved a foil-wrapped sandwich in my hands.

"Grilled ham and cheese," she smiled. "You need to have a good breakfast in the mornings. It will help you get through your day."

I suddenly realized how famished I was. I hadn't been eating much in the past few days. All thanks to Karen and her so-called "guidance." I thanked my mom. She looked like she wanted to say something more. Instead, she gave me a hug and a kiss on the cheek. I closed my eyes as I hugged her back, wishing everything could go back the way it was before Karen showed up. And before that stupid ceremony at the sorority house. I shoved the sandwich in my bag and headed out the door.

I checked the parking lot at school for Cura's car, but it wasn't there. Maybe her mom dropped her off? I checked her locker bay, but she wasn't there, either. I went to my locker, hoping she was waiting for me there. No Cura. I texted her a quick message, switched my phone to vibrate, and went to first class.

She didn't text me back.

My fear started to kick into high gear.

I texted her again. *Hey missed ya.*

Nothing.

Flushed, I wiped my hand across my forehead, suddenly hot. Something didn't feel right.

I texted again. *R u ok?*

Hillary wandered down the hallway, right in my direction. I waved her over. Maybe she'd seen Cura or talked to her?

"Hey, what's up?" she asked, all perky. While being around my aunt had left me disoriented and beyond exhausted, it had had the opposite effect on Hillary. She seemed brighter, with almost hyperactive energy.

I still found it strange that I even entertained the notion of engaging in conversation with her, but I had to tell someone, and since we were now part of a "team" as Karen put it, I had no choice.

"Did you see Cura today?" I asked.

Hillary lifted an eyebrow. "Isn't that your department?" She motioned with her chin. "Maybe your ex might know."

I turned. A group of guys, including Dylan, sans Ashley, strolled in our direction. Deep in discussion with Brandon, alias math geek, he walked right by.

"Hey, Dylan, over here," Hillary shouted. "Stephanie needs to ask you something."

"Jeez," I whispered, flushed. "Can you be any more obvious?"

Dylan came over to us. He must have seen my anxiety because his eyes looked concerned. My heart missed a beat. Maybe he still cared?

"What's up?" he asked, shifting his books to his other arm.

I swallowed, my palms feeling all sweaty. I felt like I was about to ask him out on a first date. "Uh, have you seen Cura?" I croaked out,

"No," he said. "Why?"

"She hasn't answered any of my texts," I replied, pulling my hand through my ponytail. Oh, I was definitely feeling nervous around him.

Dylan glanced at Hillary, who shrugged. "I haven't seen her either."

Wrinkling his brow, he leaned in closer and lowered his voice. "Does this have to do with another crossing? Dr. A hasn't called me—"

"No it doesn't," I interrupted, "Though things are a little different now with that."

Hillary snickered. "Yeah, you got that right."

The crowded hallway had emptied, but I still didn't feel quite right discussing this out in the open. "Is there anywhere we can talk?" I asked. "You know, in private?"

"Hang on." He stepped into a classroom across the hall, then came back a few moments later. "We can talk in there. Chess club is over for today." He didn't wait for my answer, but walked back to the classroom. I looked at Hillary, who only shrugged and followed.

Once inside, he motioned Hillary to close the door.

Then Dylan faced us. "I've been meaning to talk to you." He stared intently in my direction.

"Really?" I asked, suddenly warm. Hope surged through me. Maybe he'd tell me there was no Ashley and him, and that I'd been silly to even entertain such a notion. Although, why he'd say that in front of Hillary eluded me.

"I don't know what you two have been doing. . ." He ignored Hillary's snort and pressed on. ". . .but it's way dark."

My hopes were smashed into a bazillion pieces. I looked away, wishing I could just disappear, but knew this wouldn't help my friend. I had to come clean. Now.

I glanced back up. Questions and concern flared in Dylan's eyes.

"Well, you know my aunt's back in town," I stuttered, struggling to find the right words to explain. "We met with her and she wanted to talk to us about her side of what happened, and to teach us about the Other Side."

Hillary took a big step away from me and seemed more interested in the contents of her makeup bag.

A range of emotions flashed over Dylan's face. I waited for him to brush me off but instead he took a tentative step closer. "This is the aunt who caused that fire? What did she teach you guys?" he said. "You can trust me."

Could I?

I swallowed, ignoring the warning look from Hillary. "Stuff that she learned, but that's not the reason I need you." I quickly changed the subject. "I had a weird nightmare about Cura."

Dylan's gaze didn't waver.

"Wait," Hillary snapped her bag shut. "You're having dreams again and you didn't share this with me?"

I don't know what kind of dream it is. All I know is that I'm worried about Cura. She isn't at school today and she hasn't answered any of my texts."

"You're worried over nothing," Hillary said,

"Maybe she's on one of her thrift store shopping trips with her mom, you know how much they love stinky old clothes."

"Just shut up." Dylan whirled around, "I'm sick of all your snark." He didn't drop his gaze, almost daring her to say something.

Her eyes widened, her mouth hanging open.

Score one: Dylan.

Dylan waved his finger in her face. "If anyone knows about any of this? It's Steph. Deal with it."

Wow, just wow. I knew there was a reason why I loved this boy. Even if he was dang stubborn and yes, pushy, and yes, annoying. Then Ashley's flirty face popped into my head, drowning out my wave of hope that maybe Dylan still wanted to be with me.

I pushed that depressing thought aside because I had no time to dwell on my love life. Not when Cura might be in danger.

Then he faced me, ignoring Hillary's exaggerated pout. "What should we do?"

"We need to tell Dr. A." I shook my head, trying to take all this in. "I just hope nothing bad has happened to her."

Dylan placed his hand under my chin, lifting it. I could get so lost in his eyes. Goosebumps covered my whole body and I wished the last month or so would just disappear into the ether and we could go back to the way it had been. Me and him. For now, though, we had more pressing issues. Like finding Cura.

I just hoped we weren't too late.

CHAPTER 37

Dylan left to meet up with Dr. Anthony and fill him in about Cura.

"Why didn't you tell him everything we did with your aunt?" Hillary asked.

Exactly, why didn't I? Maybe because I knew what we'd done with Karen was wrong and I didn't want to ruin the moment with Dylan. I didn't want him angry with me. We'd gone too far to the dark side. We hadn't listened to Dr. A. I hadn't listened to my mom either. The place we crossed over to was not where the dead go. At least not the dead girls I helped to cross over. I realized that everything Karen had told us about the past was probably a lie, including the part about my mom and the fire. How could I have even entertained the notion of believing anything that woman had told us?

"There's plenty of time to tell him that. Right now, we need to focus on finding Cura." I replied.

"You're right," Hillary said, shocking me. "Look, if Cura is missing, maybe Karen knows something about it?"

I nodded, fishing around my bag for my phone. I glanced at the screen and saw that Aunt Karen had texted me. I realized that my phone was still on vibrate, so I hadn't heard the ping.

"Karen just texted me a few minutes ago."

"What did she say?" Hillary asked.

"To meet her at the sorority house."

Hillary's eyes widened. "Why?"

"I don't know." I shook my head. "But this doesn't bode well."

"Even though I hate that disgusting place, if it means helping Cura, I'm in."

Hard to remember not that long ago Hillary wouldn't have even entertained the thought of being around either one of us, let alone wanting to help us."

Although Hillary had brought her mom's Mercedes to school, I didn't want her driving me. Thank goodness, I'd borrowed my brother's car that morning. I told her I'd meet her there.

When I got there, I stepped out of my car and took in the sight of the former sorority house. Sadness wrapped around what remained of what had been, at one time, a happy place. For some unexplainable reason, I sniffled back tears.

Hillary rolled her eyes at me and I thrust my chin up, pulling on my inner resolve. Something I needed right now. Faded graffiti in a rainbow of different colors covered one of the crumbling walls. Animal feces and some other nasty things lay scattered around the property.

Wow, seeing the place in daylight totally revealed its true character.

"Ew," Hillary said, wrinkling her nose. "This place really does need to be demolished."

Right on cue, Aunt Karen opened the door and waved us in. White streaks highlighted her dark updo. Weariness etched her eyes. She looked like she'd aged since we last met.

Hurry up, we don't have time," Aunt Karen said, opening the door farther. Not waiting, for us, she went back inside.

Hillary and I exchanged looks.

"Okaaay, that was weird," Hillary said. "And what's with her Bride of Frankenstein look?

I rolled my eyes and walked inside.

Had it been only a month since we'd been here? It seemed longer. It felt like we'd been on a crazy amusement park ride.

Karen was waiting up ahead, standing in what was once the main floor common room. A few old newspapers were cluttered in the corners. I caught the date, '1990' but didn't have time to investigate. Instead of venturing up the crumbling stairs as we had when we were last here with our mothers, she turned left down the hallway.

Hillary and I exchanged glances and followed close behind.

Karen stopped at a door and opened it, picking up a lit candle that was sitting on the floor beside the door. She glanced over her shoulder to make sure we were following. On the other side of the door was another set of stairs going up. I looked at Hillary and she swallowed audibly, her eyes huge in her face. We followed Karen up the steps, the flickering light from the candle she was holding threw ghostly shadows on the walls. We went up and up. It seemed like the staircase would never end. And then we finally reached the top step. And another closed door. Karen opened the door and we stepped up into the room.

"Wow," Hillary said, stopping suddenly. She looked over at me.

"My sentiments exactly."

It looked like we were in the attic of the sorority house. The ceiling was low and the room was long. There was one tiny window at the far end. The entire space was lit with candlelight, but unlike the candles that Hillary had used in her kitchen, these were black. Dylan told me once that a black aura was very negative. Did that apply to black candles, too?

My nightmare of Cura locked in a dungeon flashed through my mind. Was Cura somewhere in the sorority house? I had to find out.

Scattered on a long, chipped, wooden table were a collection of talismans and candles including a foot-long cross. Intricate designs decorated the wood, making my own previous artwork seem amateurish in comparison.

Karen finished lighting yet another black candle, placing it back down with a group of others on the floor. She walked over to the table and carefully picked up the cross I'd been staring at, turning it in her hands. "I have another lesson to share with you."

"Do you know where Cura is?"

My aunt waved her other hand impatiently.

Hillary and I exchanged worried looks.

"I never said that she was here, did I? I just told you to come here."

Didn't I learn my lesson with Mark? Deep down a voice shrieked for me to flee. I hoped that Dylan had called Dr. A and they were both on the way. Something wasn't right with Karen.

From the moment I'd met her, she'd seemed strange, different. But I had been drawn to her because, well, we had something in common. We could both communicate with the dead. Plus, I had been angry with my mom and Dr. A for keeping things from me. But after Karen pulled us into that weird other realm, and now with Cura missing, I knew she was truly dangerous.

"Why all this then?" I pointed to the talismans. "I'm not stupid. Crosses help the dead cross over. Why are they here? Who are we crossing over?"

"Relax." She smiled, but there was nothing warm or friendly about it. She was clearly anxious. What was she covering up?

"The candles." Hillary lifted a large black one off the floor. "Why black?"

Aunt Karen stared at me. "I think you know, don't you?"

"It has something to do with calling on the dead, but not in a good way." I looked at Hillary, "She lied to us.

She doesn't know where Cura is, or she did something really bad to her and is playing games. Let's get out of here."

"You're just like the others," Aunt Karen snarled. She shot me a withering glare. "Too afraid of your own shadow. You could be really powerful. More powerful than that entire Light Bringers group."

"Whatever. I don't need this!" I glared at her. "I was stupid enough to think that we had something in common and that you actually cared about me because you're my aunt." I shook my head. "But all you care about is power. You don't care about helping the dead."

"You are so weak. Just like your mother. Just like the rest of them."

"Steph," Hillary protested, snagging my arm. "Don't forget about Cura."

I wanted to leave and take Hillary with me because I didn't trust Karen one bit, but Hillary was right. We needed to find Cura, and I had a feeling that Karen could lead us to her. "What do you want from us?"

Shadows flickered over my aunt's face, chiseling hard angles in her otherwise once flawless features. Now she looked way older than Mom. More like Mom's mother or grandmother.

An itch started at the back of my legs, slowly intensifying until I thought I'd scream.

"I think I see someone!" Hillary motioned to the back wall, close to the large mirror.

"Good, they're almost here," Aunt Karen said.

I looked in that direction, but saw nothing.

"See? You did help the other night. I needed you to bring back a couple of friends," Aunt Karen whispered, "They'll help in finding your friend."

Huh?

A cold breeze blew through the attic, scattering some old newspapers across the floor.

I jumped at my aunt's words. I wanted to flee. Now. Once again, the sensation that something wasn't right with her resonated with me.

I just prayed those spirits Aunt Karen alluded to didn't include Cura. Oh, please, God, not her. Anyone but my friend.

"Yes, here they are!" Hillary exclaimed. She jumped up and down.

Right on cue, a girl around our age materialized in the room, purpose in her stride.

Not Cura!

I blew out a breath in relief. I recognized her. She was one of the girls we'd seen just last night in that weird other realm.

Her heels tottered on the floor, making a scraping sound as she walked through the debris scattered around. I gagged at her spicy-smelling perfume.

Hillary grimaced in distaste. "Why is she dressed like a '90s music video reject?"

The girl stopped in front of Hillary and gave her a snarky look.

I would have laughed if I didn't know that this girl had been dead for what looked like a few decades. It still was hard to look at the burnt side of her face, but the left-hand side revealed a pretty girl.

Something else about this ghost felt familiar. I knew her, but how?

Then it came to me. A shiver skittered up my spine. I looked at the ghost-girl's face, at least the side that wasn't melted, and I looked at Hillary's face. There was a resemblance. "Ohmigod. She's Hillary's aunt. She's one of the girls who died in the sorority fire."

Hillary's eyes widened as she and her aunt looked at each other.

"You knew about this, didn't you?" I whirled around, confronting Karen. She only shrugged.

"You helped me bring them back." Then she

motioned to the far corner of the room." "You're forgetting someone."

At that moment, another girl walked forward. Of course! Dylan's aunt. I could see the resemblance, too.

Adrenaline rushed through my body. Karen never wanted to help us or teach us. She just wanted our help in summoning these two dead girls. But why?

I could almost hear my mother saying: *Why are you so surprised?*

That only made me madder.

The ghost-girls stood side by side. They didn't speak, but they shook their heads.

"What did you do?" I finally asked.

Aunt Karen only smirked. "Sisters on Earth. Sisters in Death. Did you really think death would separate us?"

Ohimgod, she had lost it!

"But how can that be?" Hillary asked, "They're dead."

Aunt Karen tssked. "Oh, ye of little faith. In death, they can help us even more."

"That's why you took us to the Other Side. To get them to come through." Why didn't I realize this? We'd played right into her hands.

My aunt smirked, but said nothing.

"What exactly?" I could barely say the words without choking. "Are they going to help us with?"

"They can help us find Cura." She cocked her head to the side, "That's what you want, isn't it?"

But Cura hadn't been missing when we went over to the Other Side. This made absolutely no sense.

Hillary stepped closer to me and gripped my hand.

"But first, we need to complete the circle," Aunt Karen said, waving the spirits closer.

What the hell? I wanted nothing to do with this. I whirled around, pulling Hillary along.

"Where do you think you're going?" My aunt's

voice stopped me for a moment. "I thought you wanted to help find your friend."

"Of course, I want to find Cura. But you're just playing games with the dead. You should have left these two girls to rest in peace. Instead you forced them to come back here. You're crazy."

"Stephanie, dear." Goosebumps flared up my body at the sound of her saccharine-sweet voice. "What exactly has that mentor of yours done for you? Aren't *you* the one helping *him*? He's using your abilities for his own purposes. Studying you like a lab rat and writing about you in one of his secret journals."

Ignore her. I repeated this silent mantra, trying to block out her words.

"Admit it," Karen taunted. "You liked getting a taste of the Other Side and you knew that Dr. Anthony would never approve of you strengthening your abilities. He wants to keep you as his own little minion."

Hillary whispered. "Maybe she has a point."

I glared at her.

"You don't know what you're saying," I said, even as I realized that Karen had hit close to home. I had felt a little resentful toward Dr. A and Mom. Dr. A acted like I couldn't handle anything other than what I already knew. He kept me at a certain level. Why? To protect me or because he knew what was inside me? And Mom forced me to keep my abilities a secret, even from Dad. Why? Was she ashamed of me? Afraid I would turn into her sister?

Aunt Karen seized on my moment of hesitation and sidled up to us. My nose recoiled at the whiff of her heavy musk perfume. She placed her hand on my cheek. Her eyes were soft, reminding me of Mom.

"You were able to go where no living person has gone before," she whispered. "That kind of power is so rare. And you have it inside you."

I shook my head in denial.

[265]

She pressed her hand against my face, the caress became almost painful. "Come on, Stephanie, I know how lonely you've been. No one believing in you. Being ostracized by everyone, including your own mother, who is supposed to love you no matter what. Instead she tried to destroy your gift. And that's what it is—a wonderful gift. Don't you want to know how to channel it in every way?"

I froze. Every word she said pierced through the so-called iron clan shield I'd built. I trembled at her words. She'd hit me where it hurt. I felt a strange push and pull inside my mind. A battle between what I knew to be right and a deep, secret desire to know more . . . What was happening to me?

"The so-called *good* doctor is lying to you. He didn't tell you everything, did he?"

I shook my head.

"And he won't. Trust me. I know better than anyone how he can suddenly turn on you." Karen wrapped her arm around my shoulders. "I can help you. If you'll only let me."

"Why them?" I pointed to the dead girls.

"We need a circle of five. I can be your conductor, but only if you let me."

"So you can't do this alone," I said, then my eyes widened. A horrific thought flashed through my mind. Young girls. Dead girls . . . "Cura is important to this circle."

She smiled. Cold. Calculating. She wandered back to the table and began moving the candles around in a strange pattern. She took out a vial of some liquid and poured it into a black bowl. Then she lifted one of the candles and angled it over the bowl, letting the melted wax drip into the bowl. A stench rose up in the air. It smelled like burning garbage.

"Gross!" Hillary and I began coughing. Our eyes watered.

No! I couldn't let Karen pull me in. I had to get out of there. I grabbed Hillary's hand and we carefully started to make our way to the door, hoping Karen wouldn't notice. Karen suddenly flicked her wrist and the door slammed shut. Hillary and I looked at each other. I could see the fear in Hillary's eyes. They mirrored my own.

I was stupid. Weak. Too trusting. Again. Just like with Mark, I had allowed Karen to get under my skin. To make me doubt myself and my purpose. To make me turn against my mentor, Dr. Anthony, and my own mother.

No, no, this wasn't me.

Karen glared at us and a flash of fire flared in her eyes. Evil.

"You're insane," I said, finding the strength to speak out. "What have you done with Cura?"

Hillary trembled next to me. Her usual bravado gone. She no longer seemed excited about the possibility of going to the Other Side. I didn't blame her.

I glanced at the two ghost-girls. They were standing a few feet away from us. Watching. Waiting. Their eyes looked sad.

Oh please Cura, don't be dead.

"Oh, ye of little faith." My aunt sneered at me.

I cringed hearing the word "faith" from Karen. It sounded almost sacrilegious coming out of her silicone-enhanced, pouty lips.

The familiar ring tone of Alive Zombies went off. The deafening sound startled not only me but Hillary. I yanked my cell out. Dylan's face grinned back at me.

"Put it away," Aunt Karen snapped, annoyance in her voice. "You can talk to whoever it is later. Or don't you want to find your friend?"

I hesitated.

The offbeat music went off again, echoing in the mostly deserted room. I had to give Dylan credit. He didn't give up easily. I snuck another glance at the screen.

Don't believe your aunt.

Dr. A filled me in.

Dylan

It's Mom," I lied. "She wants to know when to expect me for dinner. I'll just tell her I'm at the library studying." I texted as I spoke, hoping Karen wouldn't snatch the phone from my hands.

Sorority house. Help!

I locked it with the password and shoved my cell back in my pocket before Aunt Karen could confiscate it.

I looked at my aunt. I mean, really stared at her. I'd had my share of bad experiences with the undead, though I knew Mom's sister didn't fit that category. But I also sensed that she wasn't quite right in the head. A sinister presence resonated within her. And if I wasn't careful, it could get inside me, too. I had already felt its pull. I couldn't let it grab hold of me. Of my insecurities.

"You can't stop us. We're leaving. C'mon Hillary."

Aunt Karen's face wrinkled in confusion, then she threw her head back and laughed. She flicked her wrist again and Hillary suddenly let go of my hand.

"I can't go with you. I want to stay." Hillary looked at me oddly, like she was confused about what she was saying. She turned and walked over to Karen.

Karen put her arm around Hillary and smiled triumphantly. "You see Stephanie? Hillary is a smart girl. She wants to learn from me. She knows I can show her the truth."

Damn. What was Karen up to now? A few minutes ago, it felt like she was trying to drill into my mind, and now she was able to yank Hillary away from me. I turned and ran as fast as I could toward the exit. If I had to, I would kick the door as hard as I could to open it.

Out of the shadows, the ghost of Hillary's aunt

glided close to me. She stretched her hand and the locked door flung open, releasing a big gust of air, and nearly knocking me on my bottom.

At first, I shut my eyes tight, my whole body rigid with fear. Then I opened one, then both eyes. Her wavering body hovered just close enough that her icy breath sent a chill through me. I backed away. I'd heard about the tragedy from that night, but nothing had prepared me for this.

Sadness crumbled her features and she mouthed two words that were unmistakable: *Help us.*

I walked backward out the door and stumbled. I'd forgotten the stairs.

My arms wind-milled as I tried to find my footing, but I fell back and tumbled down.

Everything went black.

* * *

With a jolt, I opened my eyes. Where was I? The smell of burning candles reminded me.

I tried to get up, but the whole world tilted up and down. It felt like that time when I was twelve and snuck into Mom and Dad's liquor cabinet and poured half a bottle of Baileys over my bowl of vanilla ice cream. And OMG, a pain that felt like tiny needles was piercing my skull. It took every ounce of effort not to pass out again.

I had to get up or who knew what other evil my aunt might unleash? Because I knew, without a doubt, that the spell my aunt did twenty years ago unleashed an evil that not only caused the deaths of Hillary and Dylan's aunts, it also caused some kind of haunting possession of Aunt Karen.

I struggled to get up, when I felt the sharp edge of the cross press against my thigh. In all the craziness, I'd forgotten the one thing that could help me. Renewed hope surged through me.

Kim Baccellia

I sat up, trying to get my bearings. The room was pitch black. This wasn't the attic. Where was I? I heard some shuffling behind me and faint moans. The ghosts? One lone candle burned on a small table in the corner. Where was Hillary? I peered into the shadows, but couldn't see her.

"I changed my mind," I croaked out.

Silence.

My hands trembled. "I said, I changed my mind. I'll do your ceremony."

What the heck was going on? Where was Karen?

I had to play along to give Dylan and Dr. A enough time to get to us. It was our only hope.

* * *

An eerie quiet hung in the stale air of the abandoned sorority house, reminding me that death lingered nearby. Cura was missing. Now Hillary was gone, too. Although I couldn't see the ghost-girls, I felt their presence. Fear gripped me and, if I wasn't careful, whatever evil had control over Karen would over-take me too.

This was all my fault. I talked Dr. A into letting us go down this path. I thought I could handle it, but I couldn't. Karen was too strong. Well, whatever entity had taken over Karen was too strong. It had tried to take me, too. Made me question myself and my purpose. Made me resent my mom and Dr. A. Kept me from reaching out to Dylan and confiding in him. I could see the truth now. If only I had seen it sooner.

A footstep sounded behind me and I slowly stood up.

A sudden zap flickered through the air and hundreds of candles flared to life

And then I saw everything.

The circle of black candles. The triangle on the floor. The three chairs in the middle of the circle. One chair was still empty. But sitting in the other chairs were Cura and Hillary. Their eyes were wide with fear. Their mouths were gagged and their arms were tied behind their backs.

Fear and relief washed over me at once. I had to stay in control. I had to think straight or I wouldn't be able to help my friends.

"Why are they tied up?" I knew she was here too. Waiting in a darkened corner.

"You didn't listen to me. And now you have to pay the price." Karen stepped forward and, bending down, lit the fifth candle in the circle.

"Okay, you're right." I swallowed, my mouth as parched as a desert. "I'm listening now. I'm here now. Just untie them and we can do the ceremony."

"You know I can't do that."

"What the hell are you planning to do?" I croaked out.

Aunt Karen tilted her head and grinned. "I have to complete the circle," she said in a sing-song voice. "I can finally shatter the wall between the two worlds."

I gulped, fearing I'd pass out, "But we're not willing. You have Cura and Hillary tied up."

"Oh, a minor detail." Her cackle echoed around the basement. "I just said that to get you to come here. But it's not necessary."

A sick realization hit. "You're going to kill us, aren't you?"

As soon as the words were out, Hillary and Cura squirmed and groaned behind their gags. Their eyes were wide with fear.

Karen flashed her creepy smile again.

"Kill you? Well . . . I do need your blood, so it might get a bit messy."

No way! Dr. Anthony's warning flashed through my mind like a neon sign. Blood spells bring darkness and evil. Not to mention death.

"This isn't about helping the dead or moving between the realms," I said realization dawning on me. "You're looking for immortality."

Right on cue the temperature dropped to freezing. Hillary's aunt and Dylan's aunt stepped out of the shadows. Emotionless, they glided across the floor and hovered beside Hillary and Cura.

Cura squirmed in her chair so hard, it almost toppled over.

The cross pressed into my hand. I fingered the talisman, gaining strength from its shape. I knew what I had to do.

"Dear niece, please sit in the empty chair with your friends." Karen's disembodied voice floated out to me.

She stepped into the glow of the candles. In her hand was a very long, very nasty looking blade. She swung it in a series of arcs and movements. Etched on the wood handle were rune-like designs similar to circles, triangles, and squares.

I gulped, every gruesome image of every horror movie I'd ever seen flickered through my mind. My breathing sped up into short, sharp gasps. Pain gripped my chest and lungs. No, I couldn't lose it. I couldn't have a panic attack. Not now..

"Stephanie, you have to do as I say, or we're not going to get this done in time."

I had to act now if I had any chance of saving us. I didn't have time to second guess myself. My hand gripped the talisman. My heart pounded in my ears. It was now or never . . .

The sound of pounding feet echoed in the house above us.

Karen snarled and moved toward the girls with deadly intent.

I was never a track star, by any means, but at that moment, I could have won a gold medal. I rushed past

Karen, pushing her aside as I turned and stood in front of Cura and Hillary.

"You bitch!" Karen had dropped her knife. Bending down she picked it up.

I whipped out the talisman from my pocket and held it up to the light.

Karen froze when she saw it, her blade in mid-air. She hissed at me.

"Stop!"

Karen whipped around, still wielding the knife.

Dr. Anthony and Dylan rushed down the stairs.

"Karen?" Dr. A stepped forward slowly.

Karen's eyes narrowed and she backed away from all of us.

Dylan ran toward me, and seeing him, Karen flicked her wrist and he was flung backwards, landing with a thud on the concrete floor. I wanted to run to him, but I couldn't leave Cura and Hillary.

Dr. Anthony stepped closer and only then did I notice the burlap bag hanging around his neck. He slipped his hand into the bag and when he brought it out, something was clutched in his palm.

"It's been a long time Karen," he said quietly, almost gently.

"Yes, it has. Sorry I never wrote," she chortled. "Busy. Busy. Busy. You know how it is when you practice black magic."

"You always did love to walk on the wild side," Dr. Antony whispered.

Okay, what was going on here? Dr. A and Karen looked like they wanted to make out.

Dylan had stood up and had made his way over to me and Cura and Hillary. I had no idea where the ghost-girls were.

Dr. A stood before Karen. His eyes gazing into hers. She gazed back. Like she couldn't help herself. Huh? Was she still ga-ga over him? After all these years?

Dr. A leaned forward, like he was about to kiss her, then he suddenly opened his palm and blew some kind of powder into her eyes. "Depart from here!" he roared.

She stumbled back, her hands covered her face. A scream echoed around us, like a huge beast had just been wounded. A dark red liquid oozed from between her fingers.

"Go back from whence thou comest," Dr. Anthony shouted. He whipped out a vial of water and splashed it onto Karen's head. She fell to the ground. Deep groans of agony were coming from her, but they didn't sound like her. She writhed on the floor, convulsing so violently, I thought for sure she was dying. Dr. Anthony stepped back, breathing heavily with exertion. I gasped as I saw something I never expected to see. A great black beast with horns pushed itself out of Aunt Karen's quaking body. Dr. Anthony pulled out a cross, just like the one I was holding at held it up to the beast, who roared at Dr. A, like it wanted to attack him.

I don't know why I did what I did next, but somehow I knew I had to do it.

I ran up to Dr. A and stood beside him, facing the snarling demon. I held my own cross up to the creature. Together we faced the dark evil menace that had taken hold of Aunt Karen for more than twenty years.

"Begone!" I shouted. "You are not wanted here, you filthy beast."

Dr. A repeated the same words he'd said earlier.

We repeated our chants over and over again as the demon struggled to remain in our realm. And then it flashed through me: all of my anger, all of my worry, all of my fear that had built up inside me for the past month. I felt it all. I felt it flow through me. I rushed toward the demon beast, and with the talisman gripped tightly in my hand, I punched through the beast's chest with all the force I had in me.

"Begone!" I shouted again.

The creature screamed as though in agony and splintered into a million, tiny fragments before vanishing into thin air.

It was gone.

I stood there frozen with my hand still out.

Dylan ran up to me and pulled me into his embrace.

"You did it Steph," he whispered into my ear as he twirled me around. "You did it."

CHAPTER 38

Aunt Karen opened her eyes. We all stood around her in a circle, watching her.

"Anthony? Is that you?" she whispered.

His hand cupped her chin. "Yes, Karen, it's me."

"I'm s-so sorry," she said and then closed her eyes once more.

Dr. Anthony turned to me, "We need to get her to a hospital."

Chaos erupted like a scene right out of a hellish movie.

Bang!

I stumbled, trying to get my footing. It didn't help that the whole building quivered. "I think this building is about to fall on top of us."

The exorcism must have triggered it," Dr. A said. "Let's get the hell out of here!"

"My sentiments exactly."

Dylan and Dr. A carried Aunt Karen up the stairs, and I helped Cura and Hillary.

Twenty minutes later, we huddled together outside, watching the flames eat up the sorority house.

"I'm so sorry, honey." Mom was there pulling me close. She hugged me tight. It felt good. It felt like my mom was back.

Dr. Anthony supervised the paramedics as they strapped Aunt Karen onto a stretcher and placed her into the waiting ambulance. He inclined his head, letting me know he was going to ride in the ambulance with her. I nodded. I knew they had a lot to catch up on. I knew everything would be okay.

"Honey, I never thought she'd do this. Believe me," Mom said.

"It's okay, Mom It wasn't her fault. She was possessed."

Mom nodded, tears in her eyes. "I had no idea. I thought she was so mad at me. I'll go see her later at the hospital. But you're my priority now." She hugged me tight again.

"You had that talisman hidden in the attic just in case something like this happened, didn't you?"

She nodded.

"Thank you," I whispered.

I scanned the area looking for my friends. Standing a few feet away were Cura and Hillary and Dylan. Their moms were crying and holding onto them tight.

Just beyond them I saw Dylan's aunt and Hillary's aunt. They were both smiling at me.

It's going to be okay now. I heard them say in my head. *We can finally go home. You have an amazing power. Never forget that.* They waved one more time and then vanished.

I swallowed a lump in my throat and hugged my mom even tighter, if that were possible.

*   *   *

After all the excitement and under strict orders from, not only Dr. Anthony, but our mothers, we stayed under the radar for a few weeks. But even they realized that it was a given that these powers of ours weren't going anywhere, anytime soon. Which could be good or bad, however you looked at it.

I'd been forever changed, though. I had fought another evil demon that had had its grip on my aunt for decades. Another portal had been closed, but how many more were still open? I wondered if my abilities had changed too. Would the dead girls visit me in my dreams again? Would I have the same kinds of visions I used to have before all of this happened? At least I wasn't alone in this. Cura and Hillary were with me, too. And Dylan and Dr. A.

Morgan and Emily's killers had been identified and arrested. It caused a huge scandal at the college and led to the frat house being closed. Let's just say those guys wouldn't be drugging other girls' drinks for some time.

But that didn't mean, any of us—Cura, me, Dylan, and, yes, even Hillary—couldn't wait to meet up again, and when Dr. Anthony summoned us to his office, we all went.

"So, what's next?" Cura asked, between a couple of loud snaps of her overly sweet bubble gum. Some things never changed.

What was left of the sorority building had been scheduled to be bull-dozed and the city had unanimously voted to build a memorial park there. A quiet place for meditation and reflection.

Added bonus: Dylan and I were a couple again. He insisted nothing had gone on with Ashley. They were just friends. I didn't push it. I trusted him.

Mom had a long chat with Aunt Karen while she was in the hospital. I wasn't up to going, but I made her a *Get Well* card. Mom said she was touched. The Light Bringers had visited her, too. They were sending her to Scotland for "convalescence." At least that was what Dr. A had told us. Dr. A had spent some time with her, and I wondered if they would keep in touch and how things would be between them.

I marveled at everything Dr. A had done that night. The way he had mesmerized Aunt Karen in order to draw the demon out of her. That was some powerful "magic." But he said he couldn't have done it without me. He told me I had a special gift and he would help me nurture it in the right way. That made me feel good.

I knew that Mom didn't exactly like this gift of mine. And I'm sure we'd clash over it again one day. And I certainly hated keeping it from Dad. Mom had given him some excuse about a party that had gotten out of hand. But Dad wasn't stupid. He hugged me and gave Mom one of those "we'll talk about this later" looks. I hope Mom would be okay. I hope they would both be okay.

I surveyed our group—Dylan, standing beside me, holding my hand, Cura hovering by the doc as he pulled up some file on his computer, and Hillary standing a little apart from all of us buffing her nails. She rolled her eyes at Cura, but I knew better. She was one of us now.

"Well?" Cura walked over to me and Dylan and whispered to us while Dr. A was on the phone with one of the Light Bringers. "Do you think your aunt and Dr. A will get back together? After everything that happened?"

"I hope so. If anyone can help her, the Light Bringers can." Remembering how Dr. A had touched her face after she'd collapsed made me think she would be okay.

Cura glanced at Hillary. "I think it's kind of cool to be able to help spirits find peace."

"Yeah, I guess," Hillary shrugged as she continued buffing her nails.

"You can't tell me you don't want to know more," Cura said. "Why else are you here?"

"Okay, you're right." She pursed her lips. "If I have this ability, I may as well know how to use it." Then she pointed her nail file at us. "Don't think this means we're all BFFs."

I smiled. "No, that thought never entered my mind."

Cura and Dylan chuckled and even Hillary cracked a smile.

I think we might make one heck of a good Rescue Team after all.

ABOUT THE AUTHOR

Kim Baccellia has always been a sucker for the paranormal. She blames it on her families' love for such things as having picnics at cemeteries, visiting psychics, and reading her mother's copies of the daily horoscope. In middle school, Kim wrote a horoscope column for the school newspaper. It was a huge hit!

Kim's other published YA fantasies include *No More Goddesses*, *Goddesses Can Wait*, and *Earrings of Ixtumea*. All are available on Barnes & Noble.com and Amazon.

A member of RWA, Kim is currently finishing revisions on a post-apocalyptic novel where a Latina teen questions her cult's faith. She's also finishing a romance set in Tuscany, Italy. She lives in Southern California with her husband, son, and two parrots.